Braving the Storms

Strengthen What Remains, Book Three
By Kyle Pratt

CAMDEN CASCADE

PUBLISHING

Braving the Storms

Strengthen What Remains, Book Three
By Kyle Pratt

Copyright © 2015 Kyle Pratt
ISBN: 978-0-9969412-1-1
Third Edition – January 2016
All Rights Reserved

Editors: Joyce Scott & Barbara Blakey

Cover Design: Micah Hansen

Sign up for my no-spam monthly newsletter and get a free ebook.
Details are at the end of the novel.

Acknowledgements

I have no idea how many hours I've spent writing *Braving the Storms*. The life of an author is usually portrayed as solitary, but that has not been my experience.

Many authors say that their spouse is their biggest fan. My wife, Lorraine, is certainly that, but she is also my office manager, business partner and first line editor. She has read every chapter of this book several times. Without her support I would not be able to be an author.

I owe a huge debt of gratitude to the members of my critique group; Robert Hansen, Barbara Blakey, Carolyn Bickel, Debby Lee and Kristie Kandoll. They are more than fellow writers, they are friends and mentors, and they have taught me so much.

Finally, I appreciate my friend William Childress for beta-reading the manuscript and finding all the errors I made during final edits.

Thank you!

Chapter One

Rural Lewis County, Washington state, Sunday, September 20th

First Sergeant Fletcher spread the map on the hood of the Humvee and wondered where the gang might be headed.

The screen door of the nearby log home squeaked as Deputy Philip exited. He was only twenty-four years old and, Fletcher was sure, had not seen many murders. The door creaked again as Private Spencer, his skin deathly pale, followed the deputy out of the house.

"Anybody alive?" Fletcher asked.

Philip shook his head, took a deep breath and let it out slowly. "An older man and woman are inside, both dead. The gun safe is open, but empty, except for this logbook. It lists eight rifles and three pistols by make, model and serial number. It looks like the gang tortured the husband, probably to get the combination of the gun safe, and then killed them both."

"How long have they been dead?"

"Two days, maybe three. The gang could be anywhere by now."

The corporal walked up. "There's no gas in the car or tractor. The gas caps are off so, I'd guess the gang siphoned it."

"How much fuel do we have?" Fletcher asked.

"The gas cans are empty and none of the tanks are full. We have enough for today, but we'll need more soon."

Fletcher didn't want to turn back. "They're animals. I don't think they know we're hunting them, but if we don't find them quickly, they'll figure it out." He drew a circle with his finger. "All the attacks have been in this area. We've been checking homes, farms, motels and such, but they could be camping somewhere."

"They would need shelter, water and a place off the road

4

where they can hide," Philip said.

"There's a hunting lodge here." The pale private indicated a location on the map. "It was owned by a rich guy, but since he was from Los Angeles...."

Fletcher nodded. Los Angeles was nuked by the terrorists on the second day of attacks. The owner of the lodge was probably still in the city when it was destroyed. He looked at the deputy. "I think we should check it out."

"It's the best idea I've heard today."

"Private, round up the rest of the men and let's move out."

While the squad of soldiers returned to the two Humvees, Deputy Philip tried to radio in the murders, but heard only static. "We're out of range."

Fletcher looked south. "The direction we're going will keep us out of radio range. Do you want to head back to Hansen and report or—"

"No," the deputy said. "I'll drive to here." He pointed to a small town on the map. "I know that's in radio range. I'll report in, get more gas and meet you at the lodge."

Fletcher nodded and turned to the soldiers nearby. "Okay. Let's saddle up."

Two Humvees headed into the mountains south of Randle, while the deputy drove north toward the highway.

Since Private Spencer knew the location of the lodge, Fletcher had him drive the lead vehicle while he sat next to him with the map. Trees lined both sides of the road as they climbed into the Cascade foothills. Some of the land was national forest, some was owned by timber companies. Occasionally a house came in view. As they passed a meadow the first sergeant spotted a man, woman and several children baling hay and loading it on a horse drawn wagon. *Perhaps they moved here thinking this was a safe place to raise a family. It probably is safer than most cities.* He chuckled inwardly. *We used to think the world wasn't safe. We had no idea just how unsafe it could get.* He sighed and studied the map.

A few minutes later Spencer said, "That's the turn off. It's about two miles up the gravel road near the top of the hill."

"Stop here." Fletcher had the drivers block the narrow road with the Humvees. The two squads hiked on either side of the private lane through a forest of mammoth trees. The sun was low by the time they approached the lodge. Just out of sight of the building, Fletcher took one squad and circled toward the back.

Using binoculars he observed the large two-story log structure with a wrap-around covered porch. Ancient fir and cedar trees surrounded the building, some less than a yard from it. Two pickup trucks and a Mustang were in a gravel parking lot on the south side. The only sound was the occasional chirp of a bird and the rumble of a small engine. He assumed it was a generator. Using the binoculars, Fletcher checked every door and window in view, but detected no movement.

When the soldiers were in place, covering all sides and avenues of escape, Fletcher shouted. "You're surrounded by the military. Under the Martial Law decree, I'm ordering you to come out with your hands up."

Only the rumble of the engine could be heard in reply.

"Come out now or we will use force to enter."

The engine putted along without concern.

Crouching along the tree line the first sergeant moved and checked the last few windows. No one looked back at him. As he continued toward the backdoor the sound of the engine grew louder. Clearing a line of trees he spotted the generator under a carport-like structure. Next to it was a propane tank.

Looking at one of the soldiers he said, "Shut the propane off. Kill the generator. I'm going through the back." He pointed to Spencer. "Have you been in the building before?"

"Once, years ago."

"Congratulations, you're our expert. Is there cover inside that backdoor?"

"Ah, there was a bar at the back. You know, where they served alcohol, but I was young and didn't spend much time there. I think it was near the door."

Fletcher frowned at the lack of intel. "Okay, you follow me. Everyone else keep watch. If anyone shoots at us, shoot back." Then he sprinted to the back steps like an Olympian. As he put his weight on the first step it creaked and he cringed.

The generator, stuttered, backfired and died.

Silence reigned. Fletcher glanced at the rear windows, but saw no movement. Perhaps those inside didn't hear him over the generator. "You're surrounded by the military. Come out with your hands up. That's an order under the Martial Law decree."

Nothing moved.

He inched up the groaning steps toward the back door. Reaching the porch, he smelled death and worried that this wasn't the hideout of the gang, but more victims.

Behind him the steps creaked again. He glanced sideways as Spencer crept up behind. Pointing he indicated the private should cover the door. Fletcher turned the knob. *I wish I had a stun grenade.* He threw the door open and darted behind the bar.

Spencer followed.

All Fletcher could hear was his own breathing and flies buzzing. Slowly he looked over the top of the bar.

The smell of death filled his nostrils.

He scanned the room. An oversized couch was against one wall. A large rug filled the center of the room. Pictures of hunters with deer, elk and bear dotted the walls. Several stuffed game trophies hung on the far wall on either side of a large stone fireplace, but nothing threatened or even moved. "Have the soldiers out back come in this way," he said to Spencer. "Let's clear the building."

With his gun at the ready, Fletcher checked a door behind the bar. It led to a short hallway.

Spencer shouted from the porch, "Guys, in through this door on the double." He stepped back in.

"Check out this hall." Fletcher nodded his head in the direction.

The private coughed and spit and then disappeared through the door.

The first sergeant continued out around the bar, deeper into the room.

Four soldiers ran in, one after another. Several gagged and scrunched their faces as they entered.

Spencer joined them from the rooms behind the bar. "There's an office and storeroom. It looks like a lot of booze is gone. The safe is open and empty, but no people."

Fletcher directed the four who had entered to check out the east end of the building in pairs. "I'll stay with Spencer and clear out the west side." He then continued to the far end of the bar. As he moved away from the windows the room was darker. He thought about having someone restart the generator, but rejected it.

The smell of death and decay was stronger now. An alcove was off to his left. As his eyes adjusted to the darkness, Fletcher detected a shape.

Snapping his gun in that direction, the first sergeant shouted. "Hands up! Come into the light. Now!"

Nothing moved.

Spencer stood a few feet away with his weapon pointed into the darkness.

Carefully Fletcher paced forward. With each step his view became better. A man sat in the corner.

Chapter Two

Library Park, Hansen, Sunday, September 20th

Major Caden Westmore sat on the tailgate of the pickup as he read the last paragraph of the report. *It's coming and there's no way to stop it.* He slapped the folder down beside him and pressed his hand on the cover as if to hold the danger within. He was glad he was healthy and maintained the youthful assurance that he would remain so, but reason told him the future was uncertain. Millions would die in the coming months if the data in the report was correct. He wished Dr. Scott had waited to tell him until after the Harvest Festival.

The year had proved a hard one: Six cities obliterated by nuclear terrorism; the Chinese claimed they came to help, but it was a power and resource grab; amidst the turmoil the dollar collapsed; hunger and civil unrest grew. He spent much of the year battling gangs, terrorists and other Americans.

The cold winter gave way to a hungry spring, and then the long summer of work and waiting until the harvest. *Thank God it has been a good one.* There was hope that those who remained would survive the coming winter.

Music, smoke and the smell of barbeque drifted over the parking lot. His stomach growled. He inhaled deeply and smiled. *More than one fatted calf had been sacrificed for this celebration.*

Loudspeakers boomed the voices of children singing.

"Over the river and through the wood,

To Grandmother's house we go.

The horse knows the way

To carry the sleigh

Through white and drifted snow."

Like the smoke that wafted to and fro, his thoughts now floated back to the Nebraska Medical Center report. It contained many medical terms that he was unfamiliar with, but when she handed him the report, Dr. Scott summarized it in two words: "It's spreading."

Caden looked across the parking lot toward Library Park. He'd come to know many of the people who lived in and around the town of Hansen over the last year. Together they had struggled through fear and tragedy to this day of hope.

Dr. Scott was still nearby, talking with his sister-in-law, Sue, as both women admired the baby.

"You want a beer?" Lieutenant Brooks, his XO, shouted from a nearby stall as he held up a bottle of homemade brew.

"Maybe later," Caden replied.

Brooks took Lisa by the hand and the two disappeared into the crowd.

The grins that everyone displayed hid a multitude of tragedy. Brooks had been shot and nearly died. Caden's brother, Peter, did die from radiation sickness after the Seattle blast, leaving Sue a widow.

Zach and Vicki Brennon, the auburn-haired brother and sister, crossed the parking lot smiling and holding plates of food. Six months ago their mother tried to kill herself … did kill herself, but it was a slow, lingering death.

"Over the river and through the wood
To have a first-rate play.
Hear the bells ring,
Ting-a-ling-ling!
Hurrah for Thanksgiving Day!"

It was only September, but it was a day of thanksgiving. The crops were in and food stocks were the best they had been since the panic of the attacks. Caden struggled to smile.

Maria walked up and looked at the folder. "What's that?"

Not wanting to spread the depressing news from Dr. Scott sooner than he must, he answered, "Just a report Dr. Scott received on upcoming medical issues. That's all." True, but vague enough to hide the facts.

She sat beside him and, for a moment, he enjoyed her company in silence.

Maria leaned against him. "Remember when I said I didn't

want to marry you because I had to?"

Caden nodded wondering where this might go. "Yes. You said you wanted to know you didn't have to marry me…that you could walk away."

"Right…ah…well, I think this is that day."

"Are you saying you'll marry me or you're leaving?"

She shoved his shoulder. "Don't be silly. I'm saying, if you still want to, I'll set the date and we can get married."

Caden glanced at the folder beside him. Perhaps it was best to enjoy life to the fullest. Then if the pandemic predicted in the doctor's report did devastate the region, or some other tragedy occurred, he had lived life and there would be no regrets. He leaned over and kissed her. "When is our big day?"

The children's voices drifted toward them once again.

"Come to the feast,

There is room at the table,

Come let us meet in this place."

*   *   *

Sheriff's Office, Hansen, Sunday, September 20th

"Are you kidding me?" Sheriff Hoover snarled the words. "After everything else, now we have a pandemic?"

"It's a natural consequence." Dr. Scott sat in the chair beside Caden.

"Natural?" Hoover walked over to the window. "There's nothing natural about this."

"With hundreds of thousands of people still in FEMA camps, refugees living rough where they can, malnutrition, latrines and poor hygiene…we've already seen dysentery in the local camps and Hepatitis E in southern California and Arizona. The CDC reported new strains of influenza earlier this year. Under those conditions, it was only a matter of time before a pandemic strain of flu emerged."

Caden rubbed his chin. "What we really need to discuss is how to deal with it if it hits us."

Hoover looked at the doctor expectantly.

"It is spreading. It's only a matter of time before it gets here."

"I have lots of threats that are already here," Caden said. "Tell me what I need to do if this threat materializes."

The doctor sighed. "Normally the CDC would be working on a vaccine. But Atlanta…."

"Was nuked by the terrorists. I know." Thoughts of his then fiancée, Becky, shot though his mind. She had been outside of Atlanta when the attack came, but now she worked for Durant.

"Well, the University of Washington had a good medical center, but Seattle…." The doctor shook her head. "Well, you see the problem. The Nebraska Center is trying to organize a study—."

"What can *we* do?" Caden asked.

Dr. Scott shrugged. "Avoid contact with infected people, wash your hands with soap and water, avoid touching your eyes, nose and mouth."

"I've been hearing that advice for years," the sheriff said with a shake of his head. "It never stopped the flu before."

"And it won't stop this one," Dr. Scott said. "But you asked what we could do."

"Don't touch my nose?" Hoover frowned. "Wash my hands? That's what I can do?"

Caden rubbed his chin. Suddenly conscious of how close his hand was to his mouth he dropped it to his side.

"What about antibacterial soaps… will they help?" Hoover asked.

"Those soaps kill bacteria, but they don't kill viruses like the flu."

Caden snapped his fingers. "I've heard of medications that help when you have the flu. What about those?"

"Yeah. No dice. I've had the antiviral medications on my requisition list for months." She frowned at Caden. "You've never been able to get them from the supply depot."

"They may not have them the next time either, but I'll keep checking. Give me a list of those medicines. I'll see what I can do."

*   *   *

Westmore Farm, Rural Lewis County, Sunday, September 20th

Caden stepped into the house more concerned about the possible pandemic than he cared to admit.

"Good, you're here." Maria crossed the living room and kissed him. Still face-to-face she said, "Did you have your phone off?"

He fumbled in his pocket. "Ah…yes…I guess so."

She shook her head. "Are you trying to avoid finalizing the date?" She grinned.

"For the wedding? No…no, just busy."

His mother, Sarah, walked down the stairs. "Oh, good you're home. We've got to go."

"Go?" Caden asked. "Where?"

"The children are singing at the church."

Of course the children were singing. The Harvest Festival was going on all weekend and all over town. The newspaper printed the schedule of events, the radio station blared the news, and every church in the county probably had it front and center in their bulletins. This was to be the happiest time since before the first attack. He looked at Maria. It *was* the happiest time, but that joyfulness now mixed with the knowledge of what would come. Caden forced a smile. "Let's go."

His father stayed behind to work on the tractor, and keep watch on the farm, but the rest of the family surrounded the SUV.

Maria strapped Adam into their only car seat as his mother, sister Lisa, and Sue, with baby Peter, entered through other doors.

With his mind on gangs, lawlessness, war, hunger and a possible pandemic, Caden drove toward the church.

From the front passenger seat Maria looked over her shoulder at Sue. "We need to get another car seat."

"I know. I've been looking, but there haven't been any in the stores since the attack."

"I haven't seen any in the library market either," Sarah added.

"No." Maria shook her head. "Not since Caden got the one for Adam."

"Huh?" Caden glanced at Maria. "What?"

"Nothing, dear."

"I think families are holding on to them," Sue said, looking at baby Peter in her arms. "Who knows when you'll be able to buy something like that, or how much it will cost."

Caden drove on while the women chattered about many things. Minutes later he wound past groves of old apple trees, toward the white, wood-frame church that sat atop the hill.

Many families walked on the warm autumn day. Others rode horses and arrived in wagons. Someone installed hitching posts along one side of the parking lot, but several horses were on long leads tied to nearby trees.

Caden glanced at a field to the east of the church as he drove into the parking lot. The area was surrounded by a ten-foot chain-link fence. Inside were two large Quonset hut greenhouses, along with several backyard versions, and dozens of raised beds. All had been harvested and the earth tilled, ready for winter crops.

As usual, few cars were in the parking lot. Gasoline was expensive, and sometimes unavailable. Although Caden's position as area military commander provided greater access to fuel, it was limited. Still it allowed him to provide some transportation for his family. Caden turned the corner, cut diagonally across the lot, and parked in his favorite spot near the west side door of the church.

The Westmore clan strolled into the sanctuary as others flowed in filling it to capacity. After some announcements the children gathered on the platform.

"We plough the fields and scatter
the good seed on the land,
but it is fed and watered
by God's almighty hand."

Caden found it impossible to enjoy the music. Every cough, every sneeze, reminded him of the doctor's words. *It's coming and there's no way to stop it.*

Chapter Three

Rural Lewis County, Sunday, September 20th

"Hands up!" First Sergeant Fletcher stepped forward. His eyes fixed on the shadowy outline of a man in the dark corner of the alcove.

The shadow gave no response.

Private Spencer stepped backward.

"Did you hear me?" Fletcher inched closer. As his eyes adjusted to the darkness, Fletcher realized the man in the corner heard nothing. No life radiated from the open eyes. His mouth hung oddly slack, and his head leaned awkwardly against the wall. On the table before him were bottles of pills and booze. His right hand still clutched a glass resting on the table.

The first sergeant poked the lifeless man with the end of his M4.

The body fell rigid to the side.

"What happened here?"

Mouth agape, Private Spencer shook his head. "I have no idea."

The question had been rhetorical, but Spencer's answer reflected the first sergeant's own confusion. He grabbed his flashlight, but the beam quickly faded. "Dead, like this guy. Do you have one?" He asked waving his.

The young man approached with eyes fixed on the body. "Yeah. Here." He held out the light and advanced no farther.

Fletcher took it, knelt by the body, and poked and pulled at his shirt looking for fatal injuries.

Spencer stepped closer and placed a hand over his mouth and

nose. "I don't see any wounds," he mumbled. "It looks like he just died." He pointed to the bottles. "Did he commit suicide?"

Fletcher picked up the empty container. "It's some sort of medication, but I'm not sure what." He looked at the body. "I've heard the suicide rate is up, but why come all the way out here to kill yourself. He might have just been sick." Leaning a hand on the table, he stood.

A door swung open behind them, and both spun around, weapons ready.

"Just me, First Sergeant." Corporal Franklin said. "We found two bodies. No gunshot or stab wounds. They're just dead."

"How well did you check them?" Fletcher asked.

"We lifted one—with a broom, and checked under. No blood."

"How did they die? A suicide pact?" Spencer asked.

Fletcher doubted it, but had no answers. "Corporal, get the others from out in front. Station someone at every exit and on all four sides of the building. The rest of you come with me, we're going to finish searching this place. *And maybe find some answers.*

The first sergeant marched down the hallway with Spencer behind. The stench of death grew with each step. Coming to a door, Fletcher turned the knob and threw it open. He entered, leading with his rifle. A bed stood in the room without sheets, two chairs and a dusty dresser alongside it. Everything appeared undisturbed.

The room across the hall was much the same.

Farther along the smell of death hung heavy in the air.

Bursting into the third room, Fletcher nearly puked due to the stench that grated his nose and tongue.

Spencer stepped in, gagged, then stumbled back out, coughing and choking as he did.

The bodies of a man and woman lay side-by-side on the bed. A cloud of buzzing flies circled like a sky full of vultures. The nearest body had long dark hair and was curled into a fetal position. Her eyes were closed. It was hard to tell now, but she appeared to be in her late twenties.

On the far side of the bed was the bloated body of a man in his thirties or a little older. His bulging eyes stared into the heavens in fear.

The first sergeant paid them little attention.

A pistol lay ominously on the nightstand by the man. Not wanting weapons loose in the building, Fletcher grabbed it, withdrew the magazine and slipped them both in his pocket.

A dresser stood along the far wall. Jewelry and cash lay in piles on top. On either side rifles and shotguns leaned against the wall. Fletcher examined a Winchester .270 with scope, a .308, and a Remington 12 gauge.

After nearly a minute of gagging at the door, Spencer entered. "I don't know how you do it First Sergeant. This room reeks of decay, puke, and—."

"Do you have the serial numbers for the stolen weapons?"

The private retrieved a paper from his pocket then returned his hand to his mouth and nose.

After checking several guns Fletcher nodded. "These are stolen. We found the gang hideout." He looked at the two bodies on the bed. "But what happened to them?"

"I sure don't know First Sergeant, but could we figure it out somewhere else?"

Glad for the excuse to leave the room, Fletcher smiled. "Help me move these guns."

When the search was done, the soldiers assembled on the front porch of the lodge to assess the situation.

"Seven bodies total, all but one in bed, and not a mark on any of them. At least not that we found." Fletcher shook his head.

"How long would it take for bodies to stink like this?" a private asked.

"Five days maybe," the first sergeant guessed.

Spencer shook his head. "More like three or four in this weather, but the first body didn't smell nearly as much, indicating that he was probably the last to die."

Fletcher cast him a questioning glance.

"I like to read crime novels."

"This is like some horror movie," one private said.

Fletcher agreed, but said nothing. The sun had disappeared behind the trees. Long shadows covered much of the forest. He knew they didn't have enough fuel to make it back to Hansen. Since Deputy Morris hadn't yet returned with more gas, they would need to set up camp for the night. Fletcher explained it to the men. "So it looks like we'll spend the night here, by the dead bodies and the creepy lodge in the dark woods."

Spencer cast a nervous glance at the building. "If it's okay First Sergeant, I'll sleep outside."

"That smell isn't going away any time soon. I think we'll all be sleeping outside tonight," Fletcher said with a smile. "Corporal Franklin, have a couple of soldiers drive the Humvees back here. Set up a perimeter watch and have someone retrieve the MREs. The rest of you load up the bodies in bags and take them out back."

When the Humvees were parked on the north side of the building and a fire crackled in a nearby pit, two soldiers brought lawn chairs. Everyone not on sentry duty sat in a circle around the fire.

"Coffee would be nice right now," the corporal said as he finished his MRE.

"Or some marshmallows," a young man said staring at the fire.

"You know what I miss the most?" Private Spencer asked.

"Your mama?" Another replied.

Spencer tossed an empty cup at him. "Football. The season should have already started."

Nods and murmurs of agreement circled the fire.

"We should start a team. We could play against other units," one private said.

"What do you think First Sergeant?" The corporal asked.

"I think I'm going to get some sleep." Fletcher stood, grabbed his rifle, a tarp, and a sleeping bag, and strolled away looking for soft ground.

*   *   *

The first sergeant awoke with a start. Someone knelt beside him.

Private Arnold thrust a finger against his lips and whispered, "Movement in the woods."

A limb cracked.

Fletcher turned in that direction.

"It's probably a deer or elk," Arnold said softly, "but it's moving closer."

"You were right to wake me." He stood, grabbed his rifle from where it leaned against a nearby tree, and stared into the darkness.

A soft breeze blew against his face.

Another snap came from the woods.

That's too noisy to be a deer. Could it be an elk or maybe a bear?

They quietly roused the others.

Fletcher ordered most of the men back into the lodge, others guarded the Humvees. "You two, with me," Fletcher whispered. "One of you stay on my left, the other on my right. Move forward slow and easy. Let it come to us. Got it?"

They nodded.

"Okay, let's see if we can spot the noisemaker."

They moved through the forest, boots slipping over the ground, until coming upon a large fallen tree. There they waited using the trunk as cover.

Snap.

An owl hooted.

Silence.

Crack.

Certain whatever moved toward them did so deliberately, Fletcher clenched the rifle and stared into the darkness. *Could the noisemaker be human?*

He rested his M4 on the old trunk and pointed it at the sound. For nearly a minute they listened and waited.

From behind a tree a shadow moved, or was it his mind playing tricks. No. About thirty feet ahead something stirred.

"Freeze!" Fletcher shouted. "Put your hands up!"

"Don't shoot!"

The voice sounded familiar. Fletcher shined his flashlight in that direction. "Morris?" The beam quickly faded. "Is that you?"

"Yes! Hold your fire."

The two other soldiers shined their lights.

Fletcher stood. "Why in the name of heaven were you sneaking up on us?"

"I wasn't sneaking up on you. I was sneaking up on the lodge."

"Huh?" He shrugged. "Why?"

"Because, when I went to gas and report the crime at the other place, we thought there might be a murdering gang staying here."

The first sergeant laughed. "Okay. I guess that's a good reason. I'm glad we didn't shoot you."

"Yeah me too," the deputy said.

"The criminals are behind the lodge." Fletcher pointed.

"You captured them?"

"No."

Morris looked confused.

"Walk with me and I'll try to explain what we found."

*   *   *

Rural Lewis County, Monday, September 21th

The aroma of bacon and eggs roused Fletcher from a restless sleep.

Hearing the crackle of fire he rolled his head to the side. About forty feet away Deputy Morris and two soldiers cooked breakfast.

Morris banged a spatula against a pot. "Who's your favorite deputy?" he shouted. "I brought bacon and eggs back with me. Come and get it."

Fletcher's head pounded in protest as he sat up. Every joint ached like he had been in a fight—and lost. He dismissed it as the result of age and sleeping on the ground. The bacon smell curled up his nose and turned his stomach. Holding back a wave of nausea he gritted his teeth.

Nearby, Private Arnold rolled from his sleeping bag and stood with the speed and posture of an old man. Lurching forward two steps he fell to his hands and knees and vomited.

Fletcher struggled to focus his thoughts. Cold sweat beaded his brow. "What's happening?"

Chapter Four

Hansen Armory, Monday, September 21st

"The flu has been a part of my life, just as it has for everyone else. Some of the old and the very young die." Caden shrugged. "What can I do about it?"

"Read this." Dr. Scott waved the book in her hand.

"I'm busy. I don't have time to read a history book."

"Don't play the busy card with me. I've been busy, too! I've put you back together more than once." She slammed the book down on his desk and sighed. "Just read the chapter on the 1918 flu pandemic." She paused, and ended with a softer, "Please."

The friendlier tone cut through Caden's frustration. "Okay. I guess I owe you that much."

The doctor left, and Caden opened the book to the prescribed chapter.

"Both the specific strain of influenza and its origin are unknown. However, within months it had spread to almost every region of the Earth…highly contagious…Like all strains of influenza, it attacked the respiratory system, but one unusual characteristic of the 1918 virus was that it attacked and killed a disproportionate number of the young and healthy. Often death was due to a cytokine storm."

"Cytokine storm?" Caden stared out the window of his office trying to grasp what he had read. "What in the world is that?" he mumbled.

The early autumn sky shone clear and blue and the day warm, but the weather would soon turn rainy and cool. The flu often came in the fall and winter. Why? Was that ideal weather for the virus to spread? He returned to reading.

"More soldiers died of the flu in 1918 than died in battle…many doctors and nurses became infected further complicating the medical situation…imposed quarantines…closed schools, churches and theaters."

So many people worked hard over the last few months to restore the life and vitality of Hansen. Caden didn't want to imagine quarantine signs littering the town, or closed schools and churches.

"More than twenty-five percent of the U.S. population fell sick…funeral parlors were overwhelmed…bodies piled like logs…fathers dug graves for their children. The exact number of dead will never be known, but estimates range from 50 to 100 million."

Millions? He set the book back on the desk. The doctor had made her point. They needed a plan. In the past he had tried to understand all of the problems that Hansen faced, but for this one he would have to rely on Dr. Scott.

He leaned back in his chair. During this long year she'd been a tireless worker at the hospital and given good advice when asked, but she was not a leader and this pandemic would be more than a security issue. He rubbed his chin. For the community to pull through, it would need more than him…more than Dr. Scott. They would need a lot of people and things…medicine, food, fuel. Who would bury the bodies if the mortuaries were overwhelmed? Do we know for sure that it will get here? How much time will we have to prepare? Is Governor Monroe making plans? What about the Guard?

Caden found his phone under a dozen papers on his desk and called General Harwich. After fifteen minutes on hold, he made it through.

"Major Westmore, it's good to hear from you. Is everything well in Hansen?"

"Yes sir," Caden replied. "Now it is, but I'm hearing reports of the spread of a deadly influenza virus."

The General was silent for a moment. "We hoped to keep that news contained for a few more days."

"That may not be possible, sir."

General Harwich sighed. "I'll call some people in. Be at the Emergency Operations Center tomorrow at 0900."

After the call, Caden walked over to the XO's office still deep in thought. "I'm going to a meeting tomorrow in Olympia."

"This is short notice." Brooks frowned. "Is there a problem?"

Caden hadn't told him about the virus. Why bother when it might never be an issue, but now he thought he should. "Isn't there always a problem?"

Brooks shrugged.

"Well…right now I don't know much, but…." Caden told him what he knew. I'll brief you when I get back. Until then keep it quiet. There's no reason to start a panic." Then he remembered the list of medical supplies Dr. Scott gave him. "I'll do a supply run while I'm there. Add these medicines to the current requisition list and have a deuce and a half and a fueler ready first thing tomorrow."

Brooks nodded, looking over the list of medicines.

The morning sun turned the sky from black to dark blue as Caden drove to the armory the next morning. Other units would arrive early in Olympia and grab supplies before the meeting. Caden wanted to be first in line.

He retrieved the printed requisition list from the supply clerk and examined it while he headed toward the motor pool. Zach Brennon just finished fueling one of the trucks as Caden arrived. "Why aren't you in school?"

"Ah, because, sir, it's 6:30 in the morning."

Caden checked his watch. The young man was correct about the time. After the terror attacks and chaos, Zach and his sister, Vicki, caught fish along a stream near the Westmore farm to feed themselves and others. The young man dropped out of school to help find food, but insisted his sister keep going. Caden admired that about the young man and encouraged him to return. "How are you doing with your classes?"

"Good, sir. I should graduate in December."

Lieutenant Brooks entered the motor pool followed by a half-dozen soldiers.

Zach put on the gas cap and replaced the nozzle. "The trucks are fueled and ready, Lieutenant."

Brooks nodded then turned and saluted Caden. "Have a good trip, sir."

He returned the salute. "When is Fletcher supposed to report in?"

"Later this morning."

As the sun rose over the nearby trees, the convoy, with Caden's SUV, rumbled toward Olympia. Although gasoline had become more available, it was expensive. Few vehicles were on the roads during the day, and this early in the morning there were even less.

Over the summer they'd moved the supply depot closer to the port. Caden sighed as they arrived; a dozen trucks were already lined up at the gate. Two armed guards checked their identity and paperwork before allowing them in the compound surrounded by chain-link fence and topped with rolled razor wire. Several Humvees and deuce-and-a-half trucks stood idle before a line of warehouses in the parking lot.

Caden pointed to a nondescript office. "Park over there," he told the driver. Once inside, he handed the requisitions to a supply clerk.

"We've been seeing more requests for anti-viral medications." He shook his head. "If we still have them, they'll be at the medical warehouse on the end."

Caden jogged to the last building and checked with the supply officer.

"No, we haven't had these in nearly a month. Lots of meds are difficult to find."

"Thanks." Caden walked from the office. "Get everything you can," he said to the sergeant with the convoy, "and then return to Hansen. I'll head back on my own later." Caden drove his SUV to the Emergency Operations Center.

Moments later he parked outside the Wainwright building and checked his watch. "Almost 0900." He hurried into the building, found the elevator in use and sped up the stairs to the third floor.

Exiting the stairwell he stepped into a crowd milling about. Caden wondered if these people were there for his meeting or some other. Eventually he noticed a young second lieutenant giving directions and asked him.

"Yes, this is the right place. Follow me." He ushered him down the hall past the EOC. "We're merely running behind."

Hurry up and wait. Caden was familiar with the concept.

They arrived at a large metal door with a small blue label that read, 315. A keypad was on the wall beside the door. The lieutenant punched in the combination and the door buzzed.

Caden pushed it open and stepped into the entryway. Heavy double doors stood just five feet ahead. Going through into the conference room he recognized the design. Keypad at the entrance, secure metal doors, sturdy walls with no windows; he hadn't been here before, but he knew the design, this was a SCIF for classified briefings. "Sensitive Compartmented Information Facility—for the flu," he mumbled. This might be worse than he imagined.

Two tables sat in the form of a capital "T." Half of the chairs were already occupied. David Weston was seated at center top. They exchanged smiles and nods as Caden approached the tables. Several people he didn't recognize sat on either side of Weston.

Caden sat near the top of the leg of the "T." He recognized the colonel across from him, but struggled to recall his name. He had gray hair and a rough masculine face. In another time Caden would have envisioned him as a cowboy, but right now the cowboy was turned in his seat, talking to someone still standing. Caden couldn't see his nametag.

Then the roughrider turned and locked eyes on Caden. "Hello, I'm Colonel Hutchison, from the south central region."

"Nice to meet you, sir, I'm Major Westmore."

"Yes, I see." He pointed to the nametag. "Our areas of control border each other. My headquarters is in Yakima."

Caden nodded. He knew the names and regions for all the area commanders. "I believe you have the largest area."

"In square miles, yes. Most of it is farmland, hills and scrub brush." A grin spread on the colonel's face. "I read your Operation Lexington report. Your fight with the terrorists made for some good reading."

Caden smiled and for the next few minutes they discussed shared problems.

When more than a dozen people entered the room with several civilians, Weston stood. "If everyone would please be seated we will get this briefing started."

Voices subsided and everyone took a seat along the tables.

"The governor asked you all here today so we could advise you of a growing public health issue."

"Public health?" With a puzzled look, Colonel Hutchison shook his head . "I'm dealing with gangs, hunger and lawlessness—."

Weston held up his hand in a stop motion. "And soon you'll be dealing with this. Three weeks ago reports came from the Chinese zone of a deadly form of influenza the refugees call the Kern flu."

"What! Why haven't we heard about this before?" a major down the table from Caden asked.

"We requested the media hold off reporting on it for a few days while we determined the extent of the threat, attempted to contain the outbreak, and prepared useful information."

"Has it been contained?"

"No." Weston sighed deeply. "It's spreading."

The room burst into questions and talk.

When Weston regained control of the room he said, "That was the layman's brief. I'll let Dr. Eaton from the Washington state Department of Health give you the medical details."

As Weston sat an older man on his right stood. "My aide will pass out packets with the latest information and procedures for the medical personnel in your areas."

He gestured to a young woman burdened with a stack of blue folders in her arms.

"Please pass these down," she said and plopped a stack on the table next to Caden.

Caden did so as the doctor continued.

"We are dealing with a new, highly pathogenic, subtype of the H1N1 influenza virus," Eaton continued. "It is airborne and once infected the onset of symptoms is swift. For the first few hours it can appear as a bad cold, but this is soon followed by extreme fatigue, fever, headache, vomiting…."

Caden's gut tightened into a knot. Images of sick and dying people filled his mind. He shook his head and turned his attention back to the doctor.

"…this harsh cough can tear abdominal muscles and cause internal bleeding. All of this leads to a cytokine storm that can kill in less than 48 hours."

"What is that…ah, cytokine storm?" Caden asked.

The doctor rubbed his chin. "It's an overreaction of the immune system, a kind of last-ditch effort to destroy the virus, but which often kills the patient. We saw this with the Spanish Flu of

1918."

"That epidemic killed millions." A man on Caden's right said.

"Actually it was a pandemic, worldwide, and killed 50 to 100 million people," Dr. Eaton corrected.

"And the Kern flu is like that one?" Colonel Hutchison asked.

"Yes."

Again the room erupted into a myriad of questions and discussions.

Weston stood and held up his hands. "We'll get nowhere with this uproar. Everyone settle down and let the doctor continue."

Dr. Eaton massaged his forehead as attention in the room turned to him. "I heard several of you ask if there is a vaccine. No, but several medical centers are working on it."

"When do you expect the illness to arrive in this area?" a woman asked.

The doctor shrugged. "We don't know. The Chinese aren't saying anything officially, but refugees have reported widespread infection in the Oakland and Ventura area. Texas military units serving in New Mexico have reported cases. In areas we control, we've seen infections in Medford, Oregon and Carson City, Nevada. We've implemented containment procedures at all ports and airports under our control, but if an infected person drives, or flies, before they show symptoms, we could see cases in this area in the next few days."

Chapter Five

Olympia, Tuesday, September 22nd

For a moment the room was silent, and then exploded with rapid fire questions.

"When will there be a vaccine?"

Dr. Eaton shook his head. "We don't know."

"How fast does it spread?"

"The R-Naught Factor is between three and five."

"What?"

"It spreads quickly."

"What percentage dies?"

"That varies greatly depending on age, health and access to treatment." Eaton sighed. "We estimate a twenty to twenty-five percent mortality rate."

"When are you going to tell the public?"

"We've been waiting until we knew what we were dealing with. There will be a press conference later today. I suspect everyone will know about Kern flu by tomorrow."

The room fell into a hush, followed by another flurry of queries. Over the next hour the pace of questions slowed. Eventually Weston stood and glanced at his watch. "Well, I guess that concludes the medical briefing. We'll break for lunch in a moment, but first let me give you the good news and the bad. The good news is we're paying for lunch." Weston slid a stack of lunch coupons to Caden. "Take one and pass them down please." Returning his gaze to the table at large, he continued. "The bad news is lunch is at the cafeteria in this building."

Laughter arose from several around the table.

"It's not that bad," someone said.

"It's not that good either," someone else said.

General Harwich stood. "We started late and that briefing was longer than planned. Be back here at 1300 and we'll continue with security issues and the current tactical and strategic military situation.

Caden checked his watch, it was just after noon. Despite the grumbles of his stomach, he looked through the blue packet of information while most others left. As he stood, an aide projected the current sitrep map of the country on the screen.

Colorado had been a battle ground when he had last seen such a map. Now most of the United States west of the Mississippi and north of Oklahoma and New Mexico was colored blue, Constitutionalist states loyal to the new congress. Most of the U.S. east of the Mississippi was still colored red, controlled by Durant's forces.

The southwest, under Chinese control, was colored maroon. Northern Utah, Texas, eastern New Mexico, and Oklahoma were green. Orange dots with tails arcing away marked the contaminated zones.

Then he noticed a new state. The northern third of California, under Constitutionalist control, was labeled, "Jefferson."

Caden's stomach grumbled. Mulling all he had seen and heard that morning, he sought lunch. He knew about the cafeteria, but not its location. Following signs and slow moving individuals, he descended to the first floor where he followed his nose to the far corner of the building.

The smells were enticing, but the prices outrageous. A burger and fries was nearly twenty dollars or three dollars NSC.

For the first time he actually read what was on the chit. Printed in red letters was, "Limit $4.00 NSC."

"What is 'NSC?'" a lieutenant ahead of him asked the woman behind the counter.

"New silver certificate or coin. The Denver mint has started issuing them, but I've only seen them on the lunch coupons. I'm told they'll replace the old money."

Caden had heard rumors, but never seen any of this new money. He looked at the coupon in his hand. Inflation was rampant making meat a luxury. The thought of someone else paying for the beef he would eat was too good to pass up. With a smile he handed over the voucher. "I'll have the burger and fries."

He walked away from the counter still smiling.

Colonel Hutchison motioned for Caden to join him and another officer.

Hutchison gestured toward the other man, when he sat. "Major Westmore this is Major Dowrick. He doesn't talk much, says that's because he works in intelligence, but he listens well and asks good questions."

Dowrick was about ten years older with thinning hair.

Caden smiled. "Hello."

"Hello. I do work in intelligence but the reason he thinks I don't talk much is because, around him, I don't get much of a chance to speak."

Again Caden smiled and then bit into his burger. As he and Hutchison talked about families, schools and duty stations, Dowrick listened and said little.

Caden smiled as he again bit into the juicy char-broiled burger and let it roll along his tongue. More than once he tried to answer a question with meat, lettuce and tomato still in his mouth.

"So..." the colonel asked, "What do you think about this talk of pandemic?"

Caden shook his head. "I'd rather be fighting people...something physical that I can see."

Hutchison laughed. "I agree." He slapped his hand on the table. "That's exactly it. We were trained to fight the enemy, not manage a quarantine of the sick and dying." The colonel finished his burger and pushed the plate aside. "The doctors need to do their job—find a vaccine. That way we can get on with taking the battle to Durant. Fighting, that's what we do."

Caden wanted the same things, a vaccine and Durant defeated, but he sensed their motivations were different. He stuffed the last bite of burger in his mouth, chewed, swallowed, and excused himself.

Reaching the briefing room, he walked in on a dozen officers staring, pointing, and gesturing at the screen. Caden sat at the table and joined others in scrutinizing the sitrep map.

A few feet away, Weston wrote while staring at the table. When the last few entered the room, he stood. "Welcome back. If everyone would be seated, we'll get started. General Harwich will conduct most of the meeting this afternoon, but I thought I'd provide a brief political update.

"After Durant's forces were defeated in the Denver area the new congress of the United States established the temporary capital there. They've met there now for three months. Acting President Durant remains in New York City surrounded by civilian and military loyalists. Effectively, he is now a dictator in control of much of the east."

Images of Becky flashed through Caden's mind. Once they had loved each other and planned to marry, but events, both good and evil, pulled them apart. He thought of her now with fondness, but without love or regret. It was Maria that now came to mind when he thought of love, home, and family.

Weston was still talking. "...have two centers of government that aren't cooperating, or even communicating, with each other." He shrugged. "Durant has only been in control for eight months and has spent most of that time dealing with the same issues we have struggled with, food shortages and economic depression. Also, he needs to consolidate power and authority. I believe he is still working on that and will fight when he is ready.

"I'm sure you know all that." Weston waved his hand dismissively. "However, what might be news to many in this room is that this morning the congress asked the Speaker of the House, John Harper, to fill in as president until the November election."

"Harper? Isn't he like ninety years old?" a young lieutenant asked.

Weston grinned. "Seventy-eight and he only has to do the job until the election on November 8th."

Laughter sprinkled the room.

"I know my boss, Governor Monroe, hasn't been campaigning," Weston continued, "but he is still the only candidate running."

"Can he win against Durant?" someone asked.

"Yes. I believe he will win, either at the ballot box or, if no one gets enough electoral votes, in the new congress."

Caden stared at the sitrep map and did some fast math. If Monroe won every state under Constitutionalist control it would not provide enough electoral votes to win. Even with Utah and Texas it wouldn't be enough.

Durant wasn't running, still insisting the election be postponed. However, by Caden's estimate, the states under Durant's government wouldn't provide the votes he needed to win the election either.

China, with its control of California and most of the southwest, could play kingmaker, but the new congress would never recognize an election they supervised. According to the Constitution, the House of Representatives would decide if no candidate received a majority of electoral votes. Durant would never allow that.

When Caden's attention returned to the briefing, General Harwich was standing beside the sitrep map using a laser pointer as he talked.

"Both sides are reluctant to engage in full-scale conflict, but it is coming. New America divisions, loyal to Durant, are stationed around Minneapolis, Des Moines, Jefferson City, Little Rock and in central Louisiana.

"The Constitutionalist forces are centered near Bismarck, Pierre, Omaha and Topeka. The Texans control both banks of the Sabine River and western Arkansas."

"Are the Texans fighting with us?"

"Texas fights for Texas, but their governor says they will fight with us when the war comes."

"*When* the war comes, not *if* it comes?" Someone asked.

Harwich nodded. "I suspect the Kern flu will incapacitate both sides for the next few months. Millions may die this winter, but either a vaccine will be found or spring will come and the flu will wane. Then the fight will begin."

"So you think there will be full-scale war?" asked a young second lieutenant.

"I think you can count on this," General Harwich said slowly. "If you're in uniform, and survive the Kern flu, you're going to be fighting a war."

Chapter Six

Hansen, Tuesday, September 22nd

Zach strolled down the quiet streets of Hansen toward the address DeLynn had given him the evening before. She had been secretive about it, just saying that her father wanted to talk with him. Mr. Hollister's attitude had changed since the shootout at the ranger cabin, but he wasn't looking forward to "a talk" from the father of his girlfriend. And why did he want to meet in downtown Hansen?

All Zach could see were empty shelves when he looked in the windows of the hardware store. A line stood outside a grocery market several blocks ahead. Something special, like meat or fresh fruit, must have arrived.

When he turned the corner, Zach realized the meeting was at the Lewis Hotel. That just added to the mystery. The seven-story, brownstone building had once been the grandest hotel in the county. It was empty now, and had been for several years. Zach knew about a backdoor that looked locked, but wasn't. Many times he had pulled on the broken latch to open that rear door. This was one of the places he got things that he needed for trade.

He pulled on the front door and, for the first time, it swung open. The inside was dark. He scanned the lobby wondering if DeLynn might be there, and noticed a well-dressed woman sitting on a crate in the shadows. As he approached, he recognized Mrs. Hollister. On numerous occasions DeLynn had spoken of her mother's problems. As the world spiraled out of control, she had sunk in a whirlpool of despair. Like his own mother's depression, Zach struggled to understand her despondency. She had a loving husband and daughter and enough to eat. Why was she so sad? Busy with the task of surviving, he had rarely seen or asked about her lately. "Hi, Mrs. Hollister. DeLynn asked me to meet your husband here."

An expressionless face stared at him.

"Do you know where he is?"

She pointed. "Standing in the middle of the street." Her head slumped.

Zach walked out a side door and found Kent Hollister staring at the building from the middle of the road. Since there was no traffic, Zach joined him.

"I bought it." Kent said with a smile.

"You did?" The outside of the building was drab, but Zach knew the inside looked like a construction project, or perhaps a destruction one. "You think this place is a good investment?"

"Yes." The older man nodded. "The building is sound and it is near the only place in town with a thriving economy—the library park market. I needed a location near it and this was the cheapest building for sale that met the criteria."

Yeah and I know why it was so cheap. It's a wreck.

"I can tell from your face that you think it's a bad idea, but that shop there on the corner of the hotel was once a bakery. I'm going to fix it up. I know where I can buy flour. Bread and pastries will sell well." He pointed to another corner. "Fifty years ago that was a general store. It can be again. We can make this block bustle."

"Okay, sir, I'll help you fix it up." *It's your money.*

"I could use your help with the renovations, but what I would like is for you and Vicki to manage the general store. Our family will work the bakery." He spread his arms and gestured toward the two sides of the building that faced major streets. "Eventually, I want stores in all those spaces on the first floor."

"I've never run a store."

"Actually you did."

Zach cast him a confused glance. "No, I'm pretty sure I didn't."

"The fish stand at the park was a small store. You're a very resourceful young man with an innate ability to find food and other things you need."

"Vicki and I fished and I hunted, then we sold what we didn't eat. That wasn't really a store."

"Basically it was. The general store will just have a bigger inventory and there will be a couple more zeros to carry when adding up the balance."

Actually I didn't carry a balance. I ate it.

"In college I worked in a warehouse and an accounting department." Kent Hollister patted him on the back. "I'll teach you what you need to know."

"It would be nice to have an inside shop, but how much do you want for it?"

"Rent you mean?" He shook his head and silently stared at his feet for several moments and then looked Zach in the eye. "I've come to a better understanding of a few things this year. You saved my daughter's life and in this new and crazy world, you are better equipped to provide for and protect DeLynn than either her mother or me. Given the same circumstances, I would have starved—and my family as well. We'll be building a future together."

Zach felt his face flush. "I won't have a lot of time until I graduate."

"I want you to graduate and go on to college. Any future son-in-law of mine should be well educated."

"Ah…son-in-law?" Zach's face burned hot.

Kent smiled broadly. "You two seem to love each other very much, but I do want you both to wait, mature, and get some education."

Finally able to speak, Zach said, "I also want to keep working at the armory."

"I would prefer that you not join the military. I don't want my daughter to be a young widow."

"Huh?" Zach was certain he would soon burst into embarrassed flame.

Kent grinned again and then the two talked of business for several more minutes before Zach jogged on to school. First period was government class and since it was required for graduation he tried to concentrate, but he spent more time smiling at DeLynn, on his left, than at the notes Mr. Hammond wrote on the board.

DeLynn cast him a disapproving glance and nodded toward the board.

He reluctantly turned his attention to the front of the class only to be surprised by big red letters, 'Test on Friday.'

Zach sighed.

"Mr. Brennon," the teacher asked, "am I boring you?"

Why did Mr. Hammond always address students so formally. "Ah…no…well, how useful is this class when the government is falling apart?"

"How can you understand what you've lost, if you never knew what you had?"

Another student asked, "Why do you always answer questions with questions?"

"I don't." Hammond smiled. "Do I?"

Laughter dotted the classroom.

"Will there be a war?" Delynn asked.

A boy near the front turned back around. "Your boyfriend fought in the first battle. It's already started."

The guy seated behind Zach patted him on the back. A few others chanted his name. Zach stared at the desk in humiliated silence wishing he could forget his cowardly performance as he hid behind a tree and cried that day.

After school he walked toward the armory with his head hung down, kicking stones as he went. He knew he wasn't a coward. DeLynn thought he was the bravest man alive. He smiled and kicked another stone. She was brave too, and he liked that about her. Perhaps they had both been brave when they needed to be on that awful day at the cabin.

With one of his demons tucked away, at least for the moment, Zach smiled and jogged on toward his job at the armory.

*   *   *

Along the freeway south of Olympia, Tuesday, September 22nd

"So that's my future," Caden mumbled as he drove toward Hansen. He glanced at the blue folder on the passenger seat. "Die of the Kern flu or live and fight in another war." Life in the army had taught him that death would come when it did. He would not live in fear of its arrival. Still, he had danced around death's snare many times. How long could he do that before it caught him? Someday, the sun would rise and he would not feel its warmth. Life would go on, but without him.

He shook his head. Dwelling in despair and sadness was no way to live either. Life was a gift and, as long as he possessed it, he would enjoy it.

These drives up to Olympia and back always leave me too much time to think. Caden took a deep breath and tried to refocus his thoughts on something less existential. For several minutes his vehicle rolled along the empty asphalt.

Heading south out of Olympia, he reached a section of freeway lined with forest. In this area, with only an occasional home visible, he could imagine the terror attacks never took place. However, when he reached the top of a hill the freeway swept out for nearly a mile before him. He looked at his watch. Five vehicles were on the road, a fuel truck, an eighteen-wheeler, two Humvees, and the SUV he was driving, and it was rush hour.

Caden sighed and tried not to think of the growing threats to the nation and around the world. Even the problems of Hansen appeared daunting. With the collapse of the dollar, the cost of food had risen beyond the means of many people. Farming was once again a dominate trade, but many still went hungry. Law enforcement and security had been his main focus. He knew how thin the veneer of civilization was and, with war and a pandemic looming, he worried that the last of it would soon be worn away.

Governor Monroe always seemed composed. How did he manage the many issues he faced without being overwhelmed? Managing a platoon in combat seemed easier. Caden knew he was going to need help.

Rummaging in his pocket, he retrieved his phone and speed dialed Lieutenant Brooks. When he answered, Caden said, "I want to call a meeting of the LEPC—."

"The what?"

"Local Emergency Planning Committee, or something like that."

"Oh. You haven't been to one of their meetings for months."

"True, but I'm going to need their help."

"How bad is it?"

"Bad, but it isn't here yet, so we still have time. I'll brief you when I get back and you should probably come to the meeting."

"Ah, before you hang up, First Sergeant Fletcher didn't report in this morning."

"When did he last check in and what did he say?"

"Deputy Morris radioed in yesterday. He reported the location of another murder and said the patrol would be checking out a hunting lodge that might be the gang hideout. Morris said he was picking up supplies and returning to the patrol. That's the last we've heard."

"Do we have anyone else in the area?"

"No, but I have a squad ready. They can refuel with the Morton police and be at the lodge by dawn."

"Do it." Tomorrow was shaping up to be a long day. He wondered whom to call next and decided on Dr. Scott. She knew everyone on the LEPC and this was a medical situation. Poking around on his phone he looked for her number.

The blare of a horn startled him.

Caden looked up. His SUV straddled two lanes.

A huge truck filled his rearview mirror.

He swerved to the fast lane.

The eighteen-wheeler rumbled past.

Caden's heart pounded in his chest. One other vehicle traveled along the road and, because of him, they had almost collided. Right then he decided that for any future military travel, he would have a driver so he could work in transit.

Recalling the rest area a couple of miles ahead, he dropped the phone on the passenger seat and continued south. The sun was still above the trees when he pulled off the freeway into what had been a park-like rest area. However, now the grass was overgrown and about a dozen cars were stripped and pushed to the rear where shadows and trees obscured the view. Near the forest, in a makeshift camp, a few people lingered beside a fire.

Caden reached for his phone when a familiar sense kicked in. Perhaps it was paranoia, or some lingering post-traumatic stress, but he didn't feel safe. He pulled out of the rest area and drove down the highway several hundred yards.

Normally pulling to the shoulder of a freeway would be stressful but, on this empty road, he felt safe. Retrieving his phone he called Dr. Scott. "We need to talk."

"I just got out of surgery. Can it wait?"

"Not really. It's about the pandemic."

"Did you get the medicines?"

"No."

"Oh." A heavy sigh floated through the phone.

"But we still need a plan. I'm told the Kern flu could be here in days."

"Yes, it could, but I don't know what we can do other than quarantine the sick and treat symptoms."

"And pray for a vaccine," Caden added. "Let's get everyone together tomorrow morning at an LEPC meeting and see if we can come up with some plans."

Two small boys trotted out of the woods ahead of him and walked toward the car.

"Okay," the doctor replied

One of the boys pressed his face against the driver-side window.

Caden smiled at him. Into the phone he said, "Would you call them? I'm still traveling back and don't have all the numbers in my phone."

"Why me?"

"Because you're on the committee and they all know you."

The doctor sighed again. "Sure, a plan would be good."

"Great." When he ended the call Caden dropped the phone on top of the blue folder next to him.

The boys lingered in the roadway. Caden rolled down his window. "Hello. Where are you from?"

The shorter boy pointed back toward the rest area.

"We're hungry," the other said. "Do you have food?"

"My mom is sick, can you help?"

"No," Caden shook his head. "I don't have any food."

Disappointment spread across their faces.

He recalled Henry, the farmer stuck with his family in the parking lot by the freeway and wondered if he might be able to do some good, but he was concerned about the sick woman. "What's wrong with your mother?"

The boys shrugged. Their eyes darted beyond Caden's car and then, without saying a word, they backed away.

Caden stiffened. His senses went on high alert. He fingered his pistol.

The passenger door flew open.

A pistol pointed at his head. "Get out!"

Chapter Seven

Along the freeway south of Olympia, Tuesday, September 22nd

The two boys ran toward the trees.

Caught with a pistol in the face, his weapon holstered, and still seated, Caden opened the driver-side door, lifted his arms, and slid out of the car.

Another man jogged up clutching a baton-style flashlight. "Stupid kids! Why didn't they say he was in uniform? Does he have a gun? We could have been killed."

"Calm down, Jake," the armed man replied. "They did what we asked them to do. I'll keep an eye on him, get Carol into his car and let's go."

"He's got a gun in that holster. Let's get it before we go."

Caden's eyes shifted between the two. "You can have the car." He turned slightly, moving the holster out of view and making himself a narrower target for the armed man. "But I'm keeping the gun."

"Like hell you are," Jake said and took a step closer.

The situation brought back memories of Fort Rucker and the two men who tried to rob him. Maria had been the unexpected savior there. He hoped to get home to her tonight, and he just might if Jake stepped closer. Caden visualized using the angry man as cover while he pulled out his pistol.

"Shut up Jake!" the man with the pistol barked. "Get your sister."

With anger still in his eyes the man turned and jogged into the forest.

"I'm sorry about Jake. My wife, Carol, is really sick. I've got to get her to the hospital."

"Did you run out of gas?"

Pistol Man nodded.

"Why didn't you ask for help?"

"We've tried waving down cars." He shook his head. "You're the first to stop since we arrived. I couldn't risk you saying no."

A minute later Jake returned, struggling to carry a limp woman. As he neared, he stumbled and the woman slid toward the pavement.

Instinctively, Caden darted over, thrust his arms under her, and lifted. "I'll help you get her in the car." As they moved toward the SUV, Caden wondered if the woman had Kern flu. "How long has she been sick?"

"Two days," Pistol Man said.

"Where were you driving from?"

"Why do you ask so many questions?" Jake asked as he opened the rear of the car.

Caden pushed the hatch up, and they laid her gently in the vehicle.

Another woman approached, followed by the two boys. They stared at Caden as he and the men walked to the car.

Turning his gaze back to the man with the gun, Caden said, "The keys are in the ignition."

"Sorry," Pistol Man said with a nod.

Caden and Pistol Man stood staring at each other as Jake sat in the driver's seat and the others climbed in the back.

"Please just stand there while I get in the car." Pistol Man said backing away. "I don't want to hurt anyone. I just need to get help for my wife."

"There's a hospital in Hansen," Caden said. "Two exits south. You'll see the signs."

Pistol Man nodded. "Thanks." He jumped into the passenger seat and the car sped away.

Caden took in a deep draft of air and let it out slowly. *Well, if I had to be robbed, helping a woman get to the hospital is a good reason.* He fumbled in his pockets looking for his phone and then recalled dropping it on the passenger seat. He sighed, wished he was wearing more comfortable shoes, and then ambled south along an empty freeway.

*   *   *

Hansen Armory, Tuesday, September 22nd

Lieutenant Brooks hung up the phone with Maria and leaned back in his chair. Something weird was going on. First Fletcher didn't report in and now Caden didn't answer his phone. Deep in thought he stood and walked into the conference room. Staring at the map he located the position of each squad from memory. Second Squad was on the road to Morton, so he should know something about the two units with Fletcher by early tomorrow.

"Where is Caden," he asked himself, "and why isn't he answering his phone?"

"What's that sir?" the sergeant in the next room asked.

"Nothing. Just thinking out loud."

He shoved a finger against the map. Third Squad there, near Longview. Fourth Squad was northwest of town near Alder Lake. Only the new Sixth Squad remained. If he sent them out looking for Caden that would leave ten soldiers at the armory. *That's barely enough to stop a band of renegade middle-schoolers, but not enough to handle an emergency.* "This is why I get paid the big, nearly worthless, bucks," he muttered. "Sergeant!"

A chair scraped against the floor and a head appeared in the door. "Yes, sir?"

"I need Sixth Squad saddled up and ready for a search mission, ASAP."

*   *   *

Along the freeway south of Olympia, Tuesday, September 22nd

As Caden walked south along the freeway shoulder he stared up at the starry sky. On his thirteenth Christmas he had received a telescope. For several years, on clear nights such as this he would walk into the meadow carrying the heavy scope and stare at planets, stars and moons. Tonight only a sliver of the moon shined. Orion, the Big Dipper, and the North Star were easy to spot. Venus was low in the sky, often hidden by trees.

Continuing toward Hansen, he sighed. The heavens would always have an allure for him, but for the foreseeable future more earthly matters demanded his attention. Moreover, he hadn't seen the telescope in ages. It probably had fallen victim to a yard sale years ago.

Still he stared at the black vista above him as he plodded

along. In the distance an engine rumbled. It was heading north so he paid it little attention.

A minute later, headlights appeared. They were coming toward him, heading north. Only a grassy median divided the north and south lanes. Caden considered jogging to the other side and flagging down the oncoming vehicle, but thought it unlikely anyone would stop for a pedestrian walking in the middle of a dark, and lonely highway. Besides, if he continued south at his current rapid pace he would be home in plenty of time for breakfast. He smiled at his own wry humor.

As the rumble neared he realized it was a Humvee. He thrust his arm out in a futile gesture to stop the vehicle, but it zoomed past.

Of course. I'm late and not answering my phone. They're looking for me.

Listening for traffic, Caden doggedly trekked south.

Nearly an hour later he crested one of the last hills before the turn off to Hansen. As he continued down the south slope the rumble of an engine disturbed the quiet. He stopped and listened. The vehicle drove south.

Hoping it was the Humvee on the return loop of its search, he stood directly on the white line of the shoulder, stared into the darkness, and waited.

Two bright lights crested the hill.

He reached out his arm.

A semi-tractor-trailer rushed out of the darkness blaring its horn.

Caden lept backwards and, after it blew by, made sure all his fingers were still there. He decided not to wave at anymore headlights. He turned and continued his trek south.

As he climbed the next hill, the sound of a vehicle growled from the north. This time he stayed well onto the shoulder.

Standing near the crest of one hill, he had a good view as the vehicle topped the slope to the north. It wasn't a truck, but in the darkness he couldn't be certain, so he stood and stared at the headlights. As it neared he relaxed.

The Humvee slowed.

Zach jumped out as it rolled to a stop. He saluted and with a broad grin said, "We've been looking for you, sir. What happened?"

"I was carjacked. Take me to the hospital."

Zach's eyes widened.

"I'm fine," Caden said. "I think that's where we'll find my car." He took the passenger seat, Zach sat in back, as the driver, private Nelson, slipped the vehicle into gear.

Grasping the microphone, Caden used the Humvee radio to report in. "Thanks for sending out the cavalry," he said to Brooks on the other end. "I'm going to stop by the hospital and see if my car is there. Have a deputy meet us."

"Roger, and I'll let Maria know you're fine."

Caden nodded at the mic. "Thanks. Tell her I'll be home soon. Out." He looked at the two with him in the Humvee. Both were young. Still only seventeen, Zach remained a civilian, but he had learned so much, and been so useful, his age was sometimes forgotten. Less than a year older, Nelson was one of the newest soldiers. "I'm glad you guys found me."

They both smiled.

They pulled into the hospital parking lot minutes later and Caden spotted the SUV near the emergency entrance.

"I don't expect trouble from them, but at least one is armed. Be alert. Block the car from leaving," Caden ordered.

With the Humvee in position everyone jumped out with weapons ready, but the vehicle was empty. The car was unlocked. Caden's phone was on the passenger side floor and turned off. The blue folder, with information about the Kern Flu, sat open on the back seat. Several pages had been removed and lay scattered. Nothing else appeared disturbed.

Caden dropped the phone into his pocket and shut the car door as the deputy pulled into the parking lot.

"Deputy Wallace, right?" Caden asked as the man stepped from his car.

"That's right, sir."

Caden briefed him and everyone hurried into the hospital.

Twenty patients crowded the small emergency room. Doctors and nurses moved through with gurneys and wheelchairs. It took several moments for Caden to spot the beleaguered admissions clerk. "About three hours ago two men brought in a very sick woman."

"We don't get many healthy ones in the emergency room."

"One of the men was probably very agitated and—"

"Oh that guy." She pointed. "Down that hall. Room 125."

They strode away with Caden in the lead. It didn't take long to find Pistol Man. He sat just outside the designated room with his head resting in his hands.

"I'll need those keys back now, and your pistol." Caden held out his hand. "How is your wife?"

With his gaze still to the floor, he held up the keys. "She's dead."

Chapter Eight

Hansen General Hospital, Tuesday, September 22nd

Dr. Scott came out of the room. "Were you the soldier he mentioned? Did you come in close contact with Mrs. Colson?"

"Mrs. Colson? Ah…his wife?" Caden gestured toward the despondent man in the chair. "I helped lay her in the back of my SUV."

Dr. Scott's eyes narrowed. "That was her."

Caden was certain he knew the answer, but asked anyway. "Why did you want to know if I came in close contact with her?"

"We need to do the rapid diagnostic test and get a viral swab of your mouth before—"

Movement in the doorway caught Caden attention. He locked eyes on Jake.

"You knew this would happen!" Jake shouted. "That's why you were asking questions—you knew!" From his pocket he pulled a pistol and pointed it at Caden.

He heard those behind him move. Certain that weapons were now aimed at Jake by those behind him Caden thought it best to deescalate the situation. He spread his hands wide.

Jake shouted and waved the weapon wildly. "But you didn't say anything or try to help—did you?"

As Jake ranted, Caden raised one arm in a stop gesture. "We're just learning about the Kern flu."

Deputy Wallace stepped beside Caden. "Sir, put the gun down."

The husband stood. "Jake, when did you get my gun? Give it back. The lady doctor explained all that. There was nothing anyone could do."

"I don't believe that, Hugh. They could have helped. Should have helped, but nobody did anything." Again he pointed the pistol at Caden. "He knew!" He waved the gun at Dr. Scott. "She's known about it for days."

"What could they have done?" Hugh asked.

The muscles tightened in Jake's neck.

Caden had seen men snap and do crazy things under stress. Jake showed all the signs of nearing such a break. Eyes wide, veins bulging, it would come soon.

Jake gestured to Caden using the barrel of the gun as a pointer. "Soldier guy had all that information in the car, but did he help us? Did anyone help us?"

A familiar woman stepped around the corner, followed closely by a nurse and the two children from the rest area. The nurse's eyes grew wide. Clutching the two boys, she hurried back around the corner.

"Jake, don't be silly," the healthy woman from the rest area said. "Put the gun down."

"We lost our little Jessica … our home." He shook his head as tears flowed. Wiping his face he locked eyes on Caden. "We've been running … starving … and … dying. We could all die and no one would care." He seemed to stare beyond those before him. Pointing the barrel at Caden, his aim steadied. "Jessica was so little."

Caden thought of Maria.

The woman stepped between Caden and Jake. "She was my daughter too. It's been an awful year and we both hurt inside, but don't harm someone because of our pain."

Jake smiled. "I love you." He moved the gun towards his head.

"No," the woman screamed.

Caden and Wallace lunged. Together they slammed Jake up against the wall.

"Don't hurt him," the woman shouted.

The deputy grabbed at the gun.

It fired.

Dust and bits of ceiling tile rained down.

Everything stopped.

Tracing the probable route of the bullet with his eye, Caden decided the three of them were unharmed.

The deputy wrenched the gun from Jake's hand.

"We're dying anyway. One at a time. Just let me. No one cares." Tears rolled down Jake's face as Wallace cuffed and patted him down.

"I care, Jake," the woman said. "We'll get through this."

Pulling on Jake's arm, the deputy stepped away.

"Oh no. None of you are going anywhere," Dr. Scott held up her palm. "We'll need to do tests, but I'm nearly certain Mrs. Colson died of the Kern Flu."

Jake shook his head and sobbed.

"I'm sorry," Caden said, "but what can be done?"

"For her?" The doctor stepped to a phone. "Nothing. But you and the two families are the first guests in our recently-expanded, and upgraded, isolation unit."

"Isolation?" Caden shook his head. "No. A lot's going on. I can't."

"I could quote federal law, but I'll make it simple. You have been exposed. Do you really want to infect the soldiers under your command, your mom, dad, Maria, and the babies at your house?"

Caden drew in a deep breath. "So, show me this isolation unit you're so proud of."

"Deputy, please bring Jake and the others." Dr. Scott picked up the phone and tapped three numbers. "Announce a code omega. Clear the halls between emergency and the isolation ward. Tell the duty nurse to use contagious disease protocols, and bring the two boys to the ward, but she must not enter. Just send the two boys in. I'll phone her if needed." The doctor grabbed a box and handed out face masks. "Wear these."

"What's the Kern flu?" Zach asked.

Nelson shrugged.

"Are we supposed to go with you too?" Zach pointed to Ryan Nelson beside him.

"No." Dr. Scott shook her head. "Not unless you were in close physical contact with the family or Caden."

"Like in a Humvee?" Zach asked.

Dr. Scott's body wilted. "Yes. Come with us. Let's play it safe." She handed each of them a mask.

Ryan frowned at Zach.

"What do you want us to do with the rifles?" Zach looked at Caden and then the doctor.

"Bring them with you." The doctor said with a sigh. "You've been breathing all over them. You may have to decontaminate them."

"Zach." Nelson shook his head. "Why do you ask so many questions?"

He cast a wry smile. "Just curious, I guess."

The group paused in front of a deserted nurse's station. Just beyond were heavy wooden doors. The sign above read, "Isolation Ward."

The two boys came running down. One latched on to Hugh, the other to the one woman in the group.

"Spread out," Dr. Scott said with a wave of the arm. "In a moment I'll start bringing you in one or two at a time." She sat at the nurse's station and typed on the keyboard.

Zach looked through the window into the dark ward, but saw nothing but his own reflection. Tufts of his auburn hair stood in every direction. He tried to pat them down as he pressed his face to a window. "The place looks deserted."

"It is," Dr. Scott said, still typing.

Private Nelson looked around. "What, no pretty nurses?"

Dr. Scott scowled. "I don't want to expose them to Kern flu or high levels of teenage testosterone. You're stuck with me."

Caden leaned against the wall and thought of all the places he would rather be. The list grew long as the doctor brought the others in. Jake, his wife, and the deputy went in together, but most entered one at a time.

Finally, only Caden remained. He thought Dr. Scott forgot him until the wooden door swung open and she motioned for him to enter. Together they passed through two sets of doors and into a large open space with a nurse's station at the center. Along the wall were rooms numbered one to eight.

"So, this is where I'll be spending the night." Caden looked about.

"At least tonight and probably most of tomorrow, but not much more…if we're lucky."

It really hasn't been a lucky kind of a day for me. "This place looks new."

"We remodeled and expanded the old isolation ward." The

doctor pointed to the ceiling. "The ventilation system for this ward is separate from the rest of the hospital."

Caden frowned. "There aren't any windows."

"Windows leak. We're trying to restrict the flow of air. That's why I had the maintenance staff construct those heavy doors you came through. I wanted sliding ones where only one would open at a time, but there were limits on what we could do." She sighed. "I hope the wing lives up to its name."

Glancing to her left the doctor said, "I have the deputy in room eight. I'll put you in room one. That way you're both close to the door and can help with security if things get crazy."

"Things like Jake?"

"Perhaps. He's handcuffed to the bed in room three. I've read of instances of delirium, so any of you could become a problem."

"This day just keeps getting better."

"I don't think you're infected. Hope not anyway."

"Yeah." Caden nodded. "Me too."

The doctor pointed. "Zach is in that room. Ryan is in the next." She continued pointing to each chamber and specifying the occupant. "But, I don't want you, or any of the others, out of your rooms tonight. Let's keep the spread of infection to a minimum."

Caden reviewed the assignments in his head. "Are you staying with us tonight?"

"Yes. I've had more exposure than you."

"All the rooms are taken. Where are you going to sleep?"

"I'm probably not." She shook her head. "Get settled in your room. Change into the hospital gown and I'll be around to check on you and perform a rapid diagnostic test, get a swab, and a blood sample in a few minutes."

Caden watched as the doctor collected vials, tubing, and needles. *Just keeps getting better.* As soon as he was in the room he spotted the pajama-like clothing he was supposed to wear. Being sick and needles were his top two reasons to avoid hospitals. Third would have to be the flimsy hospital gowns. After changing, Caden retrieved his phone and called Brooks.

"Did you find the carjackers?"

"Yes, and they might have the Kern flu." Caden explained the situation. "When is the LEPC meeting?"

"Six tomorrow evening."

"I think Dr. Scott will let me out of jail by then. Unless you hear otherwise, keep the meeting as scheduled."

After he ended the call, Caden started to dial Maria, but stopped. He hadn't told her about the Kern flu and now there was a remote possibility that he was infected. He considered telling her he would be working overnight. Duty required it sometimes. Caden shook his head. She had said more than once that she wanted the truth.

With a sigh he phoned.

"Where are you? Are you okay?" Maria nearly shouted into the phone.

"I'm at the hospital—but I'm fine." He then explained everything that happened up to finding Hugh Colson and meeting Doctor Scott at the hospital. "The doctor thinks I *might* have been exposed to the Kern flu." He left out most details of the carjacking, Jake waving a gun at him, and that he was in an isolation ward. When she didn't ask about the Kern flu he continued. "This flu thing is spreading across—"

"I know about the pandemic."

"Who told you?"

"Lisa. David told her. She assumed I knew all about it. Imagine her surprise when I hadn't heard a word."

I'll need to review security procedures with my XO. "I was going to tell you about it."

"When?"

"Probably tonight…or tomorrow." Caden spent several minutes smoothing things over with Maria and then, since he was stuck in a hospital room with nothing to do, they had one of their longest conversations in months.

The door squeaked and Dr. Scott entered carrying a tray with vials and needles.

Caden sighed. "I've got to go, the doctor is here. I'll call you in the morning. I should know a lot more then."

After getting a swab and a vial of blood Dr. Scott attached adhesive tabs to Caden's chest that led back to a heart monitor and then clipped a sensor over one of his fingers.

"I'll never get any sleep with all these wires and beeps."

As she turned to leave Dr. Scott said, "Try."

*　　　*　　　*

Hansen General Hospital, Wednesday, September 23rd

The sound of footsteps caused Caden to wake. His eyes opened to Dr. Scott holding a syringe. "Need more blood?"

"No. I think you're fine. I'll take another swab to be sure, though."

"What time is it?"

"Nine o'clock."

"In the morning? Why did you let me sleep so late?"

"You weren't going anywhere so, why wake you up before I needed to?"

Caden grunted. There was logic to the doctor's reasoning.

When she finished he stood looking for his phone.

"Sit. I need to take your blood pressure, pulse, and temperature."

Caden obeyed. "I feel fine. When can I get out of here?"

The doctor wrapped the blood pressure cuff around his arm. "If you remain asymptomatic perhaps we can release you later this evening. It depends."

"On what?"

"The samples from last night and this morning."

"Like I said, I feel fine."

"Right now you're fine," Dr Scott said flatly. "So were the two little boys, but now they're dead."

Chapter Nine

Hansen General Hospital, Wednesday, September 23rd

Caden knew the woman had died, but news of the children came as a shock. "The two boys? Dead? When?"

Dr. Scott wilted into a nearby chair. "About four hours ago."

The words were not spoken callously, but flatly, without emotion. Looking at the doctor, Caden thought she appeared older than her years. Sadness lurked in her eyes. Of course she was tired. Death had visited the isolation ward twice in one night.

Perhaps she had seen too much death this last year or perhaps the gloom was because death had come for children. Perhaps both were the cause. "What about the others, Hugh, Jake and his wife?"

"Hugh Coulson is critical and Debra, Jake's wife, is in serious condition. We'll know in the next few hours if they're going to make it."

"What about Jake?"

"He isn't showing symptoms, but I had to sedate him during the night." She shook her head. "If he wakes up and discovers the others are dead...I just don't know what he'll do."

"What about Zach and Private Nelson?"

"They're not displaying any symptoms. If you continue to be asymptomatic, I may release them in a few hours."

"Why is their release contingent upon me being okay?"

"Because they would have been infected by you. If you don't get sick they almost certainly won't. I'll let you know soon, but right now I'm waiting on the results from the tests last night."

"How long does it take you to get a test done?"

"We flew the samples to the lab at Washington State University. They'll call us when they have the results."

"You can't do a flu test here?"

"Sure I can," the doctor's voice sounded irritated. "But I need to know if it's the Kern variant."

Caden leaned back onto the bed. "Okay, I'll wait and hope for everyone's sake I stay healthy." Alone in his room he stared at the walls and wondered who the Grim Reaper would visit next. Wanting to change the direction of his thoughts, he grabbed his phone and called Maria. He wasn't going to get caught holding back information from her again.

*   *   *

Brennon Trailer Home, Wednesday, September 23rd

"Hi," Vicki said as she greeted her brother at the door of the rusty single-wide trailer they called home. "Where have you been?"

Since he wasn't infected, Zach decided not to tell his sister, or DeLynn about his stay in the hospital isolation unit. "Armory stuff. They needed me."

"You missed school. I was worried."

"Sorry. I couldn't help it."

"Well, I guess you heard the rainstorm last night and this morning." She stepped away from the door.

He hadn't, but he had seen the puddles on the way home. "What about it?" He stepped into the trailer. Seeing buckets, towels on the floor, and a mop he stopped. "What happened?"

Vicki grasped the mop. "The roof leaks."

His sister had pushed much of the furniture out of the living room, which was a soggy mess, into the kitchen. The threadbare carpet was soaked. Parts of the home were dry, but the whole place smelled like a wet dog.

"Are you hungry?"

"Yeah, sure."

"Good I'll make us some dinner." She handed him the mop. "And you can wipe up for a while."

Zach took the handle. A huge weight descended upon him. With his father a fading memory and his mother now gone, sometimes he felt more like a parent to Vicki, instead of an older brother. However, right then he really wanted a parent with answers because the rainy season would soon be upon them and he had no idea how to repair a trailer roof or where to find the money to get it done.

*   *   *

On the road to Morton, Wednesday, September 23rd

As if waking from a long and restless sleep, Fletcher blinked open his eyes. He squinted at the sun coming through a window. He was in a Humvee moving along smooth terrain, probably a road, but why? His body protested every move with aches and stiffness. Struggling, he sat up.

"Oh, good, you're alive." Private Spencer said from the front passenger seat.

"Alive." The words came with difficulty from Fletcher's dry throat. On the seat before him was a body bag. He struggled to organize thoughts and memories.

"How is Harper?"

The private laid beside him in the rear of the Humvee. Fletcher clutched his wrist. Harper's skin was clammy and the pulse weak. "Barely alive. What happened?"

"I have no idea. Monday a lot of the guys woke up ill. We started getting people into the vehicles, to head out, but more got sick until there weren't enough healthy people to move them. Then they started dying. For more than a day most everyone was sick or treating the sick. This morning there were enough people well enough to load the sick. So, we left Grim Reaper lodge."

"Grim Reaper lodge?"

"That's what we call the place."

Feeling light headed, Fletcher slumped. "What day is it?"

"Wednesday."

"Are we on the way to the armory?"

"No," Spencer replied. "We're going to Morton hospital."

Fletcher nodded, even though no one could see him. "How many dead?"

"Six. Harper, and Deputy Morris are really sick. We weren't sure about you. I'm glad you're getting better."

Fletcher wasn't sure he was feeling better, just conscious, but he wasn't going to argue the point either.

"Report in?" he asked, breathing deeply for each word.

"We're still out of range. We'll get everyone to the hospital and then report."

"Okay," Fletcher mumbled. Gradually sleep overtook him.

It seemed like only moments later that shouts and hurried movement intruded upon his fitful slumber. As Fletcher opened his eyes, two soldiers hoisted Private Harper onto a gurney. Another two pulled the body bag from the seat in front of him.

Private Spencer offered Fletcher a hand as he slid himself out the rear of the vehicle. He waved off the assistance. Fletcher leaned against the Humvee, stood for a moment, and then shuffled toward the emergency room door.

Fletcher rested a hand on Private Spencer's shoulder. "Is Corporal Franklin okay?"

"Yes, First Sergeant. He was in the other Humvee. We were the only two that didn't get sick."

"Find him. Tell him to make sure everyone gets seen and treated."

Inside the building Fletcher found the men's room and leaned over a sink. He splashed water on the gaunt face that greeted him in the mirror and then, cupping his hands under the flow, drank.

Fletcher felt, and now knew, he looked like a zombie. People starred at him as he dragged himself across the busy emergency room. He knew he looked like the living dead, but several others in the waiting area looked as bad. *Whatever this sickness is, could it already be here, ahead of us?*

He plopped down in a corner seat. His stomach grumbled, but he didn't feel hungry. All he wanted to do was sleep until he fully recovered—or died.

Private Spencer sat beside him. "All the sick have been brought in. Corporal Franklin is staying with them. I really think you should see a doctor."

"No, I'll live."

"They cleared a ward and moved Harper and Deputy Morris in. They seemed to have some idea of what is going on."

"I'm sure they do." Fletcher slid low in the chair. "When did we last report in?"

Spencer shrugged.

Fletcher cursed, fumbled for his phone, and called the armory.

*   *   *

Hansen General Hospital, Wednesday, September 23rd

Caden awoke. He never slept during the day, but without a television, radio, or even a clock, it was easy to drift off. Wires and a tube still clung to him, but he stood and looked for his phone. *Why do I leave it in random places?* Such mysteries were unfathomable.

The door creaked and Dr. Scott entered.

"Do you need more of my blood?"

"No. Your tests came back negative." She wrote on a notepad. "You'll be fine."

Caden knew he was fine, but it felt good to hear it from the doctor. "Can I go?"

Without looking up from her writing, she nodded.

"What about everyone...?" He wasn't sure how to phrase the question.

"Hugh Coulson died early this morning. Debra is recovering. Jake is asymptomatic, but still sedated. I want his wife awake and healthy when he wakes."

"What about Zach and Private Nelson?"

"I released them two hours ago."

"Why did you keep me longer?"

"Because you were resting, and even sleeping, two things you need to stay healthy."

He shook his head, found his pants, and slipped them on under the hospital gown.

Dr. Scott walked toward the door.

"Where is my phone?" Caden mumbled.

The doctor stopped, turned to a locked cabinet, and pulled out the phone. Handing it to Caden she said, "Wouldn't want you to lose this."

"Huh?" Had the doctor purposely hid his phone? She walked from the room before he could ask. After dressing, he turned the device on and called the armory. When Brooks answered Caden asked, "Any word from the First Sergeant?"

"No, but Second Squad should be near their last reported position, so we should know something soon. Are you okay?"

Caden walked from the room. "Yeah, I'll be fine." Dr. Scott sat at the nurse's station in an otherwise dark and empty isolation ward. They nodded at each other as Caden left. As he pushed through the heavy wooden doors, he asked, "What's the situation at the … hang on I have another call coming in … its First Sergeant Fletcher."

He poked at his phone and accidently disconnected Brooks. "First Sergeant, where are you."

The words came slowly. "The Morton hospital."

"What happened? Are you okay?"

"Most of us have been sick, sir. Some have died."

Caden's heart pounded. He stopped, and returned to the isolation ward. Dr. Scott still sat at the nurse's station typing on a computer, but looked up as he entered. "I think we have a problem."

Chapter Ten

Hansen General Hospital, Wednesday, September 23rd

"First Sergeant, I have you on speaker phone with Dr. Scott. Describe what happened."

"Hello...ah sir, this is Private Spencer. The first sergeant handed me the phone. He's kinda sick...."

Caden frowned and looked at the doctor.

Her brow furrowed as she hastily grabbed a pen and notepad.

"...he was out of it for most of the last couple of days, but he is getting better...slowly. We went to this hunting lodge in the mountains southeast of Morton. We were tracking a gang that used the place as a hideout. By the time we arrived they were all dead. There were no marks on them, they all just died."

The doctor leaned over the phone. "I need to know when the onset of this illness occurred and about the symptoms."

"For the gang, I don't know, but for us...it was like crazy quick."

She slumped over her pad, rubbed her forehead, and wrote. "Did you come in contact with the bodies?"

"Yes, we put them in body bags and brought them to the back of the lodge. That night people went to bed feeling fine and woke up really sick. There was vomiting, chills, high fevers. Some were talking nuts."

Dr. Scott sighed. "I need to speak with the Chief Physician."

"Ahhhh, who?"

Caden realized the young man had no idea who, or what, that might be. He stepped closer to the phone. "Private, who's the senior healthy soldier?"

"Corporal Franklin, sir."

The corporal was just a few years older, but should be able to find the man in charge with a little help from Dr. Scott. "Stay on the phone and find him, ASAP," Caden ordered.

"Yes, sir."

While they waited, Caden asked, "Private Spencer, have you been in contact with Second Squad? They were looking for you."

"No, sir, we didn't see them. I hope they don't know the location of the place. We started calling it Grim Reaper Lodge."

Caden scowled. He didn't know if Second Squad knew the location or not, but he needed to find out. He hurried around the counter of the nurse's station and grabbed the phone receiver. He tried to dial Brooks, but when he tapped the fifth number he heard beeping, like a rapid busy signal. Caden growled at the phone.

Turning from her conversation, the doctor said, "Dial nine first."

On Caden's next attempt Brooks came on the line. "Is Second Squad going to the hunting lodge?"

"Yes, Deputy Philip reported it as the last location of Fletcher's men. Are they okay?"

Caden quickly explained what he knew about the deadly lodge. "We need to stop Second Squad."

"They're at the edge of radio range now, but I'll try to contact them."

When Caden again sat across from Dr. Scott, her eyes were fixed on the phone between them. Her brow furrowed as she spoke with intensity. "No, no, no. You've got to isolate all of them. Didn't you read the material from Omaha? This is a very contagious and infectious mutation."

"Yes, I understand that, but this is a small facility," the voice from the phone said. "We don't have an isolation ward and the entire building is on one ventilation system."

Scott threw her arms up and shouted into the phone. "Is there another building somewhere? These patients can't have any contact with unprotected individuals."

"Another building? We're barely keeping the lights on in this one."

"Now you listen to me. Those patients are viral bombs. Either you contain them or you'll see the devastation spread through the town in about twelve hours. What is your decision?"

No sound came from the phone for several moments. "We'll stabilize the two that are sick in a separate building ... somewhere ... but then can we transfer them to your facility?"

"Yes, but I doubt they will live long enough for that." Dr. Scott looked up at Caden and mouthed, "Sorry."

The voice from the phone continued. "What about the recovering patients and those that remain asymptomatic?"

"If they are stable you can transfer them to this facility." Dr. Scott said with a sigh. "What is your plan for the bodies already there?"

"We'll take final samples and then cremate them."

After several more minutes of planning and arguing with her counterpart at the Morton hospital, Dr. Scott hung up, leaned back, closed her eyes, and sank into the chair.

Caden retrieved his phone and, as the seconds ticked by, wondered if she had fallen asleep.

Finally, without opening her eyes, she said, "Well, the news about Kern flu is out now."

"How are my soldiers doing?"

"Six of your men are dead. One is in critical condition. The other five are either asymptomatic or, like Fletcher, recovering. The deputy is also critical." She rubbed her chin. "I think we're going to have a major outbreak in Morton, and probably a lot of scared people will head toward Hansen."

"The LEPC meeting is still scheduled for this evening."

The doctor cupped her chin in a hand. "Whatever we decide to do, it will need to be in place by morning."

*   *   *

Hollister Hotel, Hansen, Wednesday, September 23rd

"I want to show you something, Karen." Kent led his wife into the freight elevator and pulled the handle on the rusty grate. "We just got this one repaired, so I thought I'd show you the penthouse."

Silently, she sat on a stool in the corner of the lift.

"The structure of this old hotel is sound. The roof is good. It's the interior that needs work."

Karen nodded absently.

"The bakery and general store will provide us with cash and many of the things we need." He pushed the button for the top floor.

"People will be looking for inexpensive places to live. Over time we can remodel the hotel rooms into small apartments."

"I'm tired. When can we go home?"

He shook his head. "I'm hoping you'll like the penthouse."

"Why do you care what I think about this dump? I don't want to see it. Let's go home."

Kent sighed. "We talked about this. I didn't have much choice. The house had a mortgage. Our savings are gone. My retirement plan is devastated. The little money I earned from legal work just wasn't enough—"

She stared at him with a confused look.

"No one needs a contract or corporate lawyer now."

"What are you saying, Kent?"

"I sold the house and used the money and our investments to pay cash for the hotel. This is our home now."

Her eyes widened. "No!" She jumped to her feet. "I said no!"

"We were going to lose our home and end up on the street. At least we have a place to live."

"You sold my home…for this dump?" She slammed her fists into his chest and face as she shouted, "No…no…no."

As the elevator door slid open, she slid to the floor in tears.

*　　　*　　　*

Hansen Armory, Wednesday, September 23rd

The moment Caden walked into the office and spotted Brooks, he asked, "Has there been any word from Second Squad?"

"No, sir" The XO shook his head. "They must be out of range…."

"What can we do to stop them before they reach the lodge?"

"Zach and Private Nelson showed up not long after you called. I sent them to find the squad."

Caden started to object, but Brooks continued. "I told them not to approach the lodge. Just get in radio range, contact them, and report back."

Three hours later they still had no word from either Second Squad or the pair sent to search for them. Together the two drove to the county administrative building. Caden parked the car and stepped out. Brooks, still talking on the phone, exited from the passenger seat. "Okay. Phone me if you receive any word."

The XO walked around the car and joined Caden. "I'll leave

my phone on," Brooks said. "If the armory receives any word about Second Squad, they'll phone me."

"Good." Caden nodded vaguely. It was nearly six in the evening and almost thirty cars were in the lot. As they strode toward the building, someone stepped into the sunlight. Caden squinted and realized it was the doctor. "What are you doing lurking in the shadows?"

"I peeked in a few minutes ago. There's a storm brewing. They're arguing and debating." She smiled. "It seemed a good idea to go in with someone armed."

"The sheriff isn't here?" Caden said, looking about.

"Not yet."

As he reached into his pocket for his phone, Hoover crossed the street.

The sheriff hurried over to the others. "I've been getting calls from the media, concerned citizens, and elected officials all afternoon. What happened with your soldiers out on the east end of the county?"

Caden gritted his teeth, realizing he hadn't told Hoover about the situation at the lodge or the arrival of the survivors in Morton. "I've got some bad news." Hurriedly he briefed the sheriff on both the Morton and Second Squad situations.

"Deputy Philip lives out on the east end of the county." The sheriff's countenance slumped. "I just thought he was out of radio range with your people. It never occurred to me that they might be sick and dying."

"I'm really sorry. I'll do better about communicating with you in the future."

"I know you didn't mean to leave me out of the loop." Hoover frowned "This flu situation is getting out of hand."

"Yes it is." Caden sighed. "We better head in."

The three formed up behind Caden, and proceeded to the meeting.

All eyes seemed to focus on the four as they entered the room. Conversations died.

A "U" shaped table filled the center of a conference room. All the elected local officials that Caden could recall were present, but there were several seated at the table whom didn't recognize. Dozens of residents sat, and stood, along the walls, many wearing dust masks.

Caden doubted they were effective against viruses. Two deputies and a Hansen police officer mingled among the standing crowd.

Near the bottom of the "U" someone had saved seats for Caden, Hoover, and Dr. Scott. Brooks found a chair and pulled it near his boss.

A man stood. "My name's Bob Clark. I'm the mayor of Morton. Can one of you tell me about this Kern flu and what's going to happen?"

Hoover looked at Caden.

Caden looked at Dr. Scott.

The doctor sighed, and then began a brief that Caden had heard several times.

When the doctor paused, someone standing along the wall shouted. "Why haven't we heard of this before?"

"Yeah, why have you been censoring the news?" another man shouted.

Caden stood. "I only found out about it four days ago. We thought—."

"Four days!" a woman cried. "Why didn't you say something?"

"It does no good just to say a deadly pandemic is coming," Caden shouted over the many voices. "We need a plan for when the flu arrives. That's why we called this meeting." From every side of the room all he could see were angry shouting faces. He leaned over to the doctor and whispered, "This meeting may have been a bad idea."

"I agree, but perhaps for a different reason. We have people from Morton and other nearby towns all crammed together. This is an ideal way to spread the virus."

"What's the government going to do?" a woman asked.

"The sickness is already in Morton!" someone shouted.

Chapter Eleven

Hansen, Wednesday, September 23rd

A county commissioner pounded his gavel.

"Tonight, panic is our problem," Caden muttered.

As the bangs of the gavel fought for attention with angry shouts, Caden leaned over to Brooks. "Head back to the armory and use the radio to advise all the squads about the Kern flu. Just a short message saying it is highly contagious and deadly. Oh, have them use MOPP level four around civilians or units that have been exposed."

"That may cause panic."

"Look around. Panic is already here."

Brooks nodded and left.

When order had been restored, Dr. Scott suggested a quarantine of Hansen.

Morton's mayor stood, eyes wide, face red. "What about my people?" he shouted.

A man with a scruffy beard stepped to the table. "When we blockaded Hansen after the Seattle blast it only stopped cars and refugees along the road. The people of Morton are more familiar with the area. They'll find ways into the community across the smaller streams and through the forest."

"If someone is sick we've got to keep them out," another shouted.

The pastor from Caden's church waved his arm in frustration. As he spoke, Caden struggled to recall his name, Pastor Hugh, Humphrey, or maybe Higgins.

"The citizens of Morton are our neighbors. How can we deny them refuge?"

"The pandemic is coming," Scruffy Beard shouted. "We need to keep Hansen safe."

"The people of this entire county elected me as their sheriff." Hoover shook his head. "Even when we blockaded the town after the Seattle attack, we allowed locals in. I can't keep them out now at gunpoint."

One of the Hansen city councilors coughed, then turned and leaned toward Caden. "If we don't blockade the city, Kern flu will sweep across this town like wildfire."

*   *   *

On the highway toward Morton, Wednesday, September 23rd

Zach dropped the school book on his lap. "Slow down."

"There's no traffic, and besides, Lieutenant Brooks said to hurry." Nelson steered the Humvee through a curve, barely staying on the road. "Why did you come to the armory this afternoon? No one expected you."

"The trailer where I live is falling apart. I thought maybe my sister and I could move into the armory."

Nelson took the next curve down the middle of the road. "Do you hate your sister?"

Zach tightened his seat belt. "No. Why?"

"What is she, sixteen now?"

"In a few months. Where is this going?"

"You'd move your sister in with a hundred guys our age?"

With a skeptical glance Zach stated, "There are women at the armory."

"Yeah, but they're either married, six years old, or combat trained."

Zach laughed. "Well it is either closer to you, or wet and cold in the trailer."

"Tough choice." Nelson slowed to ten miles above the speed limit. "Try and contact Second Squad on the radio."

The two continued east along the highway for over an hour. Zach made repeated attempts to contact the unit, but heard only static.

Zach opened the textbook.

Taking his eyes off the road, Nelson looked at the book. "Are you doing homework?"

"Eyes on the road. Yes, I want to graduate in December—if

your driving doesn't get me killed first."

As they approached Morton, Zach reached for the radio to try again.

A horn blared.

Tires screeched.

Zach slammed into his shoulder harness. A sedan loaded with people passed inches from the Humvee. He turned to Nelson in exasperation and declared, "Slow down and stay on your side of the road."

"Yeah. Okay."

Just outside of Morton they encountered dozens of cars packed with people and belongings headed west toward Hansen.

Zach stared at the last of a line of cars as it hurried by. "This is weird."

"Brooks said there was a really contagious illness at this lodge."

"So?"

"Well what if it is like those movies."

"What? You mean the people of Morton are fleeing ahead of brain-eating zombies?"

"You have any better ideas?"

"Yeah, just about anything else." Zach grabbed the microphone. "Second Squad this is Search One, approaching Morton. Come in, please."

Static crackled.

"All stations on this net, this is Armory Command." The voice of Lieutenant Brooks came from the radio with urgency. "A highly contagious and deadly virus is spreading in this area. All units are ordered to use MOPP level four when around civilians or exposed units."

Zach looked to his comrade. "They want us covered from head-to-foot and use a gas mask? What kind of virus is this?"

"Search One, this is First Sergeant Fletcher. Do you read me?"

"First Sergeant this is Search One. Read you five-by-five."

"Search One, Morton has been exposed to the virus. Do not enter the town."

Nelson's eyes were wide.

Zach shook his head. "Maybe brain-eating zombies isn't so

crazy."

"I was kidding about the zombie apocalypse."

Into the radio Zach asked. "We're looking for Second Squad. They were sent to find you. Have you had any contact with them? Over."

"Negative. First and Fifth Squads are in Morton and have been exposed to the virus. Repeat, do not enter Morton. The position of Second Squad is unknown. Over."

"Roger, out."

Nelson shook his head. "The first sergeant goes out with two squads and gets exposed to some virus. Second Squad is sent out to find them and disappears and now we're sent to find them." Nelson slowed to less than the speed limit.

As the Humvee came around a curve, the sun barely peeked over the nearby hills. The town of Morton stood in the shadowed valley below.

Nelson continued at a cautious pace.

Zach leaned back, glad the highway passed just south of the town. People hurried about the streets both in cars and on foot. "Why are you going so slow?"

The private sped up as the two left Morton behind.

Zach took a deep breath.

For over an hour Nelson drove higher into the hills in a southwest direction. The sun dropped below the horizon, stars appeared, and soon the Humvee headlights provided the only effective illumination.

Using the radio, Zach tried again and again to contact Second Squad. All that came back was random static. He reached down to adjust the squelch.

"…this is Second…."

Zach grabbed the mic. "Second Squad, this is Search One. Do not approach the lodge. The occupants are dead. They were exposed to a deadly virus. Do not approach the lodge. Do you read me? Over."

Static was the only response. Zach turned to Nelson. "I don't think they heard any of my warning. We should hurry."

In their Humvee, the two climbed up narrow twisting roads higher into the Cascade Mountains.

As the Humvee lumbered up a large hill, Zach turned to

Nelson. "Pull over when we get to the top. I think that might be a good spot to contact Second Squad."

Nelson soon stopped.

"This isn't the crest," Zach said with a shake of the head.

"How do you know?" Nelson cast him an incredulous gaze.

"I've been here before. This area is great for hunting elk." He stepped from the vehicle and jogged forward several yards. Waving to Nelson in the driver's seat, he shouted, "Follow me." Zach directed the vehicle across a gravel wide spot in the road. When he returned to the Humvee and opened the door he said, "When we leave, make sure you back up."

"I could see the ledge in the headlights."

"Ledge? We're near the cliff."

"What?"

"I remember it from a hunting trip. This spot overlooks the whole river valley. If we can't reach them from here they must not be listening." Grasping the mic, Zach called out, "Second Squad this is Search One. Come in please."

"Search One this is Second Squad. I have you fivers. Over."

"Second Squad, what is your current location?"

"We're parked just off the main road below the lodge."

"You are ordered not to proceed to the lodge. Do you copy? Over."

"Roger. We copy."

"They're two miles from the lodge." Zach smiled. "That's about four miles from us."

"Tell them to standby and we'll brief them when we arrive."

"No." Zach shook his head. "We were told not to approach. Contact them, and report back, that was all."

Nelson started the Humvee. "We were told not to approach the lodge, but you said they were miles from it. It'll be easier to brief them in person."

"What about reporting back?"

"I think we're out of range, but sure, go ahead and try." Nelson backed the Humvee away from the cliff.

Zach called the armory several times without success as the Humvee dipped into the valley. Minutes later the two pulled their Humvee next to three others.

Zach spotted only four soldiers as he stepped from the

vehicle.

"Where is everyone?" Nelson asked the question on Zach's mind.

"Some are searching the woods. Others are at the lodge."

"I told you guys not to go there."

"They were already up there. We stayed, as you asked, and waited for you. What's up?"

Zach leaned against the Humvee and groaned as images of the coming zombie apocalypse flashed through his mind.

The crunch of gravel caught his ear. More soldiers came down the road.

Chapter Twelve

Rural Lewis County, Wednesday, September 23rd

Zach cringed, stepped to the rear of the Humvee, opened the back and looked for MOPP gear. The night was warm, the gear made him sweat, and look weird, but the lieutenant said the virus was deadly and the first sergeant's warning, not to enter Morton, now echoed in his head. Zach had no interest in dying, so he would take no chances with the virus. Ridiculous as it was, images from several zombie movies flashed through his mind.

As Zach pulled gear from a bag, Nelson started the vehicle. "I'm moving this Humvee back away from...whatever is going on here."

"Wait for me!" Zach jumped into the vehicle as the three soldiers from Second Squad looked on in confusion. "Go!"

Nelson slammed the Humvee into reverse. "Where do we go?"

"A hundred yards back."

When he stopped, Zach hurried out and continued putting on his MOPP gear while keeping an eye on the other soldiers.

Nelson came to the back and did the same.

"We shouldn't have come here," Zach said. "We were ordered to contact them and report back."

One Second Squad soldier edged several steps closer and asked in an irate voice, "What...why are you doing that?"

"Stop!" Zach held up his palm. "Stay back! I'll tell you in a minute." When he finished putting the gear on, Zach moved cautiously forward.

Nelson followed, two paces behind.

Eight soldiers jogged down the gravel road to where the vehicles were parked. One headed toward Zach and Nelson. "Why are you guys in protective gear?"

Zach stepped back. "The bodies at the lodge have been infected with a deadly virus."

After gasps and shouted questions, Zach continued his brief. He concluded by stating, "The order is to use MOPP level four around anyone returning from the lodge."

Nelson looked left and right. "Where's Sergeant Hill?"

"Still at the building," someone said.

Sweat beaded on Zach's forehead and trickled down. "We need to get everyone away from there. Soldiers that went up to the lodge should stay away from anyone who didn't. Anybody who hasn't been to the lodge should get into MOPP gear."

"Ah, I think we've all been up there," one soldier said as he glanced about. "Or we've been around others who have."

Zach wanted to wipe his brow, but couldn't through the gas mask. He looked to Nelson for direction.

The private stepped back and stared at him with questioning eyes.

*   *   *

Westmore Farm, Wednesday, September 23rd

Relaxing on the couch, Caden sipped a locally concocted tea while he gazed at Adam wrapped in blankets on the floor before him. Nikki rested nearby. "So, the road between here and Morton is open for now, but if the virus gets loose, the plan is to blockade the bridge just east of town." He shook his head. "It's my fault that events are spinning out of control."

Maria tossed a log in the fireplace and snuggled up beside him. "Why is it your fault?"

"Because we're still under martial law, so it's my job to maintain order." He took another sip. "The community leaders blamed the soldiers for infecting Morton and causing the panic. Needless to say, the meeting didn't go that well."

Maria shook her head. "Won't the Morton doctors contain the virus?"

"Dr. Scott doubts it." He sighed. "I should have told the men sooner."

"But Fletcher left several days before you learned about the Kern flu. They were out of radio contact."

Even though it was true, the fact didn't make him feel better. "The flu is moving faster than I thought."

"I read the report. It's moving faster than everyone thought."

He nodded. "Clearly, infected people are already in the area."

"How is Dr. Scott?"

"Fine. Why do you ask?"

"She works hard and is around sick people all day."

Caden didn't want to think about the Kern flu in a community without its lead doctor. "She looked fine earlier this evening and I hope she stays that way."

Maria sipped her tea. "Adam followed me out the front door today. He was out on the porch before I knew it."

A smile grew on Caden's face. "Walking or crawling?"

She frowned. "You need to spend more time at home. He's walking now."

"I've seen him wobble a few steps."

The two continued to talk and plan as the fire slowly died.

Caden woke to the sound of a military march. He blinked, rubbed his eyes, and tried to determine his location. He was leaning on the arm of the couch. Maria's head rested on his lap with Adam in her arms. The only light the faint glow of dying embers in the fireplace and the meager light from the lamp on the end table. But the music, what was that? He slapped the phone and the music stopped. Maria must have decided to set ringtones. He picked it up. "What? Ah ... hello."

"Hello sir, this is Brooks."

"Oh, yes, what's up, Lieutenant?"

"The armory phoned. They received a message from Zach. He and Private Nelson made radio and then physical contact with Second Squad believing that they had not gone to the lodge, but most did."

Caden cursed and then gently sat up, trying not to disturb Maria.

She stirred.

He sat up the rest of the way, and then rubbed his face. "What about Private Nelson and Zach, were they exposed?"

"No, sir. They put on protective gear as soon as they realized the risk."

"Well, that's good, but half of our squads have been exposed. They should have only made radio contact, why did they—."

"We may have gotten lucky on that, sir," Brooks replied. "I called the hospital and talked to the physician on duty."

"Dr. Scott?"

"No, she's off duty. However, according to the doctor I spoke with, the Kern flu can only live a day or two after the host dies."

Maria stood, set Adam and his bundle of blankets on the floor and stoked the fire.

"So, they should be fine?"

"He recommends a quarantine for 72 hours. If they have no fever or other symptoms by that time, they should be okay."

"Well, that's good news."

"I'll get some more wood," Maria whispered.

"Rumors about the Kern flu reached the FEMA camp south of Longview," Brooks continued. "A riot broke out this evening."

"Are our people okay?"

"Yes sir, they're just outside of town. However, we've lost touch with the FEMA infirmary, so I can't be certain about the staff, or if the flu is actually in the camp."

Remembering his thought from earlier in the evening, Caden rubbed his chin. "Let's proceed under the assumption that it is."

"Yes, sir. I'll order Third Squad to MOPP level four, have them establish a checkpoint on the freeway, and work with FEMA, the local sheriff, and any army units still in the area, to protect the city."

Nikki's ears perked and she walked toward the door.

"Are you still at the armory?"

"No, I'm actually coming up your driveway."

"Huh?"

Nikki growled.

Maria came in from the kitchen with arms full of wood. "There's a car coming."

Caden smiled, pressed speakerphone, and set the device on the table.

The XO's voice came from the phone. "I was bringing Lisa home when the duty sergeant phoned me."

Glancing at a nearby clock he said, "It's after midnight."

"Your sister is lovely sir, but I can testify that she is not Cinderella."

"What?" Lisa's voice came over the phone.

Car doors clunked.

Nikki barked.

Porch steps creaked.

Lisa opened the front door and entered.

David Brooks followed her in and slipped his phone in a pocket. He sat in a rocking chair as the two continued to discuss the worsening situation.

As he talked, Caden drew a map of the area on a sheet of paper and indicated the position of each unit. "I think we will be blockading the bridge east of town soon. Who do we have available?"

"Sixth Squad," Brooks replied as he pulled a notepad from his pocket.

"No. They're not ready." He pointed to his map. "We'll need to get Fourth Squad back from Alder Lake. Use Sixth Squad as back up."

The XO wrote on his pad.

As he continued to stare at his chart, Caden shook his head. "Most of our soldiers are outside of town and half have been exposed to the virus. We were doing policing, backing up local law enforcement, but panic is rising. This may soon become mob control and we don't have the manpower or training for that mission."

Brooks looked at his boss. "What should we do?"

Caden tried to think of a plan. He decided to call General Harwich in the morning and find out what others were doing. David looked at him with expectant eyes. Caden wanted to say something insightful or hopeful, but events portended something dire.

Brook's phone rang, followed almost immediately by Caden's.

Caden shook his head. "This can't be good."

Chapter Thirteen

East of Hansen, before dawn, Thursday, September 24th

Angry shouts and horn blasts filled the night. Caden examined the volatile situation from a nearby hillside. About twenty locals, armed with rifles, had blocked the west side of the bridge with two bulldozers. Bridges were often excellent blockade points, but the steep riverbanks here made it an obvious choice. A couple dozen cars from the east end of the county were stopped along the bridge and back.

He would need to act quickly, before shots were fired and people died. However, his only available men were a bunch of teenage recruits and their trainer, Sergeant Roy. He turned to Brooks and Roy. "I'm going down there to talk to them. I want all of you to take positions along this ridgeline. Stay visible and look threatening."

Brooks looked skeptical. "What happens if they shoot at you?"

"Shoot the shooter."

"And if they shoot at us?" Roy asked.

"This isn't rocket science, Sergeant, shoot back." Scanning the faces of the young soldiers standing nearby, Caden prayed the night would end peacefully. Then he fixed his eyes on Brooks. "Make sure they understand the rules of engagement. No one fires without your order. I'd really like this night to end without death."

Caden walked toward the men blockading the bridge. As he did, two sheriff's vehicles sped up with lights flashing.

As the deputies hurried from the vehicles, Caden held up his hand in a stop motion. He would face the blockaders alone. Nearing the bridge he spotted Scruffy Beard, now wearing a dust mask, pointing and shouting orders to others on the blockade.

Scruffy looked at the sheriff deputies standing about fifty yards away. Then he glanced along the ridgeline where the soldiers were positioned. Only then did he lock eyes on Caden.

With a pistol in hand, Scruffy strode toward Caden. "You come to arrest us and take down the blockade?"

Caden stifled a grin at the sight of Scruffy's dust mask flattened against his beard. "We need a better plan."

"Better than keeping sick people out?"

"Better than just keeping everyone out. Not everyone in Morton is sick."

Scruffy scowled. "Your people are."

Caden shook his head. "My people were exposed."

"You and your men seem to be doing a good job at getting exposed and not so good at keeping it away."

"Being exposed to nasty things happens when you're out trying to maintain law and order."

Scruffy spat. "We're going to keep our families safe and this plague out of town."

"My family lives here too. I want to keep them safe."

Scruffy stared at Caden.

"Besides … I was exposed to the virus, but didn't get sick."

Scruffy touched his dust mask. "Are you immune?"

The question seemed sincere, but Caden had no idea what, if any, immunity he might possess. He shrugged. "Some soldiers were exposed, but didn't get sick. Some were exposed and got ill, and then got better. Others died. I need to get my soldiers that aren't sick back to town. How can we keep the sick out, and let those who aren't a danger pass through, or to the armory?"

Scruffy rubbed the back of his neck. "We could quarantine anyone wanting to go into the town, but if they just want to pass through, we let them."

"That could work." Caden nodded. "How can we make sure people are just passing through?"

For the next several minutes they discussed ideas. Finally Caden smiled. "That plan would work, but call me and the sheriff if someone enters the town that shouldn't."

He nodded. "That would be agreeable."

Caden walked over to the deputies. "The situation is okay for now. I'll call Sheriff Hoover before I leave."

"He's coming here now."

Angry shouts erupted from the direction of the bridge. "Good." Caden pointed to the hill. "I'll be up there briefing my soldiers." He turned and jogged up the slope.

Lieutenant Brooks met him near the crest.

Turning his gaze to the crowd below, Caden shook his head. "Order the soldiers to remain in position. The situation here is under control, but I don't know for how long." Scruffy still talked with others near the bridge. Waving of arms and raised voices told Caden not everyone liked the new plan.

Brooks passed along the updated orders and then returned to Caden's side. "What's your orders if this situation gets out of hand?"

Caden looked to his XO. "Refugees from Morton will be stuck here for hours, some for a couple of days. More will be infected. We need to get our people back here as soon as possible before this situation gets out of control. I need to talk to Hoover." He reached into a pocket for his phone.

"Okay, talk to me."

Caden spun around at the sound of the sheriff's voice.

"There always seems to be trouble when we meet," Hoover said still walking toward Caden.

The two talked, planned, and phoned others for the next couple of hours. Before the sun rose, Caden found a volunteer nurse and EMT to work the blockade. He stationed soldiers in MOPP gear on the east end of the bridge. Two deputies and the recruit soldiers stood guard along the blockade. Officially they were there to control the refugees, but Caden told them to keep watch on the locals that remained nearby.

*   *   *

East of Hansen, Thursday, September 24th

Zach rested his head against the window as their Humvee neared the main highway. He closed his eyes. Maybe the mission had gone well. He had climbed into his MOPP gear before any of the soldiers neared him. Sure, Second Squad had been exposed, but they would be home soon and since they were convoying with the squad, Nelson was forced to drive at a reasonable speed.

"Well look at that."

Zach opened his eyes to a line of about a dozen cars, packed with people and possessions, driving in from the east.

"Where do you think these people came from?" Zach asked as the convoy turned onto the highway.

"Don't know." Zach shook his head. "There aren't any big towns between here and the pass."

"Do you think they're from some other area? Is the disease worse on the other side of the mountains?"

"Now how am I supposed to know that?" Zach shook his head. "One thing is certain, I'm not going to try and stop one of the cars to find out." He slid down in his seat, closed his eyes, and drifted to sleep.

Nelson braked and cursed.

Suddenly awake, Zach sat up. "What's going on?" A rumbling boom shook the Humvee as a gas station near the edge of Morton exploded into a red and orange inferno.

Zach blinked at the bright light and felt the warmth on his face.

Traffic slipped by on the far side of the highway.

The radio crackled. "Second Squad, this is Fletcher. Command orders you proceed to Morton hospital for tests. Further direction will be given at that time."

Sergeant Hill acknowledged the order and Second Squad turned into town, leaving Zach and Nelson and their vehicle.

Zach pressed transmit on the mic. "First Sergeant this is Search One. Are there any changes to our orders?"

Nelson frowned. "Why do you ask so many questions?"

Fletcher's voice came over the radio. "Have you been to the lodge or otherwise exposed to the virus?"

"Negative."

"Then proceed to the armory."

With a sigh, Zach replaced the mic. As Nelson angled to the opposite side of the highway and around the burning building, Zach slid low in the seat and closed his eyes.

"Wake up." Nelson thumped Zach on the shoulder. "The nurse gave us the all clear to cross the bridge." The passenger door of the Humvee was open and Nelson stood just outside.

"Bridge?" He rubbed his eyes and tried to stretch in the seat. "Where are we? What time is it?"

"Just east of Hansen and nearly eight-thirty—sleepy-head."

Nelson yawned. "See the sun? I've been awake all night. Your turn to drive." He tossed Zach the keys.

They thumped Zach in the chest. He clutched them, stepped from the vehicle and stretched. "Do we have any coffee?"

Nelson laughed. "Not a drop. Just be thankful you're alive after all the excitement last night."

Zach nodded absently and walked to the other side of the Humvee. As they bounced along the grass back to the highway, Zach noticed a multitude of cars, trucks and tents on the other side of the road, in what had once been a pasture. Many of the people that swarmed about wore dust, paint or similar masks over their faces. He pointed. "What's that?"

"Refugees from Morton that have friends or family in Hansen. The soldiers are keeping them over there while they do medical checks, then if they're not sick they'll be allowed in town. Only military that haven't been exposed to the virus are getting through right now. The nurse said we're the first to get across the bridge today. "

"I'm a civilian."

Nelson shook his head. "Just barely, and don't tell anyone until we're through the checkpoint."

"Checkpoint?"

Nelson pointed. "See the unlucky shmucks in full MOPP gear?"

Zach nodded, and looked at the soldiers stationed on their side of the bridge.

"On the east side of it they have two bulldozers forming a blockade."

As they drove along the short stretch of highway to the span, Zach recalled the other camp that had formed north of town after the Seattle nuke blast. That camp sprang into existence very quickly, like this one. Then the people of Hansen had barricaded a bridge to keep out desperate and lawless people. This new camp appeared to be full of similar people.

The crowd along the road shook angry fists at Nelson and Zach. Some cursed.

"Why can't we go through?" a woman shouted.

"What right do you have to stop us?" A balding man with graying hair and beard yelled, "Why are you special?"

Near one of the soldiers at the west end of the bridge, an older woman sat in the dirt crying. "This is crazy." Zach shook his head.

Nelson nodded slowly. "This has been a hard year."

The Humvee rumbled onto the bridge.

Gunfire erupted.

*　　　*　　　*

Hansen Armory, Thursday, September 24th

Caden didn't bother with sleep. After negotiating with Scruffy and talking with the sheriff he came to the armory and did paperwork. As the morning sun rose above the nearby hill he checked his watch and waited until he thought General Harwich might be in his office, and then he phoned. It surprised Caden when the secretary put him straight through.

When the general came on the line, Caden briefed him on the events since he left the meeting in Olympia.

"You've had a busy few days."

"Yes, sir. I wondered if there is any further guidance on containment procedures or … well, things are moving so quickly."

The general sighed. "Ah … yes, we should have passed information to area commanders more rapidly. From coast to coast the situation is tense and very fluid."

Caden felt relief at not being alone, but concern that the situation might be worse than he thought.

The general breathed deeply then continued. "You're correct to emphasize law and order. Let the medical people treat the sick and dying. The pandemic is moving swiftly and … well I can't say more over the phone, but—"

Brooks bolted into his office. "Gunfire at the bridge east of town!"

Chapter Fourteen

East of Hansen, Thursday, September 24th

Nelson reached for his rifle. "Did some trigger happy redneck shoot at us?"

Zach slowed the vehicle thinking it might be the men on the checkpoint. His eyes darted from person to person. Several guns pointed in their direction, but they didn't seem to be shooting.

Another shot rang out.

Voices clamored and yelled.

Nelson cursed and spun around in his seat.

A deputy waved the Humvee ahead.

Zach pressed the gas.

A bullet pinged off the back of the vehicle.

Others manning the checkpoint waved the Humvee forward.

A soldier in MOPP gear sprinted aside the vehicle.

"Rearview mirror," Nelson shouted.

An angry crowd surged toward them. Zach slowed the vehicle and the soldier jumped in.

"Where's the other guy?" Zach pressed the gas.

"She's dead. Someone shot her, and then they all came at me, like some crazy zombie movie."

Forty yards ahead two bulldozers formed a blockade at the end of the bridge. They formed a narrow angled opening. Vehicles had to slow to a crawl to make the sharp turn. At the speed they were going, the turn would be impossible, but if he slowed down the surging crowd would be on them. Zach sped up.

"Hey!" Nelson yelped. "What are you …?" The roar of the engine, gunfire and angry shouts smothered the rest of his words.

"Brace!" At the last moment Zach slammed the brakes.

The Humvee slid past the first dozer and stopped inches from the second.

"Run," Zach shouted as he opened the door and jumped out.

The soldier and Nelson leapt from the vehicle. "And you called my driving crazy?"

"Go!" Zach yelled and looked back at the throng. "Go! Go! Go!"

Nelson and the other soldier ran through the checkpoint with Zach close behind him.

A few feet away Sergeant Roy stood on the treads of the dozer and yelled into a bullhorn. "Under the martial law decree this is an illegal assembly. You are ordered to clear the bridge. If you do not, you will be fired upon."

The crowd continued slowly forward.

Zach climbed up on the treads next to the sergeant and peeked over. Several civilians on the blockade fired at the crowd as he did. Zach cringed at the thought of shooting neighbors. "Do we need to kill them?"

"We're firing over their heads for the moment," a nearby deputy said. He glanced at the Humvee. "Good job. It blocks most of the entrance."

"Thanks."

Sheriff Hoover climbed onto the treads and, using some sort of launcher that Zach had never seen, fired a canister near the lead edge of the crowd.

As the cloud billowed over the crowd, Zach turned to the nearby deputy. "Is that tear gas."

The deputy smiled. "Yes, it is."

Bullets pinged and ricocheted off the dozer, but the mass of people stopped and fell back. A pickup and two large cars moved through the crowd. The people slid in behind the moving cover.

Sergeant Roy set the bullhorn down. "I saw one soldier jump in the Humvee with you. Did you get both from the far end of the bridge?"

Zach looked about and spotted the guy he picked up. With his gas mask off, but otherwise still in his MOPP gear, the soldier sat against a wall of sandbags staring straight ahead. "That new guy is the one I picked up." Zach pointed. "He said the girl was dead."

Sergeant Roy's face blanched. He nodded, stumbled off the dozer, and walked to the young soldier.

Zach returned his attention to the crowd. "What do they hope to accomplish? They can't get through here."

"We just need to keep them out," a nearby man grumbled. "When they get hungry they'll leave."

"These are civilians."

Zach turned at the sound of Sergeant Roy's voice. With a hand covering one ear, the sergeant spoke into a phone. He described the situation and asked when he should order the men to fire.

"Most aren't armed," Roy protested into the phone. All blood seemed to drain from his face. "Yes, sir," he mumbled.

The last plume of tear gas cleared.

The cars on the bridge surged forward with the mob right behind them.

*   *   *

Morton, Thursday, September 24th

First Sergeant Fletcher pulled his gas mask up and breathed heavily. He still didn't feel well and what Lieutenant Brooks said only made him feel worse. "Are you kidding me?" he mumbled.

"What was that First Sergeant?" Brooks asked.

"I was saying sir, that between the looters and the sick and dying the situation in Morton is lousey."

"Are you under fire?"

"We have been, but no sir, not at this time."

"Well, our people here are being shot at right now," Brooks said with frustration in his voice. "We're shorthanded and the situation is growing worse."

"That would be my assessment of this place also."

"I'll advise Major Westmore of your appraisal."

*   *   *

Hansen Armory, Thursday, September 24th

"Yes," Caden shouted into the phone. "Shoot at the mob if they're shooting at you." He hurried toward two waiting Humvees. "I'm on my way, but I won't reach you before they do. Don't let the rioters breach the checkpoint. Stand your ground and fire."

"Yes, sir," Roy mumbled.

Shouts and the sound of gunfire boomed from Caden's

phone and then the connection ended. "Brooks!"

The XO came around one of the vehicles. "Yes, sir?"

"Let's hurry. How many soldiers do we have?"

"Ten. That's everyone but the sick and wounded."

"Twelve counting us." Caden looked over the assembled young soldiers. They weren't ready for combat, and the conflict before them looked like the worst kind, neighbor killing neighbor. With a sigh he wondered how he would react fighting someone he knew. "Everyone needs to be in full MOPP gear. There will be infected people in the mob. Defend yourself and the checkpoint. If a rioter surrenders try to take them prisoner, but do not unnecessarily expose or endanger yourself or your fellow soldiers. However, we must keep the virus out of Hansen."

As the two climbed into the vehicle Caden shouted to the driver, "Go!" Turning to Brooks he asked, "When will Fourth Squad arrive from Alder Lake?"

"They're still an hour out."

"What about Second Squad?"

"They're healthy and I ordered them back from Morton, but they're thirty minutes out. Fletcher isn't happy they were pulled. He believes the situation there is deteriorating."

Caden nodded grimly. "The situation is deteriorating everywhere."

*   *   *

Morton, Thursday, September 24th

First Sergeant Fletcher ordered Second Squad to pull out and head for Hansen. The smoke from burning buildings irritated his nose and throat. No more could be done on this street. It would burn to the ground. Looters would move on. The dead would be cremated and the sick … well, they had rescued as many as possible. The few firefighters still on duty in Morton fought another blaze near the hospital. "Move to the next street," he shouted to nearby soldiers and then repeated the command over the radio. He returned his gas mask to its proper position on his face and moved forward with his men.

The elementary school, which now served as a large isolation ward, and the hospital, were behind them as they moved east through the town. Ahead on his left stood city hall, a red single story building with an American flag still fluttering above. It appeared undisturbed, but nearby stood several shops with broken windows and doors.

Fletcher could understand, if not condone, stealing food from a grocery store, but why had looters broken into the coffee shop? It seemed a senseless act of an increasingly senseless mob. Months ago the beverage had disappeared even from the black market. What were looters looking for in the coffee shop? Scones?

He waved his arm, signaling the soldiers to follow him.

Shots echoed off the nearby building.

"Where did that come from?" Fletcher shouted as he scanned nearby buildings.

A soldier pointed to the next street.

More shots rang out.

Static crackled over the radio, and then a voice, "First Sergeant, looters on Division Avenue."

"You two," Fletcher barked, "guard the intersection of Main and Second. You four follow me." Leaving Private Spencer and another behind, Fletcher and the others ran toward the shooting.

Nearing an intersection, Fletcher held up his hand signaling those behind him to slow. Corners were always a hazard.

Shots rang out.

Fletcher dove behind a nearby car. Then he noticed blood.

*　　　*　　　*

East of Hansen, Thursday, September 24th

Rapid gunfire, angry shouts and screams, greeted Caden as he stepped from the Humvee. He drew his pistol and gestured with the other arm for the soldiers to follow as he sprinted the last yards to the checkpoint.

Like medieval soldiers climbing the walls of a castle, some of the mob reached the tops of the dozers, but not much farther. Most were killed; a few lucky ones were captured.

Veteran soldiers avoided such a direct daylight assault. But these were not experienced soldiers. They were desperate and afraid civilians. Caden knew from experience the spirit of the attackers would quickly fade, but until then all he could do is defend the position.

Townsmen, deputies, and soldiers stood shoulder-to-shoulder on the treads of the bulldozers. The dozers wouldn't be moved. The gap between the two heavy machines was the weak spot. There, in the place where cars could have driven through, someone had wisely stopped a Humvee, blocking most of the space between the dozers.

But rioters were still getting to the vehicle, using it for cover, and some got past.

Kneeling behind a line of sandbags Caden noticed a lone soldier next to the Humvee firing rapidly, and keeping most rioters pinned down behind the truck. "Help protect that spot," Caden shouted. Then he pointed to nearby sandbags. "Get behind cover and protect the gap."

Only as he moved closer did Caden realize the lone soldier was Zach.

Several armed men broke through and fired.

A soldier beside Caden screamed and collapsed.

A man grabbed Zach's rifle, attempting to wrench it from him.

Another aimed a shotgun at the boy's head.

Caden fired on the armed man.

Rapid gunfire thundered.

Boom.

A flash blinded Caden. His ears rang. His eyes couldn't focus. He stumbled and fell to the pavement.

Chapter Fifteen

East of Hansen, Thursday, September 24th

Sheriff Hoover and Lieutenant Brooks each held out a hand. Caden grasped both and stood.

"You okay?" Hoover asked.

Caden did a quick check. He blinked blurry eyes and his ears rang, but he spotted no blood. He nodded. "I'll live." His voice sounded muffled. "What was that?" he said louder.

Hoover grinned. "A flashbang grenade. They're really good for stopping this kind of trouble. Fortunately, we still had a few."

"Where did you throw it—at my feet?"

"You were closer than I wanted, but if I didn't use it right then a lot of people were going to die. Including you."

"Thanks." He shook his head trying to clear it. "I guess. Is the fight over? Did we lose anyone?"

"Fight's over," Hoover said. "For now."

"Three of our soldiers were wounded." Brooks nodded toward the medic as he walked by. "Nothing serious. We believe Private Suzanne Moore was killed at the far end of the bridge, but we haven't recovered her body. Also, we don't know the status of the nurse working with the sick at the camp on the other side."

"How many civilian casualties?" Caden looked around.

Brooks shook his head. "We're still figuring that out. One wounded from our side of the bridge. There were losses among the rioters, but it looks like more were injured than killed."

Caden nodded, thankful that deaths had been limited. "No one enters the town until Private Moore and the nurse are returned to us."

"That may take some time," Brooks said.

"So be it." Ears still ringing, Caden stode off to talk to his soldiers and inspect the checkpoint.

Thirty minutes later he stood over five pale and shaky recruits. They were in shock and would soon be headed to the hospital, but were otherwise unhurt.

Brooks walked up beside him holding several pages of notes. "Forth Squad arrived from Alder Lake. Second Squad will be here soon."

"Has everyone been accounted for?"

"Yes." Brooks glanced at the papers in his hand. "The nurse is shook up, but fine. The sheriff says none of his people were injured. Sergeant Roy is with the wounded members of Sixth Squad at the hospital." Brooks listed their names. "And, we recovered the body of Private Moore."

She was so new Caden struggled to remember her face. "Do we know who killed her?"

"No." Brooks shook his head.

"Tell the sheriff. I want an investigation. The guilty must be punished." Caden rubbed his chin. "I saw Zach here defending the checkpoint. Is he okay?"

"When I checked with the armory, Nelson said he walked home after the conflict."

Walking and hiking were known Zach traits. Caden figured he was fine. "I need to talk to the prisoners."

Caden approached a group of handcuffed men sitting in a semi-circle. Three soldiers stood behind them in full MOPP gear and with rifles in hand. Caden stopped about twenty feet away. "The nurse was checking you for the virus. If you were healthy, we would have let you through. Why did you attack the checkpoint?"

One man coughed. "My wife died this morning."

The men on either side of him scooted away.

After a resigned glance to each, he continued. "If I don't get treatment soon I'll die, but that nurse was never going to let me in town." He laughed. "I'm closer to the hospital now then I was an hour ago."

For several moments no one spoke. Then, in an angry voice, a man with dark hair and rough, stubble filled face said, "You wouldn't have let any of us into town. You would have let us die or killed us just like they did in Yakima."

Colonel Hutchison's area? Caden had an uneasy feeling. "What happened in Yakima?"

"You know." He spat on the ground.

Caden shook his head. "Pretend I don't. Tell me."

"I'd heard rumors for days that they were killing people and forcing others out."

"Rumors," Caden said. "Just rumors."

With hate-filled eyes, he stared at Caden. "Then my wife got sick. An ambulance came and took her away. An hour later soldiers arrived dressed like you." He pointed to a guard in full MOPP gear. "I asked where my wife was. They said she was dead."

"Are you saying they killed her?" Caden asked incredulous.

"It had only been an hour. She wasn't that sick." He shook his head. Tears filled his eyes. "Me, my kids and wife, we left Las Vegas a couple of months ago. The Chinese control it, and if you don't cooperate, you don't eat. We packed what we could into the car and left." He shook his head. "That's what we've been living in—our car, but we thought it would be better in the American-controlled states."

Caden nodded. He would have done the same. "The soldiers that came to your house, did they do anything else?"

"They waved guns at us and told us we had one hour to leave town. We loaded everything from our campsite back into the car. I kept asking about my wife. Where is the body at least, so that I could bury her? They said the dead were being buried in mass graves. That just ain't right. They followed us to the edge of town, to a checkpoint just like this, and told us to just go away. You asked why I attacked." He spat again. "You soldiers killed my wife. My family is sick. What choice did I have?"

*　　*　　*

Morton, Thursday, September 24th

Pain surged after Fletcher spotted the blood. He leaned back against the tire of the car, carefully pulled aside the jacket and pulled up the shirt. With the fingers of one hand he spread the wound and, using the other, he wiped the blood.

The medic came alongside him. "You okay First Sergeant?" Several other soldiers huddled close to him.

Fletcher carefully inspected the wound along his abdomen.

He sighed. It was only skin deep. It would hurt and need stitches, but he would live. "Yeah, just another scar for my collection."

The medic opened his pack. "Let me look at it."

Fletcher turned. "How many guys are shooting at us?"

"Sit still," the medic commanded.

A soldier, with his M4 resting on the hood of the car, looked down a scope. "I see three guys in the electronics store across the street, one on the first floor and two on the second. I'm guessing they were looting and got caught off guard by our patrol."

Another soldier grinned as he loaded rounds into a magazine. "Apparently they don't want to pay the penalty for looting."

Several laughed.

The First Sergeant grabbed his radio. "Fifth Squad this is Fletcher. Report."

The radio squawked. "We've got two guys firing on us from the east side of the electronics store."

A young soldier laughed. "We can take on five looters."

"No." Fletcher shook his head. "We can wait. We have food and water. They have televisions and radios."

As the medic finished bandaging Fletcher, smoke blew over the position.

The radio crackled. "First Sergeant, this is Private Spencer at Main and Second. We need to move. The fire is sweeping this way."

*   *   *

East of Hansen, Thursday, September 24th

Barely aware of others helping Caden to his feet, Zach stared at the man who tried to wrestle his rifle away. Young, perhaps just out of college, he wore jeans, and a button-down shirt. His neatly cut brown hair matched his polished brown shoes. Why had he attacked them? Why had he tried to wrestle Zach's rifle from him? Was he sick?

It didn't matter. Zach had killed him.

He didn't know how long he sat there, but when he stood, he walked aimlessly for an undetermined time. Nelson walked with others in the distance. Zach walked alone. Seeing Sergeant Roy, he nodded and continued moving. Gradually Zach became aware that he strode along the highway toward town. The rifle weighed on his arms, so he flung it over a shoulder and continued his slow plod.

Vehicles passed.

The image of the man with neat brown hair dying before him remained fixed in his mind. Again and again he watched the life drain from the man's eyes.

Zach walked onward.

Just a few months ago he had wanted to kill Bo for getting his mother hooked on drugs. In the end Cruz killed Bo, but Zach had wanted to do it. Later, he did kill one of the thugs holding DeLynn. Why did this shooting trouble him?

He kicked a stone.

Would he have killed Bo? He hated the man, but would never know if he would have ... could have, killed him. Later, when he shot the thug, it was to save himself and DeLynn. This day two men struggled. One lived. One died. He looked to the sky. What cosmic or spiritual forces chose him to live ... chose him to kill? It had been a senseless attack, a senseless death. The clouds echoed the darkness and cold that lingered within him.

A Humvee stopped beside him. Nelson opened the driver's door and called over the top. "Hey, Zach, I've been looking for you. Jump in."

"No." Zach shook his head. "I ... I need to think." He opened the passenger door and set the rifle inside. His school books were on the floor of the vehicle, but they didn't matter. Nothing mattered. "I'll see you later."

"You okay?" Nelson asked.

"I'll live."

Nelson nodded and then drove on toward town.

Clouds billowed over the nearby hills. He didn't know how long he had walked when he felt the first drop of rain. Only as he approached his trailer home did he realize his clothes were soaked through. Recalling a verse from the Bible, he looked into the cloudy sky. *He sends the rain on the just and the unjust.* As the memory of the man he had killed fluttered back into his mind, Zach knew the guilt rested on him.

As he opened the door of the trailer the smell of wet carpet and mold assaulted his nose. Droplets formed on the ceiling, fell, and added to the disaster of his home. Tears welled in his eyes. The day began with a riot, then a battle, and ended with ... the man. The man he killed. The dying eyes flashed in his mind. Now a wet and smelly home. He shivered. *Why, God, why?*

Although drops fell from several places on the ceiling, his mother's old recliner had been moved and now occupied a dry patch in the far corner of the living room. An old blanket lay across it. He undressed, dropping his wet clothes on the wet carpet. Naked, he collapsed into the chair, pulled the blanket over him and drifted to sleep.

When Zach's eyes fluttered open, no light came through the nearby window. A log crackled in the woodstove and cast a yellow glow across the room, but he didn't recall starting the fire.

Giggles brought him fully awake.

Vicki worked at the kitchen sink, but DeLynn stood at the kitchen counter with filleted fish spread before her. However, she wasn't working. Her head rested on one elbow as she leaned across the counter and stared at Zach with a huge smile.

He looked down. The blanket had slid off and now barely covered his groin and one leg. He yanked it up to his chest. "How long have you guys been here?"

DeLynn's grin grew even larger. "Oh, us gals, we've been here for a while."

Zach's face burned with embarrassment.

Chapter Sixteen

Brennon Trailer Home, Thursday, September 24th

Zach stood, turned away, and tied the blanket around him like a Roman toga. "I should get dressed."

Still grinning, DeLynn nodded.

Each step went squish as Zach grabbed the wet clothes from the floor and made a hasty retreat to his bedroom.

The room remained relatively dry, but they couldn't go on living like this. He had to find a solution. Earlier he had considered getting permission for both of them to move into the armory. Nelson thought it a bad idea for Vicki to live around a hundred young men, but what choice did he have?

While Zach dressed in a dry shirt that he hoped didn't smell of mold, a struggle raged in his mind. The armory seemed the only solution, but from the battle earlier in the day, images of the man he had killed pushed into his thoughts.

The soldiers treated him like a member of the Guard, but he had never enlisted, and now he didn't want to join. His desire to learn about guns and to fight in battles seemed childish.

The armory might be bad for him and Vicki, but it remained better than a winter in a cold and damp trailer.

He pulled on underwear and jeans with a sigh, unable to find a better solution. As he tied his shoes, the memory of walking to see Mr. Hollister at the hotel flashed through his mind. DeLynn's father had wanted Zach and his sister to run the general store on the first floor. The building needed a lot of work, but if they fixed it up and ran it, perhaps they could live in the back.

Zach walked to the living room. "I'm going to talk to your

dad about business stuff. I'll be back in a few minutes." He reached for his coat.

"My dad's not at the house. He sold it."

Zach's arm stopped in mid reach. "What? When did that happen?"

"A few days ago. He said we couldn't pay the mortgage anymore."

Zach sighed. "Everyone is getting poorer."

"Apparently everyone except the guy who bought our house."

"Does your dad still own the hotel?"

"Yeah. We're living there now."

Zach looked out a nearby window and spotted the Hollister car. "Good, I need to talk with him about hotel business. Can you take me to him?"

"Sure. Grab your coat."

"You guys go ahead," Vicki said. "I'll stay here."

*　　　*　　　*

Morton, Thursday, September 24th

Fletcher sat behind the car and wondered how many people remained in Morton. Wind blew smoke and flames across the downtown area, and he heard several vehicles race away. "We need to pull back. Stay together and rendezvous just north of the highway near the hotel." He repeated the message to Fifth Squad over the radio.

Fletcher shifted his weight to get a better view of the situation. A stab of pain from the wound in his side caused him to stop. Holding the bloody bandage he inched cautiously up, hoping to shout to the looters across the street.

Bang! A bullet whizzed past his head and imbedded in the wall behind him.

He cursed and fell back behind the car. Sitting there, Fletcher tried to shout for the looters to surrender before the fire killed them.

More shots rang out.

"I think they're hoping we'll leave so they can escape." The soldier peeked around the car.

"We are going to leave." Fletcher gestured for them to move back, around the corner.

"Are we letting the looters go free?" another asked.

Fletcher shook his head. "Either the fire gets them or we will, but I don't want to be cooked while they're deciding what to do."

The squad jogged north one block, closer to the fire, but away from the gunmen. They joined with Spencer and the other private left to guard the intersection and then move away from the growing flames.

Fletcher's side ached. Gently he pressed a hand to his wound, and wondered if he would be able to keep up. He moved cautiously east with the soldiers, at a slower than normal pace and told himself that it was to avoid ambush by looters, but he knew better.

The soldiers crept east along deserted streets. Finally they turned south, away from the fire, and toward the other squad.

Shots boomed as they neared the rendezvous point.

The radio crackled. "Fletcher, this is Fifth Squad. We've engaged five shooters."

"Roger. We are headed south along the main street."

"That should bring you behind them."

Fletcher and the men of Second Squad jogged along the side of a large hotel. Flames leaped to the sky from buildings a quarter mile to the north. Smoke choked the air.

Reaching the parking lot, Fletcher spotted several men behind two pickups shooting at Fifth Squad. The trucks were loaded with food, electronics, clothes, and an assortment of other items. Fletcher turned to his men. "Spread out and move forward. When I signal, stop and find cover, but hold your fire. I'll give them one chance to surrender."

When they were twenty yards from the shooters, Fletcher signaled the soldiers to stop. He waited for them to find cover. "You're surrounded. Cease fire and lay down your weapons."

The looters turned and fired.

The soldiers shot back.

In seconds the fight was over. Fletcher stood over the body of a middle-aged man with a bullet hole in his chest. "Why didn't you just surrender?"

*　　　*　　　*

Hollister Hotel, Thursday, September 24th

As they turned the corner toward the hotel, Zach noticed lights shining from several windows and the portico. DeLynn parked in front and frowned. "Where is the valet? It's so hard to get good help these days."

Zach was confused. "You hired a...?"

DeLynn laughed. "No, of course not. Let's go find Dad."

Inside they followed the buzz of the circular saw and found Mr. Hollister in what would someday be a bakery. Covered with sawdust, he stood with his back to them, cutting two-by-fours.

"A year ago my dad wore a business suit to work. Now he wears a T-shirt and jeans." She sighed. "You guys talk business. I'll be with Mom."

Zach walked into the room. The walls were roughed-in. A used glass and steel-display counter nearly divided the space. A cash register sat on the floor wrapped in clear plastic. Hollister appeared to be cutting boards for the counter. He waited for him to stop and set the saw down.

"Ah, Mr. Hollister?"

He spun around. "Oh, hi, Zach. I didn't hear you come in."

"Could I talk with you? I have a problem." Zach explained that the trailer needed a new roof. "The carpet is soaked from the recent rains. In half the house water drips from the ceiling."

"That's an electrical hazard."

A weight settled on Zach. "I didn't think of that. I don't know how to fix a trailer roof and I couldn't afford it anyway. I don't know what to do."

Hollister rubbed his chin. "I'm not sure I can help with the roof, but I might be able to solve your housing problem."

Zach cast him a confused look.

"I own a hotel." Hollister spread his arms wide. "Follow me to the freight elevator."

A few minutes later Zach stood in a dark room.

Hollister screwed in a lightbulb. "This is the north penthouse."

Zach walked around. The interior walls had a few holes and had been stripped of paneling, trim, and electrical switches, but were otherwise intact. A hint of dust lingered in the air, but he detected no smell of damp or mold. "Do you have a flashlight?"

Hollister handed him one.

Using it, Zach inspected the ceiling. *No stains.* Moving to the bathroom he discovered there was no toilet or faucet.

"I've got a faucet, but I haven't had time to install it, and I need to find a toilet."

"We can use the one from our trailer."

"Good thinking. You'd need to do the renovation and installation work, but the roof is good. It was the first thing I checked."

Zach nodded. "On the way here, DeLynn said you lived in the penthouse."

"There are two apartments on the top floor. We live across the hall, in the south penthouse."

The thought of living so close to DeLynn intrigued Zach. He grinned.

Mr. Hollister gave him a disapproving glare. "Living in the hotel is contingent upon you accepting my offer to run the general store."

"I think we have a deal."

Kent Hollister held out his hand and the two shook.

As DeLynn drove Zach home, the weight of worry regarding how he and his sister would live that winter lifted. Sadness and regret seeped into its place. The image of the brown-haired man he had killed returned to his mind. He shook his head. Perhaps they had both made bad decisions earlier today. Zach resolved to make better choices in the future.

"What's the problem?" DeLynn asked, turning up the driveway to the trailer.

"Huh?"

"You haven't spoken a word since we left the hotel."

"Oh, just a lot to think about, I guess." Zach kissed her and stepped from the car. She drove off as he entered the trailer. Vicki came from her bedroom.

"Did you find Mr. Hollister and get your business done?"

"Yeah." Zach motioned for his sister to sit at the kitchen table. "We need to talk."

Vicki sat in her usual spot, across from Zach. "Is there something wrong?" She looked around the disheveled trailer. "Well, more wrong?"

"No. Hopefully things have turned for the better. How would you like to move into the penthouse at Mr. Hollister's hotel?"

Vicki looked skeptical. "Move into a penthouse? I don't think we have ten dollars between us. How would we pay him?"

"I'll get to that in a minute. The penthouse is nice, but it needs some work, well, a lot of work, but compared to this dump, it's great. Not like in the movies great. I'll need to take the toilet from here, but it's dry and warm."

"Is there room service? I'm not moving to a penthouse that doesn't have room service."

"What?" Zach looked at her, confused.

"I'm kidding, brother." Vicki grinned. "Move from this place into a dry hotel penthouse. Sure. Can we do it tonight?"

"There's more. I've been meaning to talk to you about this ... how would you like to help me run a store?"

"How would we buy a store?" Her eyes grew wide. "You haven't done anything stupid have you, like sell drugs, or maybe use them?"

"No, Sis, this is not a drug-induced hallucination." Zach explained how they would run the store and share the profits with Mr. Hollister.

"Why is he doing all of this for us?"

"I think he's decided that DeLynn and I are serious, and he wants me away from the military and where he can keep an eye on me."

"Good." Vicki grinned. "I want you away from the military."

"I think I do, too." He sighed deeply and stared at the floor.

Vicki touched his arm. "What's wrong?"

In a voice just above a whisper he said, "I killed a man today."

Chapter Seventeen

Brennon Trailer Home, the night of Thursday September 24th

As they talked into the night, Zach poured out the story of the battle at the bridge to Vicki. Several hours later, when the siblings gazed at each other in thoughtful silence, there were no more tears for the brown-haired man in the button-down shirt, only resolve. They would move out of the broken-down trailer and into the hotel. Zach would quit at the armory and together they would run the general store. There would be no more killing.

"Will you be okay?" Vicki rested a hand on his shoulder.

He nodded.

Vicki yawned and stumbled off to bed.

Several more hours passed before Zach managed a fitful sleep.

As DeLynn pulled to a stop outside the trailer the next morning, Vicki turned to Zach. "You should tell her what you told me last night."

"Somethings are easier to say to you." Zach nodded. "But I will ... someday."

Zach and Vicki stepped from the trailer and together, the three went on to school.

*   *   *

Morton High School, Friday, September 25th

Sitting in the lobby of the high school that now served as a barracks, Fletcher stared at a map of Morton. Fires still smoldered, but a combination of firefighter efforts and an overnight drizzle largely put them out. Still, that left a third of the downtown as a charred monument to lawlessness and panic.

Sergeant Garcia walked into view. "The soldiers are ready."

Fletcher nodded and then returned his gaze to the map. Most of the people still in Morton were either sick, barricaded in their homes, or both. The hospital, police, and fire department were the only functioning public services. Only about a dozen individuals still served in those areas. They were heroes in his mind, but he wondered how long they could continue.

He still felt weak and his side ached, but he had a job to do. Fletcher stood. "Okay, we've been ordered to establish a checkpoint at White Pass. Let's saddle up and head out."

"Saddle up? Are we going there on horses?" Garcia smiled and rubbed his chin. "Seriously, First Sergeant, why do they want us to make a checkpoint way out there?"

"Haven't a clue." Fletcher walked toward the door.

*   *   *

Hansen Armory, Friday, September 25th

Brooks stepped into the office holding several pages in one hand.

Caden hung up the phone. "General Harwich called a meeting of all the area commanders."

"When?"

"As soon as we can get there."

"That doesn't sound good."

"No." Caden shook his head. "It doesn't. In addition to my own car, he also wanted me to bring two Humvees and a squad of soldiers."

"Why?"

"He didn't say." Caden glanced at the pages Brooks held. "What have you got for me?"

"First and Fifth Squads are in route to White Pass, but … is a checkpoint that far out a good idea?"

"They will be out of radio range, but they are our two best squads." Caden walked to the map in the conference room next door. "I think refugees from Yakima might have caused the Morton outbreak and, by extension, the fight at the bridge. That's not going to happen again." He pressed his finger to the map. "The top of White Pass is the eastern edge of my authority. Until we can build a radio repeater and establish reliable communications, I want our best on the pass. We are not going to be a dumping ground for Colonel

Hutchison's sick and dying. I intend to stop the spread of Kern flu there. Let him deal with his own problems."

"Yes, sir," Brooks said hesitantly. "I'll have the motor pool get the vehicles ready for your trip to Olympia."

*   *   *

Hansen High School, Friday, September 25th

Zach stepped from class as the last bell of the day sounded. Nearly every teacher warned him not to miss more anymore classes. He looked down at a fist-full of make-up assignments and sighed. Today might be Friday, and Sunday would be his eighteenth birthday, but he would spend the weekend on homework, installing a toilet, and other renovations.

DeLynn hurried down the hall. When she reached Zach's side she thumped his arm. "Vicki just told me you two are going to be living at the hotel. We're going to be neighbors again!" A mock frown crossed her face. "Why didn't you tell me that this morning?"

Together they walked down the hall.

"I had a lot on my mind and I didn't sleep well last night."

"Is there something wrong?"

"There was." Zach stopped at his locker. "But I think things are going to be better."

"No, you don't get away that easy. What's up?"

Zach looked about at all the people in the hall. "Not here. Tonight, maybe?"

"Okay." She smiled. "Tonight for sure. Do you feel well enough to pack? We can have you moved in today."

He spun the dial on the lock. "Could you and Vicki start? I've got to go by the armory."

"Vicki said you were quitting?"

"I am, but I left my school books in a Humvee. I need to find them."

This time a serious frown appeared. "I'll take you."

Zach slammed the locker shut, threw his backpack over one shoulder and followed her to the school parking lot. If the problems in his life were gradually being resolved, why did he feel pulled in different directions?

As they neared the Armory front gate, a dark blue SUV hurried down the hill.

"That was Major Westmore in the backseat." Zach turned

and followed the car with his eyes. "He only uses a driver when he's going out of the area. I wonder what's up."

"It's not really your concern anymore."

He sighed. "No, I guess not."

Zach left DeLynn in the car and went in search of his books. It didn't take long to find them on the floor beside Nelson's bunk. He placed them in his backpack and went looking for First Sergeant Fletcher. Telling him he was quitting would be hard. The first sergeant would ask why he wanted to leave and Zach didn't want to look like a quitter when he answered. He rehearsed the words he would use, but none seem to right. He liked the guys here. He wanted to be a part of it, but the faces of those he killed haunted him.

There didn't appear to be anyone in the armory office when he arrived. He was about to leave when Lieutenant Brooks stepped in.

"Hi, Zach, do you need something?"

"Ah, yes sir. I wanted to talk to the first sergeant."

"That'll be difficult. He's at White Pass by now. Can I help?"

"Ah … I need to quit my job here."

Brooks sat at his desk and motioned for Zach to sit. "What's wrong?"

People seemed to be asking him that a lot lately. "Nothing … not really." Zach shook his head slowly. "I need more time to study and I've had another job offer."

"Well, in your case this is just a job, you didn't enlist, but your work here has been great. The soldiers accept you as one of their own. I'd be sorry to see you go." Brooks sighed. "But, if that is your decision, I'll let Major Westmore know when he returns."

As he walked from the office, Zach felt like a coward turning his back on friends in danger. He told himself quitting was the right thing to do, even though it didn't feel right.

*   *   *

Olympia, Friday, September 25th

The sun cast long shadows across the parking lot near the Wainwright building. Caden walked briskly to the multi-story stone structure and up the steps. He entered and a soldier stepped forward and saluted. "Are you here for the meeting with General Harwich."

"Yes."

"Please speak with the nurses, before proceeding to the

meeting." He gestured to his right.

A nurse directed him to a small cubicle created with partitions and plastic sheets. One nurse took his temperature while another asked him questions about his health and condition, such as age and weight.

Without looking up from the tablet she asked, "Have you ever been exposed to the Kern Flu?"

"Yes. Three days ago."

Her head popped up. "Did you get sick?"

"No."

She turned to the other nurse. "What's his temperature?"

"Normal."

She took a deep breath and wrote quickly. "Are you experiencing nausea, dizziness or lightheadedness?" After a few more questions and negative answers from Caden, she said, "You appear to be fine. General Harwich has asked all meeting participants to proceed directly to room 315."

Caden knew right where to go. He had been briefed about the Kern Flu, and met Colonel Hutchison in room 315 just three days earlier. It had been a long and stressful period with refugees coming over the mountains from Yakima, riots at the FEMA camp near Longview, and the chaos in Morton. He hoped the colonel would be there, Caden had a lot he wanted to discuss with him.

Two guards stood by the heavy metal door at the entrance to room 315. They checked Caden's identification before admitting him. The windowless room still had two tables set in the form of a capital "T." A whiteboard occupied one wall. Ten officers in ACUs stood in small groups just inside, but neither General Harwich nor Colonel Hutchison had arrived. Caden walked idly about, saying hello to those inside. Caden smiled as he passed by two officers discussing the military situation. Major Dowrick stood nearby listening.

A lieutenant pointed to a small table near the whiteboard. "There's an agenda there and some briefing papers."

"Thanks." Caden collected the pages and sat down. Most of the agenda items dealt with the Kern Flu. The other matters were on the national political and military situation.

Caden glanced as another group entered the room. He recognized most of them, but quickly returned to his reading. A few minutes later someone sat across from him. He looked up from the papers and into the eyes of Colonel Hutchison, the commander of the Yakima region, just to the east of Caden's region.

"Major Westmore, I have a problem I need to speak with you about."

"Oh?" The colonel's brusque tone surprised Caden. "I need to speak with you also."

They moved to an empty corner of the room.

"Refugees from your area are pouring over the mountains into my area." Hutchison's manner was that of a disappointed parent. "Some are sick, a few are dying." He stabbed a finger to within an inch of Caden's chest. "You need to get control of the situation."

Caden's skin warmed, as anger blazed within him.

Chapter Eighteen

Olympia, Friday, September 25th

Caden wanted to break Hutchison's finger. He clenched his fist and considered using it across the colonel's jaw. "I interviewed refugees from your area. One said his wife was sick. An ambulance picked her up and hours later he was told she was dead."

"Does he think we killed her?"

"He said she wasn't that sick. Then he told me soldiers forced him and his family out of town."

Hutchison shook his head. "Sure, we pick up sick people, but we don't kill them. Are you isolating the sick? So am I. Are you trying to keep infected refugees out of populated areas? So am I."

"Refugees from your area infected Morton."

Hutchison smirked. "Who lives in Morton?"

"Just about no one—now."

"Attention!"

"At ease, gentlemen." General Harwich strode into the room. "Let's be seated and get this started."

Without another word, Hutchison walked away.

Immediately behind Harwich a general and admiral entered the room. Caden didn't recognize either of them. They were followed by Dr. Eaton, the man who had given the Kern flu briefing just a few days earlier. All of them sat along the top table except General Harwich. He remained standing.

"This will probably be the last face-to-face meeting until the pandemic is over." The general slowly scanned the room. "Realistically, we knew containment of the Kern flu would be impossible. Unfortunately, we were entirely correct in that

106

assessment."

The general nodded at a young lieutenant. The lights dimmed and a map appeared on the whiteboard. "As you see, we have a growing number of confirmed cases in Vancouver, Longview, Yakima, Pullman, and Spokane. In addition, there are many suspected cases in a dozen other cities and towns. The only town that has gone from red to clear is Hansen. Dr. Eaton is certain that will remain a rarity."

Caden smiled broadly and glanced at Colonel Hutchison.

The general moved to the other side of the whiteboard. "Beyond our state ... ah, next slide please ... the flu is entrenched in all the larger cities under constitutionalist control ... Portland, Boise, Denver, well, you see the state of affairs."

Caden studied the map. Red dots pinpointed all the cities Harwich mentioned and many others in the constitutionalist area, such as Boise, Salt Lake, and Omaha.

"It's only been a few days," someone said.

"Yes." The general nodded. "We appear to have consistently underestimated both the speed and the deadliness of this flu."

"Is there any progress in making a vaccine?" the captain beside Caden asked.

"Not yet." Dr. Eaton rose. "Several medical centers are attempting to grow the virus in the lab, but that has not yet been accomplished."

"Shouldn't you be trying to kill the virus, not make more of it?" the captain replied.

Eaton smiled. "We need a controlled supply so we can find ways to kill it."

The officer across from Caden shook his head. "So, this is why we're here? For an update on the flu?"

"Actually, no. We have a potentially bigger problem. The spread of the flu has not been as great in the eastern portion of the country. While this will change, our source inside the Durant administration tells us that during this period, when our forces are more seriously affected, he will launch a major offensive, codenamed Operation Hellhound, to eliminate the new congress, kill acting president John Harper, and Governor Monroe."

Gasps and murmurs filled the air.

"Why would Durant want to kill the governor?" Hutchison

asked.

Caden faced the colonel. "Governor Monroe is a leader of the political opposition to Durant and the likely next president in the constitutionalist states—that's why." He looked back to General Harwich. "Durant would need it done before the November election and have plausible deniability of his involvement."

"I agree." Harwich nodded. "Our source indicates that Durant loyalists are working with a traitor in this area to coordinate an attack, but that is all we know."

"So we don't know when?" someone asked.

"No." Harwich shook his head. "However, we have indications that it will be soon."

Hutchison tapped a pen on the table. "What are those clues?"

"Those 'clues', as you call them, are on a need-to-know basis. However, we can reveal some that concern us, here in the northwest. I'll let Admiral Wallace begin that portion."

The admiral stood and looked to the back of the room. "Would you put up the Pacific tactical map?" He pointed to a course plotted on the chart, and continued. "One of our attack submarines is following a Chinese navel battlegroup on a course that will lead it to the Strait of Juan de Fuca. The battlegroup includes five type 71 and 72a amphibious warfare ships. They could have 4,000 marines onboard along with tanks and other vehicles."

Tension filled the room and churned in Caden's stomach. "What do we plan to do?"

"Nothing for right now." The admiral sighed. "President Harper in Denver has warned the Chinese not enter the strait."

Caden wondered how threatening the words of a seventy-eight year old acting president of half a country would be.

The admiral continued. "We're no longer in a position to challenge the Chinese navy on the open seas. However, both the air force and navy will monitor the Chinese as they approach our waters.

"The Canadians have pledged to keep all Chinese ships and subs out of their waters. As the battlegroup approaches our coast they will enter the Strait of Juan de Fuca and hug the American coast. When that occurs we will challenge them."

Hutchison rubbed his chin. "What if they make their attack from off the coast?"

The air force general leaned forward. "If the Chinese launch any sort of attack our forces will respond appropriately."

The meeting had been going for nearly two hours when Caden stifled a yawn.

General Harwich stood. "If there are no more questions, I'm going to call it a night. Oh, one more thing. Governor Monroe will be leaving tonight for an undisclosed location. He will remain there until this current situation is over."

Caden rubbed his face as he left the room. It had been that kind of meeting—things were bad and they would get worse. He felt drained. When he noticed Hutchison up ahead, he hung back. He had made his point and had little desire for more conflict.

Outside, Caden spotted the three vehicles from the armory. As he walked toward them he wondered why General Harwich had asked him to bring the extra Humvees and men.

Five men stood in a tight group between the Humvees. One carried a large steel briefcase. Caden could see only two faces, but didn't know either. He tensed and glanced about. His men seemed relaxed. He continued toward the five. As he drew one turned and saluted.

"Governor Monroe requests you join him in your vehicle."

A bit confused he opened the back door of his car. Immediately he recognized the governor's chief-of-staff. Caden smiled, stepped inside and thrust out his hand. "Hi, David. What's going on?"

Weston clasped his hand. "Congratulations, you're the winner. I'm playing governor tonight and going home with you."

"What? But you're not the—."

"Let's get this convoy moving. I'll explain on the way."

The driver headed south as Weston continued. "Governor Monroe and his family will leave later for Colorado Springs. If Durant launches an offensive the governor will work with the military from there. Meanwhile, I'm the decoy if something happens here."

"So you want people to believe the governor is still here and with me?"

Weston nodded.

"How can you be sure the traitor will learn that you ... that is, Monroe ... left with me?"

Weston gave him an incredulous glance. "First of all it's easier to leak something than keep it secret and, did you notice anyone else arrive for this meeting with three vehicles and a squad of soldiers."

"The general asked me to bring them. I don't know ... oh, you planned the decoy before the meeting."

"You're catching on." Weston smiled. "You probably noticed the steel case one of the soldiers carried."

Caden nodded.

"That is a KY-68 secure phone so we can keep in better contact with command."

"Well, that'll be helpful, but how do you know I'm not the assassin?"

Weston smiled, but Caden thought he saw sadness mixed in. "Someday I hope I can tell you how I know you're not the traitor."

*　　　*　　　*

Hollister Hotel, Sunday, September 27th

Zach slapped at the windup alarm clock. When sufficient blows had silenced it, he rolled to a seated position, yawned, and walked across the cool room. He grabbed his clothes from a chair and dressed quickly.

Vicki and DeLynn would have to set the fish traps this morning. With most of his homework done, the toilet installed, and at least one light working in each room, he would spend his birthday on a hunting trip. He could almost taste the fresh meat and, what they didn't eat, he would sell. If Vicki and DeLynn wanted a party, they could have it tonight.

After dressing in brown trousers and a pale green shirt, he stumbled to the kitchen to find something to eat, but instead found an unfamiliar lunch box. A yellow sticky note hung from the side with a smiley face and read, "Love, DeLynn." Inside he found a thermos with soup, two sandwiches, and a cell phone with another sticky note. This one read, "Call me, if you get bored."

Where did she get an extra phone? He searched the device to set it on vibrate just in case DeLynn got bored, and called at an inopportune moment. As he fumbled with the phone he discovered it belonged to DeLynn's mother, Karen. He considered returning it, but he knew no one would be awake. Finally he set it to vibrate, slid the phone into a pocket, and the lunch box into his backpack.

With a smile on his face and feeling much warmer, he stuffed an orange hunting vest and flashlight into his pack. Then, near the door of the penthouse, he grabbed the antique lever-action 30-30, he had traded venison and fish for earlier in the year.

As he hiked from town he considered his exact destination. In the past he had noticed that hunters seemed to prefer downhill treks. He would proceed uphill in the general direction of the armory. To avoid getting shot by inexperienced hunters, he put on the hunting vest as he entered the forest. Vicki, DeLynn, and even some guys he knew, would be nervous walking in the woods before dawn, but it never bothered him.

A twig snapped to his right.

He stopped and listened for a moment, but heard nothing. He recalled coming across a pack of wild dogs nearby. *Okay, I almost never get nervous.* Certain the twig had not been a dog pack, he continued.

Fifteen minutes later, Zach came out of the woods into chest high grass along a muddy path. A stream splashed a few yards ahead, but in the predawn darkness, he couldn't see it.

Something rustled against the nearby grass.

The breeze was gentle and in Zach's direction. He kneeled, slid the rifle from his shoulder, and breathed slowly.

Thirty yards ahead a large buck lifted its head from the grass.

Since the animal foraged in his general direction, Zach waited for a closer shot.

The buck ambled back and forth along the path, casually eating.

Visions of venison steaks filled Zach's head.

The buck's head jumped into the air and looked back, the way it came. Ears twitched. The animal galloped forward.

Startled Zach fell backwards.

A yard from him, the animal reared up.

Hoofs danced inches from Zach's head.

Then the animal spun and raced into the trees.

What in the name of heaven just happened? Why did the buck charge? Was that a rut behavior?

He sat there for a moment, trying to figure it out, when he heard more rustling in the grass. Cautiously he lifted his head.

A squad of camouflaged soldiers crept toward him.

Chapter Nineteen

Hansen Armory, Sunday, September 27th

David Weston opened his eyes and reached for the phone that vibrated and hummed on the nightstand beside him. "Weston here."

"The individual has been identified."

Weston recognized the voice and sat up in bed. From the cryptic phrase he knew they had identified the spy. "Who is it?"

"They're not yet in custody, so I'd rather not say."

"Okay. When can I return to Olympia?"

"Not right now. Operation Hellhound is in full swing. The Chinese are near the strait and, we believe, a special ops unit has deployed to kill the governor."

Weston rubbed his face. He knew that any unit out to kill Governor Monroe would actually be on his trail and, if they found him, most likely kill him. "I understand." He grabbed his pants and shirt from the back of the chair, and went to find Caden.

*   *   *

Near the Hansen Armory, Sunday, September 27th

For just a moment Zach thought he should announce his presence, but he didn't and slid down into the grass while he considered what to do. The pre-dawn glow did not provide enough light to identify the soldiers, but they were in standard army ACUs—they had to be from the armory. He must have stumbled into some sort of exercise. No. He quit two days ago and there hadn't been any maneuvers planned.

Zach knelt and stretched until he could see through the tops of the grass. The soldiers weren't following the path. He dropped his head down below the stalks. Perhaps they didn't know about the trail. Their course would take them a few yards south of him. Using the trail, he moved away.

When he reached the cover of rocks and trees, Zach lay between two boulders and watched. Eight soldiers moved through the grass almost without a sound. The only squad scheduled to be at the armory this weekend was Sixth Squad, a bunch of recruits. The men Zach watched didn't move like newbies. Except for the rustle of grass and an occasional snap of a twig they crept forward with stealth.

Whoever these soldiers were, they advanced ever closer to the armory, less than a mile away.

Zach's stomach churned so much that he worried the soldiers might hear. He needed to do something, but what?

In the distance he spotted more soldiers crossing the meadow, and counted a total of sixteen, but doubted he saw them all.

This had to be an exercise.

He continued to watch when someone stepped from the tree line several hundred yards downstream. In the soft morning light Zach could only be certain the person had a rifle and wore civilian clothes.

Two soldiers moved toward the hunter with rifles at the ready.

The man held up his hands with the rifle in one.

Another soldier came up behind him, whipped out a large knife, and slit his throat.

Zach struggled to breathe as he slid backwards, and around bramble and brush, until the forest bush surrounded him. He wanted to run in panic, but that would get him killed. As he fought to control both his breath and emotions, he recalled a nearby gully. With slow, steady movements he removed his backpack and orange hunting vest. Then he stuffed the vest in the backpack. He planned to crouch low, reach the gully, and head away from the soldiers.

No.

These killers were the enemy and his friends at the armory were, almost certainly, their target. He had to warn them.

But how?

As he watched, the soldiers reached the tree line. The closest would soon pass ten yards from him and he still had no idea what to do.

Then he recalled the phone DeLynn had passed to him. Holding his breath he slid the backpack from his shoulders and pulled out the phone inch but slow inch. Breathing quietly he stared at the device unable to do anything. He never owned a cell phone, and rarely used one. They didn't even have a landline at the trailer. He didn't know any phone numbers. Panic rose within him again.

He did know one number, DeLynn's. He rolled into a ball and punched the numbers.

"Zach? Is that you? I didn't expect you to call so early?"

"What's the number for the armory?" He could barely hear himself.

"Why are you whispering? I can't hear you."

He tried again, but she still couldn't hear and he dared talk no louder.

A text box appeared on the screen with a click. He immediately turned the sound off. "R U OK? What do u need?"

He started typing his reply but changed his mind. "Need # 4 Caden Westmore."

"Why?"

"Tell u later. Pls hurry."

His stomach churned and every sound of the forest caused his heart to race. Finally, the number appeared on the screen. Then another box, "What's going on? UR scaring me."

"Later. Got to go." Zach hung up and texted Caden.

* * *

Hansen Armory, Sunday, September 27ᵗʰ

Caden sat on the bunk in his office, wiped an eye with one hand, and squinted at the message with the other. Word that the base would soon be under attack didn't surprise him, but that the news came from a Karen Hollister somewhere in the nearby forest, did. Using his thumbs he typed out a quick reply. "Who R U?"

"FM Zach. Borrowed a phone. I'm 1/2m WNW of Armory. 16 soldiers moving ESE toward base. They killed a hunter."

"RG. Stay on phone & both u and Karen get out of there."

Weston burst into the room, still buttoning his shirt. He looked pale and disheveled, not at all like the man Caden had seen so often before. "Operation Hellhound ... they're coming."

"Actually, they're here." Caden said flatly.

Weston moaned.

Caden stood, arched his back, and wished for coffee. "Sergeant!"

Rubbing his eyes, the soldier stepped into the doorway. "Yes, sir."

"Get everyone awake and ready for combat. Do it quick but quiet. The armory is going to be attacked. This is not a drill."

The sergeant closed his mouth and swallowed. "Yes, sir." He turned and ran down the hall.

*   *   *

Near the Hansen Armory, Sunday, September 27th

Zach needed no further encouragement than Caden's order to leave. Staying as low as possible he crept to the gully and moved north, away from both the soldiers and the armory. When several hundred yards separated him from the threatening soldiers, Zach turned in the direction of a nearby road.

His stomach churned less now and breathing came easier. He pulled out the phone DeLynn gave him.

Caden had left several messages asking his location and if he were okay.

Zach started to type out a reply, but stopped. He couldn't leave. His friends were in danger and he could provide valuable intel about the enemy position and strength. He would use a wide arch route to reach a rock outcrop that would serve as a good observation post.

He typed a new reply. "Heading toward rock outcrop NW of armory. Will signal when close. The moment he sent it he knew it was a foolish plan. The soldiers in the forest would kill to keep their presence unknown and, if the armory soldiers spotted him, they might shoot. Friendly fire was rarely friendly.

Caden's reply vibrated the phone. "No! Get out of area. That's an order!"

"Not in the military and, XO shud have told u, I quit job on Fri. Will tell u when

115

I'm in position." Then he hastily added. "Pls don't shoot me." Zach stuffed the phone in his right trouser pocket and stepped up the hill.

Loose gravel gave way and he fell hard, scraping his right arm and leg.

Great start to my heroic plan. He held his breath for several seconds as he listened to the world around him. Only the breeze rustled in his ears.

Carefully, Zach stood and climbed the hill toward the rocks and trees that he knew would hide him. Still, every twig or mat of fir needles would shout his presence if he stepped wrong.

He wasn't a military strategist, but as the light grew Zach wondered if the soldiers were behind schedule. In every war movie he'd ever seen, the sneak attack came at night, not after dawn. He continued up the hill aware that, as dawn drew near, the cover of darkness faded for both the soldiers and him. Even when the granite boulders and ancient fir trees came into view, he worried the morning light might reveal him.

Between his own steps a twig snapped. The sound came from the east, not from the west as Zach expected. He dismissed it as an animal, but then another twig broke and another. Creeping to the top of a nearby knoll he peered over. Five soldiers stood in a group just ten yards away. They appeared to be consulting a map. Zach grinned at the thought of them being lost, but then they turned and headed in the direction of the armory.

As he slid below the top of the knoll, he spotted another soldier advancing west. Panic surged within him. Like a vise, one group of at least five soldiers advanced from the east, another group of sixteen came from the west. If he didn't get to cover, he would be caught and killed as the vise grip of soldiers grew ever tighter.

He took several deep drafts of air and moved with all the stealth he could muster toward the rocky cover.

*　　　*　　　*

Hansen Armory, Sunday, September 27th

Caden studied the topographical map of the area spread out on the conference room table. He looked up when David Weston returned with Lieutenant Brooks.

The XO studied the map. "What's the situation?"

"Zach reported sixteen soldiers advancing on our position

from the northwest. About here." He tapped the chart.

Weston looked at the map. "Are you sure they're out there?"

"Yes." Caden nodded and returned his gaze to the map. "The boy is reliable. I just hope he's safe."

"What is he doing out there?" Brooks sat at the table. "He quit on Friday. Sorry, with this Operation Hellhound situation, I forgot to tell you."

"Yes, he mentioned that he quit, but apparently that's a difficult concept for him. He's acting as a spotter."

"Where exactly?" Brooks leaned in closer to the map.

"I don't know." Caden shook his head. "He said he was going to a rock outcrop northwest of the base, but I've never explored these woods. I don't know where that would be and the call ended several minutes ago. We've had no word since."

Chapter Twenty

Hansen Armory, Sunday, September 27th

"You could call him," Weston suggested.

"And risk his phone ringing, beeping, or whatever?" Caden shook his head. "We'll have to wait for his call." He turned to Brooks. "How are we doing for manpower?"

"We have everyone back except the first sergeant and his men." He looked at his watch. "They should be here soon. I just hope it's before the shooting starts."

"Does everyone have their gear? Are they in position?"

Brooks nodded. "Yes to both, sir."

"Good." He wanted to inspect the defenses, but that would reveal many of them to those outside the fence. Caden sighed. "I can't figure out their plan."

Weston peeked through the blinds of a window. "I'm no military man, but isn't the idea to attack this place, kill the governor and, since I'm pretending to be him—kill me?"

"Attacking the armory anytime would be difficult, but they should have done it an hour or more earlier, not this late. The best way to do it would be when we were traveling down here or when we leave. Unless they have mortars and RPGs to force us out of the buildings and defensive positions, we can hold this base for a long time with the soldiers and supplies available."

Brooks rubbed his chin. "Maybe they do have mortars and RPGs."

"With the perimeter defenses we've set up, we could still hold the armory for a couple of hours. Remember we have the SINCGARS radio and now the KY-68 phone. We can get reinforcements from Olympia."

Brooks rubbed his chin. "But it would take at least an hour."

"Perhaps they don't plan on attacking," Weston said with a hopeful grin.

"Then why are they here?" Caden stood, intending to inspect the positions inside the buildings and on the rooftops, when his phone beeped.

*   *   *

Observation Post WNW of Armory, Sunday, September 27th

Encircled by boulders, giant fir trees, and bramble, Zach collapsed at the top of the knoll, let out the air in his lungs, and tried to breathe normally. After several moments, he eased his head above the nearby rock and vegetation. About ten feet above the surrounding forest, his position was good. He couldn't see the armory through the brush and trees, but the soldiers were moving into a line only thirty yards ahead.

He reached into his pocket and cut his finger. Biting his lip, he eased the phone from his pocket. Blood dripped on a maze of cracked glass across the screen.

Zach sighed inwardly. He must have broken the screen when he fell. For several seconds he poked the device trying to launch the text app. When it appeared he turned and looked over the positions of the enemy. As he counted the men before him he noticed something unusual off to the right. The soldiers had a tripod and a weird contraption. He didn't understand what they were doing, but knew it must be important.

Tapping his thumbs on the cracked glass Zach struggled to compose a message. Because of the damage, he turned the phone on the side to type some of the letters. As he sent the message he realized he'd been holding his breath. Silently he forced himself to breathe in and out.

*   *   *

Hansen Armory, Sunday, September 27th

Caden grabbed the phone from the table and read the message.

"Zach here. 10 Soldiers 100yds WNW of armory. Set up a tripod. Pointing something at u. Doesn't look like rifle or mortar. Squareish, more like camera."

"Is it Zach?" Brooks asked.

Caden nodded and read the message aloud.

Brook's eyes shot wide. "What are we going to do?"

"Huh?" Weston's looked confused. "What is that thing the kid saw?"

"It's a laser targeting device. They're guiding a missile to this building."

Weston stepped toward the door. "Ah … shouldn't we get out of here?"

Caden slammed his fist on the table. "That's what the other soldiers are here for. It only takes a couple to set up the laser. They want to kill all of us. If we try to leave they'll use suppressive fire to keep us bottled up until the missile strikes." He rubbed his chin as he thought. "Phone the lookout on the roof. Ask them if they can spot the laser."

After conferring, Brooks shook his head. "They don't see soldiers or anything unusual."

A soldier ran into the room. "The first sergeant is five minutes away."

Caden rubbed his chin even harder. He sent a message on his phone and smiled at the reply. "I have a plan."

*   *   *

Observation Post WNW of Armory, Sunday, September 27th

"If we provide cover fire can you shoot the laser?"

Zach tapped out his reply. "Yes."

"Get ready. In 1m we fire. After u shoot-leave."

He took a deep breath, rose slowly and rested his rifle on the rock. With the laser off to his right, he had a good angle for the shot. For the next several moments he focused on sighting in the device and waited.

A branch snapped.

He looked down and to his left, into the eyes of a soldier about his age.

*   *   *

Hansen Armory, Sunday, September 27th

Caden stood in the hall by the main entrance dressed in combat gear. The doors faced east toward the parking lot and main gate. He looked to Brooks and the sergeant. "We only get one chance to do this right. Does everyone understand what they have to do?"

Heads nodded.

Caden patted the pistol on his side and gave his M4 a quick inspection. Behind him were twenty young soldiers with nervous and worried faces. Caden's stomach churned. Good men would die today. Anxious, he glanced at his watch.

Gunfire erupted from the roof of the building.

"Go!" Caden burst through the doors.

Immediately they came under fire from the forest to the east.

The soldiers from the armory fanned across the parking lot and returned fire.

Caden slid behind a car and fired off a three-round burst.

Brooks did the same five feet to his left.

The sound of rifle fire boomed in Caden's ears. Bullets pinged and ricocheted. The windshield beside him shattered. Blood trickled into his eyes. He wiped his face with one arm and noticed more cuts on his hand.

Brooks slid down the vehicle and curled into a fetal position with a phone to his ear.

"Are you okay?" Caden shouted.

Brooks nodded.

Caden continued to shoot.

Squatting low the XO scooted close. Blood from several cuts ran down his face. "The first sergeant reports he's coming up behind soldiers east of the armory. He'll be in position in one minute."

Caden smiled. That was good news. If the missile hit they were still too close but, hopefully, Zach had taken care of that and the noise of their gunfire had covered his shot. "Ceasefire. Pass the word."

While the gunfire gradually stopped from Caden's men in the parking lot, it continued in other directions from the roof and defensive positions on the north and west of the armory. He waited hoping the traitors in the forest wouldn't notice the change of gunfire.

Caden worried as the seconds ticked along. Then he heard gunfire erupt from deeper in the forest. The blasts told him Fletcher had engaged the soldiers on the east.

*   *   *

Observation Post WNW of Armory, Sunday, September 27th

The soldier's M4 fired a three round burst.

Zach felt a blazing hot burn as one bullet cut along his cheek. The others kicked up stone and dirt into his face. Zach fired a single shot from his 30-30.

The soldier stumbled back.

Zach fired again and the young man fell limp to the ground.

Even with the noise of gunfire from the armory, several soldiers turned.

Zach shot the laser.

It fell.

For good measure he fired another round into the device.

Bullets slammed around Zach, throwing dust and dirt into his face. Gunfire filled his ears as he bolted from the hill. Like a cheetah he shot through the forest only wavering to avoid obstacles in his path. Death and fear filled most of his thoughts, but as he sprinted he recalled the day he tried to catch DeLynn's kidnappers. If he ran hard he could lose these soldiers.

Then the realization hit him, he couldn't outrun a bullet. He changed his strategy. Using the natural features of the forest for momentary cover he ran from tree to bramble to gully and rocks. Each time he came from behind something, Zach cringed, expecting a bullet to slam into him. His lungs burned but he dared not slowdown. The soldiers might be right behind him.

At the top of a slope he slid on loose ground and tumbled over and over, down a steep embankment to the creek below.

He splashed into the shallow water and jumped to his feet.

Pain shot through both legs.

Zach collapsed to his hands and knees. He glanced up the slope. No soldiers were in sight. His heart still pounded, but he slung his rifle on his back and dragged himself to the cover of nearby bushes.

Now hidden, he examined his wounds. Blood stained the right thigh of his jeans. Glass snagged denim threads as he eased the phone from his pocket. Pain shot down his limb. Several pieces of glass were missing from the bloody screen. He knew for certain where they were.

No hope of calling for help remained. He dropped the remnants into his backpack. With great care he pulled his pants down to mid-thigh and hoped he would remain undiscovered. He didn't want to die with his pants down.

He pulled his shirt off and used it to brush blood and small pieces of glass from his leg. Then he swept across another spot and pain surged like an electric shock.

A deep moan rose in his throat, but he choked it back. Footfalls!

Zach stifled a groan as he looked through the bush.

Six men scrambled down the embankment.

Were they looking for him? No. These soldiers sprinted as they passed on both sides. He sat frozen, barely breathing; convinced he would soon die with his shirt off and his pants halfway down his legs. He sighed inwardly remembering that today he turned eighteen. Afraid he would die on his birthday he remained still until they disappeared up the far bank.

Shots boomed in the woods and distant voices sounded in the air. A helicopter flew low over the gully. Shouts arose in the forest, but no one came close enough for Zach to identify. So, he remained hidden in the brush, staring into the blue sky. Gradually he realized the only sounds were the gentle ripple of the creek and the breeze.

Again he examined his legs.

As he pulled the sliver from his limb, Zach wondered how he would pay for Mrs. Hollister's phone. Examining the two inch long-shard he was thankful it cut at a steep angle and not directly into his leg. The wound would be painful and need a few stiches, but he could walk.

His left ankle still throbbed. He hoped it wasn't broken, but the pain indicated at least a sprain. He might be able to hobble along. With a smile, he recalled the saying first sergeant Fletcher often said, "What doesn't kill you makes you stronger." He was growing very strong today.

Now high in the sky, the sun indicated a time around noon. Were there more enemy soldiers in the woods? He didn't know. But if there were, he couldn't outrun them. Still he felt like a coward hiding in the bushes. He had run while his friends fought. How many died had died after he ran away?

Hours passed before he could bring himself to eat the lunch DeLynn had provided. Over the next few hours he drank from his water bottle, but other than that, hardly moved.

The sun cast dark shadows across the gully before he left his hiding place. He filled his water bottle from the stream, and found a long branch to use as a crutch. The embankment loomed too steep to climb in his condition, so he followed the creek to a nearby road. There he hoped a car would come along and offer him a ride, but no one passed.

The moonless night overtook the day while he trudged the side road. The stars were beautiful, but the darkness made his hobble all the more difficult. He seemed to stumble over every rock in along the path. He retrieved his flashlight, but used it only sparingly. Batteries were expensive.

As he neared the main highway his foot kicked something soft and he fell across it.

The softness moaned. "Help us."

"What?" Zach, on his hands and knees, turned back at the sound of a woman's voice. He patted for what he barely saw.

A hand grabbed his collar with unexpected force and pulled him close. "Help us. They stole our car."

Zach felt her breath as she spoke. He pulled back and fell on another lump of softness. In near panic he scrambled painfully toward the road. Clutching his branch like a weapon, but still on his knees he used his other hand to turn on the flashlight.

A woman and two small children lay huddled along the roadside.

Chapter Twenty One

East of Hansen, Sunday, September 27th

"Are ... my girls ... okay?" The voice came as a whisper.

Zach crawled back between the mother and girls. The two children were inches from the woman, so close that Zach, had to be careful not to kneel on them. They both felt cool and he found no pulse. "Ah ... they're okay." He lied.

"Help us."

Zach could barely help himself. He had been hobbling down the road all night. He had no idea how to assist this poor woman. "What happened? What can I do?"

"Do you have ... a phone? They took mine."

Zach grasped the phone in his bag. But as he pulled it out he recalled its sorry condition.

She smiled at the sight of it. "Call 911."

The shattered screen told Zach no call could be made. He smiled at the woman. "Of course." He tapped the screen once. "Ah, they'll want to know what happened."

"Sick. We were going ... to the hospital. Carjacked. We've been walking."

"Okay. I'll tell them." Zach wanted to run from the woman and the illness that he knew might be Kern flu, but he stayed. He tapped the broken screen three times and then faked a conversation with the emergency operator. When he ended the call he forced a smile. "They're coming." But he had done nothing to help her, and the longer he stayed the more likely he would be exposed. "I should go down to the main road. I could stop a car. They might be able to help."

"No. Stay with me … please."

He nodded, and cradled her head in his lap.

"Do you have any water?"

"Yes." He pulled the bottle from his bag and offered all she wanted.

As the next twenty minutes past, her breathing slowed, and then stopped.

He checked her carotid artery for a pulse and found none. Rarely had Zach sought answers from God, but as tears welled, he lifted his face to the sky. "Why? Why bring me here if there was nothing I could do?" He set her head on the earth and stood.

"God, what good have I done here? I couldn't save this woman. I couldn't save my own mother. What good have I done anywhere?"

Zach grasped the crutch-stick and continued along the road, but a after a few yards he collapsed to the ground, stricken by both exhaustion and despair. He had no idea how long he sat there mulling his physical and emotional distress.

When the eastern sky turned shades of purple and pink he rose, leaned hard on his branch, and resumed his slow hobble. By the time he reached the city limit the sun shone over the nearby hills and seemed unusually warm. Zach drank deeply from his half-full water bottle.

*   *   *

Hansen Armory, Monday, September 28th

Caden watched the growing splendor of dawn from the window of his office. It was good to be alive.

Weston entered, talking on his phone. "Well, that's all great news. Thanks. I'll see you shortly." He slipped his phone into a jacket pocket. "The troops from Olympia will take the prisoners for interrogation and Governor Monroe says I should head back."

"Are you going to Olympia or joining the governor in Colorado?" Caden turned away from the window.

"Olympia for now, but events are moving fast. I'll probably join him in Colorado soon."

Caden yawned. He had been up all night. "You found the traitor?"

"Yes. We were watching a few people certain one of them was the spy. We simply waited to see who acted on the false information we gave them."

Caden thought for a moment. "Is the spy Colonel Hutchison?"

"Hutchison?" Weston smiled. "No, he's a pain in the backside, but he's an old-fashioned patriot."

"Who then?"

"You probably don't know him." Weston shook his head. "Until recently, I didn't know him. He works ... worked, in the intelligence department, but didn't have the kind of personality that stood out. His name is Major Dowrick."

The name seemed familiar, but Caden struggled to recall the face. Then it came to him. He had met Dowrick one week ago in Olympia. Colonel Hutchison had joked that Dowrick didn't talk much, but listened and asked good questions. Caden nodded. Of course Dowrick listened well. That was his real job. "What will they do to him?"

"Treason is a capital offense." Weston stepped across the small office, but stopped in the doorway. "I'll pack my toothbrush and underwear." Still in the entryway, he hesitated. "That kid in the forest who warned us ... did you ever find him?"

"Zach? No. We're still looking." Caden prayed no harm had come to him.

*   *   *

Hansen, Monday, September 28th

Zach drank the last of his water as the sun blazed over his head. A few cars passed him, but none stopped. He realized that with a cut along one cheek, blood stained jeans and hobbling along using a branch he probably looked like a refugee from a FEMA camp or a bum. It didn't matter. He would soon reach the hotel and home.

When he turned the corner he saw the hotel, but stopped. He couldn't go there. The woman he helped probably had Kern flu. If he had been exposed he might infect DeLynn, Vicki, and others. The girls would be upset when he didn't come home, but if he had the flu they would live and, if he wasn't sick, he would explain and apologize profusely.

He wanted to tell someone about the bodies of the woman and her children, but he didn't see a way to do that without exposing others. Tomorrow, when he knew he wasn't ill, might be the best he could do.

Zach turned north and limped out of town. He thought about going to the hospital. Even if he didn't have the flu the doctors could treat his leg that throbbed with each step and stitch his hip and cheek.

His head ached and stomach churned. On crippled foot, the journey to the hospital would take two hours, but the place that had been home for many years would take only thirty minutes. He turned off the main road and headed for the rusty blue trailer. Hot, tired and thirsty, he spotted the end of his old driveway on schedule.

As he shuffled up the gravel lane he heard a car and looked over his shoulder. A deputy drove by. He shouted and waved, but the car had already passed. He grumbled at his bad luck, retrieved the key from the bush where it was hidden, and stumbled into the trailer.

*   *   *

Observation Post WNW of Armory, Monday, September 28th

Caden followed First Sergeant Fletcher into the woods northwest of the armory.

"I'm sure this is the place Zach used." Fletcher pushed bramble aside with his elbow, and climbed to the top of the small knoll. "I discovered it a couple of years ago on a hike in the area."

Caden spotted the dark red stain on the stone just ahead. Stepping close, he ran his fingers along the now dry blood.

"Yeah, I noticed that too." Fletcher stepped to a nearby bush and moved a few branches. "We also found this." He pointed to four 30-30 cartridges on the ground. "We found two bullets in the laser targeting device and a dead soldier just over there." He pointed. "All of this tells me he didn't get away cleanly. He may have been captured. But if not, he may have crawled off somewhere to hide and ah … well, he might be so weak now that he can't signal us."

"We'll keep looking," Caden ordered.

"Yes, sir."

As he walked from the hill, Caden prayed the young man still lived.

*   *   *

Brennon Trailer, Rural Lewis County, Monday, September 28th

Zach awoke. Light shone in through a small window. Boxes were stacked along one wall. The bed was gone, but this had once been his bedroom. He struggled to recall what task had brought him there. He leaned back in the ancient recliner that now served as a bed and pulled the blanket high on his chest. How long had he been there?

Nausea swept up from his stomach. He stumbled from the recliner and hurried to toward the bathroom. Pain in his ankle and exhaustion brought him to his knees. He vomited on the carpet near the recliner. Sweat ran down his face, but he couldn't stop shivering. Slowly he returned to the chair and pulled the blanket tight around him. Thoughts came in hazy disjointed bits, but he put the pieces together and realized the cause of his symptoms—Kern flu.

Zach pulled the blanket tight around him and smiled. Turning away from the hotel had been the right choice. He had stopped the spread of the virus.

He would die, but DeLynn and Vicki would live.

Chapter Twenty Two

Hansen Armory, Monday, September 28th

About noon, Caden walked across the parking lot still thinking about those who died and the one still missing—Zach. Caden pushed from his mind the thought First Sergeant Fletcher had brought up, that the boy might be wounded and dying, concealed somewhere in the forest.

Caden intended to go home, eat, wash up, and return to the search. He also needed to talk with Sheriff Hoover. Explaining a battle at the edge of town would best be done in person.

He fumbled with his keys and looked up as he approached his vehicle. Three holes punctured the windshield with cracks crisscrossing the rest. A pool of oil threaded off to one side and two tires were flat.

He stared at the car wondering how he might get a replacement.

A nineteen year-old private pulled alongside. "Do you need a ride, sir?"

Caden rode to the sheriff's office listening to rap music.

Hoover stood in the lobby talking to a deputy. "We'll deal with the consequences as they appear." He turned as Caden neared. "I'm glad to see you're okay. What was all that shooting this morning? I tried to get close with two of my deputies, but your people warned us off. Half the town called 911."

Caden explained what he could. "So, we had to pull our soldiers from the checkpoints to defend the armory and counterattack."

Hoover nodded. "A couple hours after your people left, the

refugee camp outside of town rioted. I think they knew the soldiers were gone. We couldn't hold it alone, so I pulled the deputies. The refugees flooded into town. I'm trying to locate the sick people, but it's probably too late."

"So, Kern flu is now in Hansen." Caden sighed. "Do you need my soldiers back on the checkpoints?"

"I suppose we should regain control of them."

Caden nodded and made a call to Brooks.

A minute later the squad car rumbled up the driveway to the Westmore home.

As Caden climbed from the vehicle, his dad stepped from the barn. "I thought we were done with the days of deputies bringing you home."

"I thought so, too." Caden grinned and waved as Hoover drove away. Turning to his father he asked, "Did you hear the shooting last night?"

"A couple thousand gunshots will rouse even a deep sleeper like me."

"Well, I'm going to need a new car."

"You all right?"

He nodded.

"I can't help with your car problems, but I'm fixing the well-house door. Join me in the barn and tell me about last night."

Caden followed his father to the old tack room which he'd converted into a tool room or, as he called it, the "man cave."

Caden sat in an old wooden chair.

His dad picked up a screwdriver. "That wasn't an exercise last night."

"No." Caden explained what he could about the soldiers surrounding the armory and trying to guide a missile in. "But Zach shot the laser targeting device and we were able to stage a counter attack. Some got away, but we captured a few."

His father put down the screw driver and rubbed his chin. "What I can't figure out is why they attacked here and no place else in the state."

"I don't think I can explain that part."

"Are you telling me you know, but can't say?" His father measured the bottom width of the door.

"I know why we were attacked." The chair creaked loudly as

Caden leaned back.

His father nodded and changed the subject. "The news on the radio said Kern flu spread out of St. Louis to the surrounding counties. Durant forces attacked Missouri this morning. Do you think all these events are somehow connected?"

"Yes, they are, but that's all I can say." Caden wished he had a cup of coffee.

"Well, aren't you a fount of information."

"Sorry. You're asking good questions."

That seemed to please his dad.

Caden rubbed his face. "Attacking now won't work to Durant's advantage for long, but it will spread the disease and misery quicker."

"Well at least those Chinese ships off the coast turned around." His father sanded the edge of the door.

"I hadn't heard. That is good news." But he wondered why the ships had been there to begin with.

"You better get inside and tell Maria about this morning. It was all I could do to keep her from phoning you right in the middle of the shooting."

As Caden entered the house he felt something wrap around his leg. Looking down he saw Adam gazing up at him with a wide-mouth grin, both arms wrapped around his leg. Caden reached down and lifted him. "Hi, little guy."

Maria burst from the kitchen. "Oh, there he is." Then her tired eyes settled on Caden. "I was worried about you."

He nodded. "Come sit with me and I'll tell you everything I can." He felt he would be explaining for the next few days. As he started his story Adam fell asleep in his arms. Minutes later, as the baby stirred, Caden finished.

"Why did those soldiers attack the armory?"

He shifted Adam to Maria. "That's the part I can't tell you."

"And you still haven't found Zach?"

"No." He shook his head. "We're looking. Some of the soldiers got away on a helicopter. I hope they didn't take him with them. If they did, we may never know what happened to him."

Maria stared at the floor. "The news reported that the Chinese ships turned around this morning. Could the helo have flown out to them?"

"No. They were still too far away."

"Everybody was watching those ships, but they turned out to be nothing." She shook her head. "Sort of like the magician who says, 'Watch here,' but then tricks you with the other hand."

Caden's jaw dropped and then he laughed.

Adam awoke.

Maria frowned.

"Sorry, but I think you might have figured it out. The ships may have been a distraction." While he thought Maria had the right idea he wondered why the Chinese would mount such a big, expensive, diversion. If this were a huge sleight-of-hand was the trick complete or would there be another?

*   *   *

Brennon Trailer, Rural Lewis County, Monday, September 28th

A scream roused Zach from blissful darkness. His eyes opened, but were unable to focus. Frightened voices of two girls, both somehow familiar, came to him. He wondered what scared them. Then darkness returned.

*   *   *

DeLynn gasped at the smell of vomit and the sight of Zach so deathly pale. He looked dead, but then his eyes fluttered.

Vicki screamed and tried to push by.

DeLynn grabbed her arm. "No!"

"He's hurt or sick. All that gunfire this morning! He could be dying."

DeLynn shut the door and blocked the knob with her body. "I didn't see any blood. I'm guessing he has that Kern flu everyone's talking about."

"But we've got to do something."

"We will." DeLynn didn't budge from the door. "Find a towel and wet it so it's damp, not dripping, and bring it to me."

Vicki still looked confused, but did as requested.

With the damp towel wrapped around her nose, mouth and head, DeLynn cautiously approached Zach. His skin felt cool and clammy. She turned his head and discovered a nasty cut along one cheek. It would require stitches, but wasn't life threatening. Moments later she discovered a bloodstain on his hip. It felt weird to unbutton and pull down his jeans, but she needed to see the wound. She found another bad cut, but not the cause of his comatose state.

Next she struggled to roll his limp body to one side and check his back. He felt damp, but no blood stained her fingers. DeLynn moved toward the door. "He's sick. There're two wounds, but neither are serious. I think he got in a fight with someone who had the flu."

"Should we take him to the hospital or call an ambulance?" Vicki asked from the doorway.

DeLynn dropped the towel just inside the bedroom, exited and shut the door. She pulled her phone from a pocket and dialed 911. She expected an ambulance to come with siren blaring but, several minutes later, two Humvees rolled up the driveway. Four soldiers wearing gas masks and peculiar raincoats jumped out. They grabbed a stretcher and first-aid kits and hurried to the trailer.

DeLynn stepped toward the door to open it, but before she could they burst in.

"Where's Zach Brennon?" the lead soldier asked.

Vicki pointed to the bedroom.

DeLynn followed the strangely-dressed soldiers. She wanted answers, but they were frightening in those outfits and didn't seem inclined to respond to questions. She heard another vehicle drive up and looked out the window. Caden Westmore stepped out of an old farm pickup. Zach told her he was some sort of high-ranking officer, and his boss when he worked at the armory. His familiar face and standard camouflage uniform made him less intimidating than the alien looking soldiers in the house. Intent on asking him why the military showed up at a 911 call, she strode across the living room.

Caden stepped just inside the trailer and motioned for her and Vicki to join him outside. "If Zach has been exposed to Kern flu it's probably best to keep as much distance as possible. I'm very glad you found him. We've been searching since the battle yesterday."

DeLynn gazed toward the bedroom door. "Why?"

"That young man saved everyone at the armory yesterday."

"Huh?" DeLynn shook her head confused. "He went hunting."

"Yesss." Caden smiled. "At just the right place to save a lot of people." He told her how Zach spotted the soldiers, passed intel, and shot the laser device.

The medic stepped into the doorway. "He's weak, but we're ready to transport."

"Do so." Caden turned back to them. "We'll make sure he has the best of care."

"Thank you." DeLynn grabbed Vicki's hand. "We'll follow them to the hospital in my car."

*   *   *

Zach awoke flat on his back as they wheeled him down a pastel blue hall on a gurney. Everyone around him wore either Mopp gear or a biohazard suit. Harsh lights blazed in his eyes and a methodical beeping throbbed in his ears. Everything hurt. Intravenous bags hung on either side of him.

A man in a white smock pointed. "Get him in treatment room one."

An alarm roared as the darkness fought to engulf him.

A woman shouted, "His blood pressure's falling."

Chapter Twenty Three

Westmore Farm, Rural Lewis County, Saturday, October 3rd

Caden sat in the living room after breakfast listening to the radio.

"... those already infected. Wash often with soap and water or alcohol-based hand rubs ... if you can find them. Avoid touching your eyes, nose, or mouth. Cover your mouth with a tissue ... again if you can find some ... and then throw the tissue away. If you experience nausea or vomiting and your temperature is over 100 degrees stay inside. Avoid contact with others, and call 911 for medical assistance."

When he heard the voice of Becky, his former fiancée, speaking as Durant's press secretary, he turned the radio off and tried to think of something else. In the last few days Caden made several trips to the hospital, first with Zach, and then a growing number of ill soldiers. When they lost control of the checkpoints several thousand refugees poured into Hansen. Perhaps only a few hundred were sick, but the flu spread. The hospital seemed darker now, a place where death lingered.

Caden's attention drifted back to the radio.

"Yesterday, Dr. Scott, chief physician at Hansen General Hospital, announced that until further notice the facility would only handle Kern flu cases and other life-threatening emergencies. The Morton hospital has closed as of this morning. All personnel and patients have been transferred to Hansen."

Caden walked outside in the cool morning air. He'd taken the weekend off to relax and try to forget about matters of life and death.

He'd done a lousy job of it so far.

He strolled aimlessly around the barn, past the chicken yard, and paused at the greenhouse he and his father rebuilt earlier in the year. Caden ran his fingers along several of the boards he'd cut and nailed into place. Their family had eaten well from the bounty of the building.

Nikki galloped over the nearby hill, with tail wagging, followed by his father. Caden wondered where they had gone so early in the morning. Standing in the shadows of the greenhouse, his father didn't appear to see him.

At first Caden thought his dad had been on a walk with the dog, but they didn't return to the house. Instead his father went to the man cave in the barn.

Caden stepped into the converted tack room. "Hi Dad. What're you up to?"

"Making a new gate. Some cows pushed down the one by the creek." He picked up a 2 x 4.

"Some cows? Not our two?"

"No. They must be from a neighboring farm, but I'm not sure which."

"Where are they now?" Caden asked sitting in the old wooden chair. Nikki curled up on a blanket in the corner.

"Last I saw the four of them were chomping grass along the stream. When I've finished the gate I'll try to find their owner." He turned on a small radio and grabbed the tape measure.

"… mass burials and burial at sea will now be conducted by the Texas National Guard and the Coast Guard."

His father turned to him with a worried look "Will you be doing that? Is that what will happen here?"

"I have no idea." But he feared they would soon.

*　　　*　　　*

Hollister Hotel, Saturday, October 3rd

DeLynn heard the door squeak and turned to see Vicki enter the room.

"Any change?"

She shook her head. "No, but he's breathing well and his temperature is normal. I just wish he'd wake up."

Only Zach's shoulders and head stuck out from the covers. Stubble of his red beard covered much of his face.

Vicki nodded. "I heard on the radio that the school is closed until the flu crisis is over. That'll make it easier to care for him."

Delynn stared at Zach and prayed that he would soon wake. Still seated, she squeezed Vicki's arm. "Well, you better go set the fish traps or none of us will eat tonight." As Vicki trotted off, DeLynn slid down in the chair. Already exhausted from a night of fitful dozing, she quickly fell asleep.

*   *   *

Zach's eyes fluttered open. He moved his head from side to side taking in his surroundings. Two large windows let ample sunlight flow into the spacious room. Freshly painted white walls reflected the light, giving the room a bright appearance.

DeLynn sat beside him, softly snoring. He remembered going to the trailer home, so how did he get to his bedroom in the Hollister Hotel?

Zach sat up, feeling dizzy as he did. He thought about waking DeLynn and asking how he got there, but decided to let her sleep. Besides, he had more urgent business. He slid his feet out from the covers and noticed a clean bandage on his hip and one ankle wrapped in gauze. Above the window hung a homemade banner declaring, 'Happy Birthday.' Two colorfully wrapped presents sat on a nearby table.

He smiled, and stood, slowly testing both his balance and stance. The joint still hurt, but not as much as it had. He limped to the bathroom wearing just a T-shirt and underwear.

He flushed the toilet after completing the most critical task and then downed a glass of water. Zach recalled his most recent clear memory, falling and vomiting on the carpet at the trailer. He still felt weak and a bit unsure on his feet, but decided he would live.

As he made his way to the kitchen he wondered how long he had been unconscious. His recovery certainly took more than a day, but beyond that he had no idea. He opened the fridge looking for food and found one fish fillet. Zach shook his head. He neither wanted to cook fish nor eat it, so his search continued. After finding bread and a half eaten apple he sat at the counter to eat.

A stifled scream came from the bedroom.

*   *   *

Westmore Farm, Rural Lewis County, Saturday, October 3rd

The gate consisted of a 2 x 4 frame with wire mesh fencing

attached to one side. Caden smiled as he finished helping his father make it. The last three weeks had been tense, but at that moment he felt reinvigorated. Most days he moved papers across his desk, but today he had created something for the farm. It was just a gate, but he and his father had made it. "Are we going to stain the wood?"

"I'll do that later. Right now we need to hang it. I've just got a few strands of barbed wire closing the gap at the moment. After I find the owner of the cattle I'll stain the thing."

With a laugh, Caden grabbed one end of the gate. "Okay, let's get going."

Leaving Nikki behind, they climbed into the farm truck.

As his father drove to where cattle had broken the old gate, Caden checked the time and decided to call Brooks. "What's our status this morning?"

"Two possible new cases of flu and three deaths last night." Brooks listed the names. "Otherwise all is normal and calm."

They had lost two or three soldiers every day since the refugees flooded in from nearby towns. Caden had expected just such a report. "Call me if anything changes." With a sigh he slid the phone back in his pocket.

"You better give that young man a few days off or Lisa will be livid." His father smiled at him.

"Brooks is going out with her on Monday—if things don't go crazy between now and then."

His father stopped the truck and the two quickly hung the gate. His dad pointed toward the nearby creek. "See our two Jersey cows there and the four on the other side of the stream munching away?"

"A nice little herd." Caden climbed back in the truck. "Which farm do we visit first?"

*   *   *

Hollister Hotel, Saturday, October 3rd

Zach ran toward the bedroom as fast as he could with a sore ankle, but before he got to the door it burst open.

DeLynn stared at him with wide eyes. "You disappeared. Where were you?"

"Ah, the bathroom."

She continued to stare at him.

"And then the kitchen."

"You're awake!" DeLynn ran to him and hugged tight.

She leaned so hard on him he stumbled backward, putting more weight on the sore ankle. He grimaced. "How long was I asleep?"

"Four? No, this is the fifth day."

"Wow. That would explain the need for the bathroom."

She laughed.

He recalled walking away from the hotel so he wouldn't infect anyone. "How did I get here?" Worried and weak, Zach slumped in a nearby chair. "Are Vicki and your parents okay?"

"Everyone in the building is fine." DeLynn sat beside him. "We heard the shooting around the armory that day and expected you to come home right away. After the battle, when you didn't return, we went looking for you. Eventually, Vicki and I found you at the trailer."

"And you're all okay?"

"I was careful." She explained how she used a damp towel around her mouth and nose.

"How did you know to do that?"

She shrugged. "I saw it in a movie. Then we called 911, but your old boss, Mr. Westmore, and others with gas masks and weird ponchos, showed up."

Zach smiled at her description of MOPP gear.

"They had you in the isolation ward but moved you here last night. The doctor said you would live and weren't contagious."

"Really?" He raised an eyebrow. "I'm surprised they sent me home while still unconscious."

"Mr. Westmore said a medic would come by and check on you twice a day. Oh, and the hospital needed the bed. The place is full of Kern flu patients."

He nodded slowly considering all that he heard. "Just one more thing, would you bring me my pants?"

*   *   *

Rural Lewis County, Saturday, October 3rd

"Third time's a charm, isn't that what they say?"

Caden wasn't sure that applied to finding the owner of lost cattle. "Or we could have a really nice barbecue."

His father glanced at him with a suspicious eye.

"Just kidding, dad."

"Yeah." His father grinned and then pointed ahead. "I've been meaning to go by the Wilson place. I haven't seen Bob in several days and, well, he's getting up there in years."

"I don't remember him as anything but old. How old is he?"

"Eighty-seven, I think."

"Yeah, that's starting to get up there."

"His wife has dementia."

Caden shook his head. "I'm surprised he's still on the farm." But what options did he have? There were no assisted living facilities or residential care homes still operating. The people in them were either dead or back with relatives. He looked at his father, glad that family surrounded him and his mother, and that they were still healthy.

His father glanced at him. "Why are you staring at me?"

"Oh, sorry. I'm just thinking about Bob Wilson's situation. Does he have any children?"

"One son. He lived in L.A."

"Oh." The terrorists destroyed Los Angeles on the second day of attacks. By dawn of that day few residents had left the city, but just hours later the survivors poured out. Since their son never came home to Washington, Caden assumed he died that day.

The truck bounced up the driveway to a white two-story farmhouse with a covered porch. Caden remembered that it extended to all sides of the house. As they stopped, he noticed the front door was open and the screen slightly ajar. He moved his hand to where his pistol should have been, but wasn't. He hadn't planned to leave the farm, so he never put it on. Cautiously, he followed his father up the steps.

His dad knocked on the doorframe. "Bob, this is Trevor. Are you home?"

"Listen." Caden turned an ear to the screen. "I hear someone humming."

Caden followed his father into the house.

"Liz is that you?" His father paused in the middle of the living room.

An old woman appeared in a doorway wearing an apron and holding a knife.

"Hello Liz. Remember me?"

She stared at him blankly.

"I'm Trevor. I'd like to talk to Bob. Could you tell me where he is?"

At the mention of her husband, she smiled. "Oh, I was just slicing an apple pie for him. Would you like some?"

"Maybe later, right now I need to talk to Bob. Where is he?"

"He's eating lunch on the veranda." She pointed to the south side of the house.

Caden led his father out the door and breathed easier as he hurried along the creaking porch. Turning the corner he spotted Bob. The man sat about halfway along the side of the house on a wooden bench with a food tray in front of him. His chin rested on his chest as if asleep. Flies buzzed about.

"Bob are you okay?" Fearing the worst, Caden took a deep breath, stepped close, and knelt to check his pulse. As he did the old man crumpled forward into Caden's arms.

"What did you do to my husband?" Knife still in her hand Liz lunged.

Chapter Twenty Four

Hollister Hotel, Saturday, October 3rd

Zach leaned against the glass near the corner of his bedroom. From his perch atop the hotel he viewed city hall from one window and Library Park from the other. The park had been the center of the community economy for nearly a year. Now it stood empty as the Kern flu burned through the town.

Still weak, he pulled a chair over and sat, staring at the deathly quiet city below.

A knock came at the door.

"Come in." Zach looked over his shoulder.

Sergeant Hall stepped into the room with his medic bag. "Vicki told me you were awake." He smiled.

"Awake, but weak." Zach started to stand.

"No. No, sit." Hall pulled a chair beside him. He checked Zach's temperature, blood pressure, pulse, and throat. "I think we can safely say you're on the mend. I won't be coming to see you again unless you need me. About half the armory has the flu. We've even set up our own isolation ward."

Zach's mouth gaped. "Have guys died?"

"Eleven, and there will be more. Hundreds have died in town." Hall shook his head. "This whole year has been like the pale horse of tribulation."

He didn't understand the reference to a horse, but decided not to ask. Zach stared out the window after the sergeant departed, feeling a strange mixture of thankfulness at being alive and sadness for his friends and neighbors that perished. Only when the sun shone in his eyes did he turn back to the room.

Again there came a knock at the door. Mr. Hollister entered the room holding a tray. "I come with bread and fish. Biblically inspired foods for a time of tribulation and pestilence."

Zach didn't understand the Bible allusion, but he knew about tribulation and guessed at pestilence, and nodded. Hungry, he ate the warm bread. "How are the building renovations going?"

"Good. The bakery will be done soon. That's where the bread came from."

"Really? This is good, but Library Park is vacant. I don't think we'll get any customers walking over from there."

"I still have some money-making plans for this building, but with the sickness ravaging the town, and the world, I want to turn this place into our own personal life preserver."

*   *   *

Rural Lewis County, Saturday, October 3rd

His father hurled himself between Liz and Caden, then shrieked in pain. Caden struggled to stand under the dead weight of Bob Wilson. His father pushed Liz away with his left arm, then stumbled backwards and fell to his knees.

"Did I do that?" Liz, her eyes wide, backed away. "Why are you here?" She dropped the bloody knife, turned and ran.

Caden pushed Bob's body to the side. "Dad, are you okay?"

His father leaned against the rail and looked at him with wide eyes. Blood stained the right side of his shirt.

Leaving Bob face down on the porch, Caden hurried over. "We need to get you to the hospital."

His dad nodded and then tried to stand, but toppled forward.

Caden helped him up. With his father's left arm over his shoulders they hurried toward the pickup. "Come on, I want to be gone before Liz shows up with another knife."

After opening the passenger door, Caden helped his father into the truck. Then he took a dirty towel from the back of the cab, ripped open his father's shirt, and pressed it against a four-inch slash wound. "Hold this against the cut. Keep pressure on it." Caden darted to the driver's side and sped away.

"We should tell your mother," his father muttered as they passed the family farm.

"I'll phone from the …." He had headed toward the hospital out of habit, but now wondered if he should go to the armory. The hospital had actual doctors, but also hundreds of Kern flu patients. The armory had only a few patients waiting for a bed at the hospital. The medics weren't doctors, but had specific training on knife wounds. Ahead, the turn toward one or the other loomed larger. "Ahhh."

"Hospital. It's closer and Dr. Scott will treat me." With a moan his father slid down in the seat.

Caden pressed the gas. "Stay with me Dad. It's not that bad of a cut."

"Rag's soaked. Shirt's ruined and my side hurts."

Caden pulled into the emergency room entrance and ran to find help. Patients filled every seat inside. They sat on the floor, or seemed to wander aimlessly. He looked for a doctor or nurse. A large sign with a bright red arrow directed those with Kern flu symptoms to another room, but there were no directions for other patients. Several nurses in biohazard suits hurried through the lobby, one pushed a patient on a gurney. None slowed enough to speak. He regretted not taking his father to the armory.

"Sure is busy."

He turned at the sound of his father's voice. "Dad!"

A few yards away his father wobbled toward him.

"How did you get here?" Caden shoved past two people to get to him.

"It's easier to get down out of the truck, than it is to get up and in." His father stumbled. "Walking hurts a bit though. I need to sit down."

But there were no seats so, with his father leaning on him, Caden continued on toward the examination rooms. As they turned a corner, a nurse blocked their path.

"Why are you back here?"

"Looking for help," Caden replied. "My father was stabbed."

The nurse looked at the torn and bloody shirt. She pointed to a wheelchair. "Use that and take him to room six." She turned. "I'll inform the doctor and be there shortly."

As he helped his father onto the table, the older man let out a moan. "Come on Dad, lean toward the bed. You'll be fine. That cut isn't the worst I've seen."

An old, pale man looked at him with a weak smile. "No, but it's the worst *I've* seen."

Caden forced a smile in return. He took a deep breath and tried to relax, but as the seconds ticked by and the blood-soaked cloth dripped onto the examination table, his worry grew.

The nurse returned two minutes later. She removed the rag and tossed it in the trash. Then performed a quick exam and placed a large bandage over the wound. She turned for the door. "The doctor will be here soon."

"Wait!" Caden jumped to his feet. He hadn't used his position as military commander to secure favorable treatment for himself or his family in the past, but now he would. "Inform Dr. Scott I'm here with my wounded father. I'd like her to treat him."

"She's in the isolation ward."

"Well, get her."

"You don't understand."

Caden stepped closer to the nurse, anger ready to erupt.

"Look, I know you're concerned about your father, but you don't understand."

"Don't understand what?"

"Dr. Scott is a patient. She has Kern flu."

*   *   *

Hollister Hotel, Saturday, October 3rd

"Use the building to preserve our lives?" Zach rubbed his chin. "How do you plan to do that?"

"First we keep unwanted people out. The exit doors are old, but they're solid wood. I'm going to install new door frames, strike plates and deadbolts."

"Strike plates?"

Hollister laughed. "I sometimes think I should have stayed a carpenter. It certainly has been more useful than my law degree this year."

Zach smiled, still confused.

Mr. Hollister placed a hand on his shoulder. "I'll get started, you just get well, so you can help me."

The next morning, after a breakfast of fish, bread, and an apple slice, Zach made his way to the first floor. The smell of fresh bread enticed him to the bakery where he found DeLynn, kneading bread with a flour smudged face.

"Hello beautiful."

She cast him a doubtful glance and continued her work. "I'm

glad to see you up and about."

Zach sat in a chair. "Thanks to everyone, I'm getting better." He inhaled the smell of bread. "Have you seen Vicki?"

"She set the fish traps this morning so I could bake."

"I can see Library Park from my bedroom. It's empty. No one is going to be coming here for food."

"Of course not." She shook her head. "We go to them. People pay us in cash or trade for home delivery."

Zach thought of DeLynn handing a bag of food to someone at their front door. Then he imagined that person with Kern flu. "Isn't that dangerous? I mean with the flu and all?"

"Maybe." She shrugged. "Dad does the actual delivery and he wears a mask. The person leaves money, or trade, on the porch and we drop off a box of food. We never actually see the people."

"You started this while I was sick?"

"Dad thought of the idea. There are a lot of hungry, desperate people out there. More than we can supply."

*　　　*　　　*

Hansen General Hospital, Saturday, October 3rd

"Oh." Caden sat, stunned by the news of Dr. Scott's illness.

He had no idea how long he sat there, worrying about his father and Dr. Scott, before the nurse returned. A young man with dark hair followed. Caden would have thought he was fresh out of high school, or perhaps a college undergrad, but he wore the white coat of a doctor.

The nurse briefed him as they entered. "This is the knife wound I mentioned. It's about four inches in length along the upper abdominal quadrant and reaching into muscle tissue."

The doctor walked directly to Caden's father. "How long ago did you get cut?"

"About 90 minutes ago." His father turned to Caden. "Call your mother."

Caden wanted to listen to what the doctor said, but stepped out. As he walked along the hall he pulled out his phone, thinking of what to say. He reached the lobby and looked around. Several people were perspiring. The room smelled of body order and vomit. A few lay on the floor asleep or unconscious. Death inhabited the room.

Caden felt sure several had Kern flu. Couldn't they read the sign directing them to another room? Were they in denial? He held his breath and hurried through the room.

Outside, he inhaled deep drafts to cleanse his lungs of whatever might have infiltrated them, but smoke and the scent of trash came with the air. Looking about he observed more families camped along the lot than before. Families cooked with camp stoves or over open flames. A mountain of trash bags stood in the far corner of the lot.

He had been in such a rush going in that he hadn't noticed. Still he knew his mother, and the rest of the family, needed to be told of his dad's condition, but he didn't want any of them to come to this place.

Reaching the truck, he opened the driver's side door. The smell of blood greeted him. He rolled down the window. Caden ran his hand along the still moist seat and shuddered at the thought of his mother riding to the hospital while sitting on the blood of her husband.

After several minutes he pulled out his phone and called his sister. "Lisa, where are you right now?"

"In my room at the house, why?"

"Are you alone?"

"Yes. What's going on weird brother?"

"First, Dad is okay."

"What!"

"Stay where you are, and hear me out." He told her what happened earlier in the morning and about taking his father to the hospital.

"We need to tell Mom," Lisa cried, tears in her voice "We should be there."

"No. I'm sure Dad will be fine. I don't want Mom to rush over here. There are a lot of sick and dying people and he isn't one of them."

"You won't be able to keep Mom away."

"I can't imagine they'll keep Dad long. They might release him tonight." Caden sighed. "All I need is a little help from you."

"What do you want?"

"You have the only vehicle at the house. Go visit Brooks at the armory. That way Mom won't have a car when I tell her about Dad. I'll say that I'm staying with him until they release him and that he'll be home soon."

"Did you say Dad was attacked while you were at the Wilson farm?"

"Yes. Why?"

"There's a big cloud of black smoke coming from that direction."

Chapter Twenty Five

Hansen General Hospital, Saturday, October 3rd

Afraid the fire might spread through the dry grass and trees to their farm, Caden phoned 911 from the hospital parking lot.

Instead of a human voice, he heard a recorded message. "Due to the high number of calls and a shortage of personnel, please use the following menu. If you, or someone you know, has Kern flu symptoms, press one. To report a death, or for the removal of a body, press two. To report a felony crime, press three. To report a fire, press four. For all other ...."

Caden pressed four.

"Please hold." After that only silence.

For once in his life Caden wanted to hear elevator music or something. After a while he hung up and phoned his sister back. "Where are you?"

"On my way to the armory—like you said. Why?"

"Can you stop by the fire station and report the fire?" He told her about his 911 experience.

"Well, someone got through. Fire trucks are coming down the highway toward me."

He heard the wail of the sirens over the phone.

When the trucks passed and they could talk again, Lisa sighed. "Are you sure we should be manipulating Mom like this?"

"Like what?"

"Me pretending to be on a date just so Mom won't have a car to take her to the hospital."

"If it keeps her alive, we've done the right thing. They're working on Dad right now and he'll probably be home soon. I really don't want Mom here if it can be avoided." Caden looked at the hospital entrance. "I should get back in there with Dad."

He knew it didn't make much sense, but he held his breath as he passed through the lobby. As he entered the examining room he noted that his father had more color. Several intravenous bags hung above the table with tubes stretching down to his father's arm. The doctor continued to work on the wound, but his dad smiled when Caden walked in.

The doctor finished, and looked at both father and son. "The injury is deep enough that I'd like to keep you overnight to ensure there is no further bleeding."

Caden tensed as the doctor spoke. "Ahhh." He glanced at his father who seemed resigned to the idea. "I'd want my father to have a private room."

"You're kidding right?" The doctor laughed. "Everyone is doubled or tripled up."

"I could take him to the armory." Caden stepped close to his father. "We have medics there."

"You're worried about the flu aren't you?" His father squeezed Caden's hand. "You have flu at the armory. It's sweeping through the town. If God has determined it's my time...." He shrugged.

The doctor wrote on a pad. "We have a wing of the hospital for non-flu patients." The doctor wrote on a pad. "He'll be there."

"I'll be fine son. Come get me in the morning."

The doctor passed his notes to the nurse. "We work hard to isolate our regular patients from those with the flu."

Caden frowned. "We all breathe the same air."

The doctor shrugged, and left the room.

Back in the parking lot, Caden pulled out his phone. He had planned on phoning his mother and then avoiding her so she wouldn't have a car to take her to the hospital, but perhaps Lisa was right, such tactics were just manipulation. If a soldier were injured or killed, he would visit the family. His mother deserved the same respect. As he slid the phone back in his pocket, it rang.

"Where are you two?"

Caden sighed at the sound of his mother's voice. "I'm on my way home now. I'll explain everything when I get there."

"What do you mean? Where are you? Is Trevor okay?"

"Ahhh." Caden bit his lip. Earlier he had wanted to do this over the phone. Now he preferred to do it in person, but if his mother kept asking questions, she would pry it out of him. "Yes, I'm fine. Dad will be fine."

"What? What happened?"

As he drove toward home he explained the morning events.

"What?" she nearly shouted. "I should be with him."

Caden had anticipated that statement. He didn't want to mention Kern flu at the hospital, certain it would add to his mother's worries, as it did his, but he still needed to answer her. "The place is crowded and the staff is very busy."

"Don't give me that. You're worried about the Kern flu. Isn't that right?"

"Ahhh, Yes, Mom, but he'll probably come home tomorrow morning."

"Good."

"I know what you're thinking right now and I don't want you to do it."

"Do what?"

"Just call and talk to him."

"I will," she said flatly, "and I'm going to see him."

Caden sighed. "There are hundreds of Kern flu patients at the hospital. They have Dad isolated, but there is a chance of exposure for anyone going in or out of the building."

For several moments silence passed between them. "Okay, I'll call Trevor and see what he says."

That would have to do for now.

When he turned on to Hopps Road, he noticed a sheriff's car about a quarter mile ahead and decided to follow. As he expected, Hoover turned in at the Wilson farm. Only smoldering black wisps still drifted into the sky. The firefighters packed their equipment. Half of the home had collapsed in on itself leaving burned lumber and a blackened chimney where a once proud home had been. A deputy stood next to his patrol car along the house.

The smell of smoke greeted Caden as he stepped from the pickup.

Twenty feet ahead, Hoover smiled a greeting. "I suppose you knew them."

"Yeah." Caden nodded. "Sad day. How is Liz? She was pretty

confused and upset earlier."

"Dead, I think. The firefighters reported two bodies in the rubble. You were here earlier?"

"Yeah. Four cows got loose last night. My dad and I were looking for the owner. We arrived here about eleven this morning."

Hoover pulled out a pad and wrote as they walked toward the charred rubble. "So you were probably the last ones to see them alive."

"I think Bob was dead when we arrived. Liz was alive when we left."

Hoover nodded. "Stick around. I'll need to ask you more questions." The sheriff turned his attention to the deputy. As they spoke, Caden retreated from the acrid smoke and smell of burnt flesh. Finding a bench upwind and far enough from the house that it remained unburnt, he sat. He didn't know the Wilson's well, so it didn't take long for his thoughts to return to his father and what to do if his mother insisted on going to the hospital.

Hoover called him over several minutes later. "I just need to ask some questions and then you can go. Do you mind following me around?"

"No."

The sheriff turned toward the house. "Tell me again what happened. Don't leave anything out."

As Caden explained the morning events, they entered through the still blackened front door. He paused just inside the house. Crime scene tape blocked entry to the kitchen. The deputy stood nearby.

Hoover's head swept back and forth as they proceeded through the living room. "Liz attacked Trevor with a knife?"

"I'm sure it was an accident. She seemed to think I hurt Bob and tried to get to him. Dad got in the way."

The sheriff pursed his lips. "Okay." He continued the slow walk around the room. "Why would Liz burn down the house?"

The comment had been no more than a mutter, but Caden decided to answer. "She had dementia. It might have been an accident."

The lawman nodded and continued his walk until he stood outside the taped off kitchen.

The deputy pointed. "She's just inside."

Hoover knelt under the tape and bent over the badly charred body.

Only a shoe told Caden he looked upon the remains of Liz Wilson. Such sights and smells were familiar to him, but he had spent years pushing them to dark, rarely visited corners of his mind.

Hoover looked up at the deputy. "Give me gloves." When he put them on, he knelt and examined the body up close.

Caden hung back.

The sheriff lifted the body slightly, and put his face near the ground. A moment later he stood. A serious look covered his face. "That looks like a gunshot wound. This might be murder."

*   *   *

Hollister Hotel, Sunday, October 4th

Bright sunshine poured through Zach's window from a clear blue sky. He buried his face in the pillow. "Curtains," he mumbled. "I need curtains."

As he lay in bed trying to ignore the sun that warmed his sheets, he assessed how he felt. Hunger seemed to be the strongest sensation. After several minutes, a combination of sunlight and stomach growls drove him from the bed.

He paused to sit as he dressed. Putting on clothes had never been so strenuous. He breathed deeply. While he felt tolerably well, clearly it would take some time to regain his strength.

When he stepped from the bedroom, a familiar, but recently uncommon, smell greeted him.

"We have eggs!" Vicki smiled. "Well, we've always had eggs for the bakery, but today we have enough for breakfast."

"Do you have bacon?"

"Don't be silly. Breakfast is eggs, apple slices, and bread. Oh, and water."

"That's all?"

"Would you like some fish? I learned in social studies that in Japan they eat fish for breakfast."

"No fish." Zach shook his head. "When this is over, I'm never going to eat fish again."

After breakfast he headed toward the door.

"You should rest." Vicki collected dishes from the table.

"I'll take it easy." Zach opened the apartment door. "I just want to get out and earn a bit of my room and board."

Vicki nodded. "Mr. Hollister said he would be working on the first floor all weekend."

"Thanks." Zach stepped from the penthouse into the short hallway. DeLynn's mother stood at the far end, staring out the window. "Good morning Mrs. Hollister."

She barely nodded.

He pressed the elevator button and the doors opened. Zach stepped in wondering why the woman always seemed so sad. As he rode down to the first floor his thoughts turned to the day before him. Knowing his strength hadn't returned, Zach felt resting in the penthouse would be letting Mr. Hollister down. The man had given him a home. Even if he just worked part of the day, it would be better than taking the whole of it off.

Sheets of plywood, 2 x 4s, several sawhorses, a circular saw, and lots of dust, greeted Zach as he exited the elevator at the lobby. From one corner of the hotel the sound of hammering echoed.

As Zach entered the store, Mr. Hollister turned and smiled.

"It's good to see you up and about. If you're well enough to help, the work will go much faster."

Zach took a deep breath and smiled.

A routine quickly developed. Zach helped Mr. Hollister and he showed Zach what he did, how he did it and why.

Nearly an hour later, DeLynn and Vicki walked through the lobby pulling wagons filled with food.

Tired, Zach sat on an old wooden chair. He looked over the wagons full of corn, tomatoes, onions, beans, jars of honey, apples, pears and various canned goods. "Where'd you get all that and why aren't we eating it?"

"You do eat some of it," DeLynn said.

Mr. Hollister joined them. "I've been buying food from local farms and selling most of it for the lumber and tools we need to get the stores up and running. The remainder we eat, but I admit there is not much left for us."

"That's why we still fish," Vicki added.

As the morning progressed, Zach assumed more of each task, cutting and hammering lumber into place according to Mr. Hollister's direction. In the lobby, as Zach finished cutting several boards, he felt a hand on his shoulder. Turning, he expected to see Mr. Hollister, but DeLynn's mother stood beside him.

Her face appeared relaxed, peaceful, almost serene. She smiled. "You're a good young man. I hope you never lose that quality."

Zach dropped the saw on the bench. Rarely did she speak to him and she never smiled—at least not at him. "Ah, thanks."

She turned and walked toward the lobby.

A bit confused, Zach returned to his work.

Near noon DeLynn arrived holding two lunch plates. Passing them to Zach and her dad she asked. "Have either of you seen Mom? I can't find her."

Chapter Twenty Six

Hollister Hotel, Sunday, October 4th

Zach searched part of the building and then returned to the lobby. DeLynn and her father were already there. "I didn't find her or any clues."

"We didn't either."

Vicki soon joined them. "No sign of her in my part of the building."

"Did your mom take any clothes or food?" Zach asked.

"Not that we can tell. She just disappeared."

His last conversation with DeLynn's mother, and now her sudden disappearance, seemed real spooky, but Zach decided not to say anything.

DeLynn turned to her father. "Where do you think she might have gone?"

He rubbed his chin. "She never accepted moving here. She might be headed back to our old house."

That seemed reasonable. He mapped out the route in his mind. "On foot, it would take her at least three hours to get there."

"Longer." Mr. Hollister shook his head. "She has an abysmal sense of direction and has never driven, or walked, from here to the house."

DeLynn stepped toward the exit. "Let's take the car and head that way. We'll probably spot her."

The four moved toward the door, but Mr. Hollister held up his hand. "This won't take all of us. Vicki, would you prepare the food boxes?"

She nodded.

"Zach, would you continue framing the wall we were working on? Just keep doing what I showed you. DeLynn and I should be back in an hour or so."

*   *   *

Sheriff's Office, Hansen, Sunday, October 4th

Caden looked at his watch and shook his head in frustration. "I explained what happened when we were at the Wilson farm. Then, I answered the same questions in your interrogation room—"

"Only so it could be recorded," Hoover interjected.

"—after waiting forever. Now you want to do it again in your office?"

"I just have a few more questions." Hoover sat at his desk and picked up a pad of paper. "Do you or your father own a .270 rifle?"

"I'm sure Dad does."

"I'll need to examine all your guns. I'm also a little concerned about why, after Liz stabbed your father, you didn't call 911, me, or your family, until after you were at the hospital."

Looking back on the situation, Caden knew he should have done so. "Have you called 911 lately?"

"I am aware of their problems. Did you call them?"

"No."

Hoover tapped his pen on the desk. "You should have called or told someone."

"I guess I wasn't thinking clearly."

"Rational decision making under stressful conditions is something you're trained to do." Hoover wrote in the pad.

"My father was bleeding out beside me." Caden leaned forward, palms on the sheriff's desk. "You sound suspicious. Do you really think I shot Liz Wilson and burned down the house to cover up her murder?"

Hoover set down the pad and pen. "Ultimately, it doesn't matter what I think, but no, I don't believe you killed her. However, in any normal investigation, you and Trevor would be the prime suspects. I have to do my job and for both our sakes, I need to do it properly."

Caden sighed. "As military commander, I could take over this investigation."

"If you do, some people will always believe you killed her and covered it up. Let us do an inquiry and find who really committed the crime." Hoover stood. "We recovered the bullet that killed Liz. Your guns should go a long way toward clearing this up. I'll send a couple of deputies to over to check calibers, serial numbers, and registrations."

Knowing his father, Caden wouldn't have been surprised if none of the guns were registered. "Someone will be there, but I'm not going home." He stood and together they walked toward the door of the office. "I've got to pick up Dad at the hospital. I'll have Maria meet the deputies." Caden stopped at the door. "Do you want to interview my father?"

"I already have."

"Really? When?"

Hoover smiled. "Remember when you sat in the interrogation room for so long?"

"While you kept me waiting you were talking to him?"

Still grinning, Hoover nodded. "I needed to know what he would say before you two talked."

"Cunning, very cunning." On the way to the pickup truck Caden phoned Maria and explained about the deputies that would soon arrive. "Show them all the guns."

"All of them? He has a lot. I doubt he's shown me all of them."

"Ask Mom for help and just do your best. I'll be home soon with Dad. Bye." His confidence grew as he reached his destination. His mother hadn't visited the hospital, the Wilson investigation would reveal the truth and his father would be fine. He pulled into the lot and parked near the main entrance of the building.

As he walked toward the door, he looked again at those camped along the edge of the lot. Were they all refugees? Did they have family members in the hospital?

Caden sat in his father's room as frustration grew within him. Why did discharging patients always take so long?

After Caden missed church and lunch, a doctor finally arrived and discharged Caden's dad. Father and son then waited for a nurse to come with a wheelchair.

"I can walk." His father wobbled to the chair by the door and plopped down.

Caden grunted, but otherwise remained silent.

The nurse arrived wearing an industrial breathing mask with filters on both sides of her mouth and nose, along with gloves. She offered a home variety mask to Caden's father.

"I don't need it." He nearly fell into the wheelchair.

"Dad, put it on please. For me and Mom. At least until we're out of here."

He complied with a "humph."

Unprotected, Caden walked ahead to clear the route.

As they neared the exit door, a man stumbled in. Sweat rolled down his face and his body sagged. His mouth gaped, as if ready to sneeze. Caden stepped aside and hurried past. A cough thundered behind him. He turned and saw his father make a face.

Just outside Caden asked, "Did you get sneezed on?"

"I don't know." He ripped off the mask and handed it to the nurse. "Let's go." With the aid of Caden, he stood, walked to the pickup, and they were soon on the way home.

When they parked in front of the house, the two deputies were on one end of the porch logging the firearm's serial numbers, checking registrations and calibers. Caden half expected his father to recite the second amendment, and then order the deputies from the property. Instead he allowed Caden to help him into his favorite chair in the living room.

Caden's mother immediately sat beside her husband and grabbed his hand. "Are you alright?"

"Don't fuss. I'm sore, but I'll be fine."

Maria motioned for Caden to sit on the porch swing with her. He did and she leaned close. As they gently rocked back and forth the two watched Adam in a nearby playpen and the deputies with the firearms. Caden talked about his day.

"Are they going to take the guns?" Maria asked.

"I'm not sure."

As they continued to talk, Caden's eyelids grew heavy.

Two shotgun blasts boomed over a nearby hill.

A woman screamed.

*　　　　*　　　　*

Hollister Hotel, Sunday, October 4th

The sound of an engine caused Zach to look up from his work. Mr. Hollister's car turned into the hotel parking lot. Father and daughter exited the vehicle and with heads slumped, returned to the building.

When they entered, DeLynn, near tears, spoke first. "We drove out to the old house and then slowly back toward town. We had to wait in line at the bridge checkpoint. I thought sure we'd see her there, but we didn't."

Her father shook his head, a worried look on his face. "I don't know where she might have gone."

Later that afternoon, Zach decided to do his own search. He didn't have the energy for a long walk, but felt he owed it to DeLynn. Donning a light jacket, he exited the hotel through the main door, and walked in the general direction of the old Hollister home. As he strode away from the hotel he hoped to find the woman soon and not have to hike all the way out of town.

Piles of bulging plastic bags dotted both sides of the street. Apparently trash collection stopped during his bout with the Kern flu. Many bags had been torn and the contents strewn along the sidewalk. Rats, mice, and feral dogs tore at some of them. Zach made wide circles around the dogs. The smell of rotting garbage dominated the air. Knowing that Mrs. Hollister would not have stayed here, he pushed onward. Few people walked the street and even fewer vehicles rolled past. The rare person he spotted moved quickly away from him.

An hour later, he reached the edge of town. Two tents stood near the North Road Bridge. The larger one had a red cross emblazed on the roof. The smaller tent had a shower at one end. Sandbags formed a checkpoint nearby, with a squad car and two Humvees parked alongside. No vehicles waited to enter or leave town. As he approached the bridge a large sign read, "Attention: Medical clearance required for anyone entering Hansen. Think before you leave."

A camp had sprung up on the far side of the river. Smaller than the sprawling one that emerged after the Seattle nuclear blast, this one, Zach estimated, still had a couple hundred campsites. Some were elaborate tents or RVs, others were single cars.

Zach walked up to the four soldiers on his side of the bridge. Three were new, and he didn't know them well, but Sergeant Hill greeted him as a friend.

"Why are people camping over there?" Zach pointed across the river.

"Either they're sick or someone in their family has been exposed." Hill shook his head.

Zach stared across the river. "Then they should be in the hospital."

"They will be as soon as there is a bed for them—if they're still alive. I've heard talk of turning the high school gym into a makeshift ward." Hill shrugged. "Nothing has happened yet."

Zach leaned against a girder of the bridge as he considered the sergeants words. After a moment, he sighed and shook his head. "Have any of you seen a middle-aged woman with brown hair, about my height cross the bridge? She would have been headed out of town on foot."

"A woman alone, and on foot, headed out of town?" The sergeant shook his head. "With the sickness killing so many, most people just stay inside."

"Yeah." A private nodded. "A few trucks have come into town and left, but no one has left on foot."

"We came on duty about two hours ago," another said. "When would she have been here?"

Zach looked at the camp on the far side of the bridge. "She might have reached the river before then."

"Ask the deputy." The sergeant pointed to the tent. "He's been here all day."

Just inside the shelter, the doctor and the deputy ate dinner from a Styrofoam cooler. Using a boxy clear plastic tent, most of the space had been turned into an isolation ward. On the other side of the plastic barrier, a nurse worked with about a dozen patients. Zach turned to the doctor and deputy and described the woman and his need to find her.

The doctor shook his head. "Unless she was trying to get into town I wouldn't have seen her."

"I don't see many people out walking nowadays so, I remember those that do." The deputy nodded. "No one has left in days—until today."

"So, you saw her?"

"I saw a woman matching that description cross the bridge about three hours ago." The deputy pointed north. "We have orders to do medical checks on everyone trying to get in, but anyone can leave."

Zach sprinted to the bridge.

The sergeant shouted as Zach ran across. "Most of the people in the camp are sick. If she is with them ...."

Zach decided to worry about her health if and when he found her.

On the far side of the bridge a sign warned people to stop and receive medical clearance before crossing the bridge. Twenty feet ahead, trash had been piled and burned. It still smoldered and stank. Zach slowed to a walk as he came to the first vehicle. Breathing deeply he hiked through the middle of camp. Having nothing but the clothes on his back he feared no harm. From a nearby car someone eyed him suspiciously. A woman looked out the window of an RV. Several men seated around a camp fire glanced at him. Others looked away.

At the edge of camp, a tarp had blown off five bodies, laid out side-by-side, a woman, a man and three children. An entire family, or just random people joined together in death? Flies buzzed about. Zach gathered stones and replaced the tarp.

When they were again covered, he moved several yards upwind, sat and stared at the ground. How many more would perish before this deadly year ends? He lifted his head several minutes later, and there, at the edge of the trees, she sat.

Chapter Twenty Seven

Westmore Farm, Rural Lewis County, Sunday, October 4th

The two deputies turned in the direction of rapid gunfire mixed with shotgun blasts.

Caden jumped from the porch swing.

Maria clutched his hand and held tight.

Leaving his father's guns behind, the deputies ran for their vehicle and jumped in. As the two sped away, the patrol car kicked up stones in the driveway.

Caden took a step.

Maria tightened her grip. "Let them do their job. You don't have to save the world."

Adam, still in his playpen, stopped tossing toys out and turned toward the speeding patrol car.

Caden stared into the darkness for nearly a minute and then sat. Perhaps he should be less involved until Hoover solved the Wilson murder.

Gunfire thundered again, followed by shouts.

Adam cried and Maria picked up the baby.

Gradually, the stillness of the night returned.

Caden remained seated, but his thoughts were over the nearby hill. He tried to remember the name of the family that owned the farm.

The door squeaked. His father stepped onto the porch, followed by his mother.

"Who owns the farm over there?" Caden pointed.

"Walt Harper." His father looked concerned. "The deputies headed over there?"

Caden nodded.

Maria stood. "It's getting cool out here. I'm taking the baby in."

His dad and mom followed.

Caden secured the gate across the driveway and then brought the rifles in the house. With a final look over his shoulder, he stepped inside, and locked the door.

*   *   *

North of Hansen, Sunday, October 4th

Zach stood and inched forward. "Mrs. Hollister, we've been looking for you!"

She darted into the woods.

Zach shook his head. He would never understand DeLynn's mother. Mustering all his energy he sprinted after her. For nearly an hour she hid and ran while Zach followed and searched. Catching her would normally have been easy but, after only two days recovery, he remained weak. He struggled to stay close to her.

Finally, he decided not to try and catch her, but anticipate her destination. Most people running away would go downhill and into deeper forest, but she wasn't doing that. She headed generally uphill and stayed near the main road out of town. He had never heard of Mrs. Hollister going into the woods. As far as he knew, she only traveled in a car and, now on foot, still followed the road toward her old home. Zach smiled. He knew just where to cut her off.

Hiking deeper into the forest, Zach traveled in a roughly straight line over a hill that the road went around. Wiping sweat from his brow, for a moment he stopped, and leaned against a tree. On the far side, the road crossed a large stream. This time of year the water could be forded in several places, but she didn't know that. He pushed on.

Zach hid in the bushes near the north side of the culvert. One car rumbled over by, and he heard another in the distance, but otherwise only the rustle of the breeze in the trees disturbed the quiet. The sun dropped behind the nearby hills, casting the valley into deep shadows. This would aid his ambush.

Out of the growing darkness came the sound of heavy breathing. Zach held his position, watching and waiting. As she stepped onto the bridge, Zach spotted her. She walked with a weary droop to her body. Afraid that it might be someone else, he waited until he could see her face. When she passed within arm's reach he stood. "Mrs. Hollister—"

She screamed.

"—why did you leave?"

She turned to run.

Zach grabbed her wrist.

She slapped and kicked.

He fended off most of her blows, and held her tight.

Finally, she collapsed to the ground.

"Everyone is worried about you, DeLynn, your husband, Vicki and me." Zach knelt beside her more confused by her actions than worried. "Why did you run off?"

She sat on the ground in silence.

Over the next few minutes, Zach gently tugged on her arm several times, and finally sat on the ground still holding onto her. He didn't know how long he sat there with her when, after more gentle urging she stood. Holding her wrist, Zach led her back toward the bridge.

They walked several minutes in silence, but then, in a voice just above a whisper, Mrs. Hollister spoke. "My mother, brothers, and sister all lived in Los Angeles. I have more aunts, uncles, nephews, and cousins that lived in the city. I've tried to remember them all.

"For months after the attack, I held on to the hope that some of them would come and knock on our door. I know they're probably dead, but in the house we owned, I clung to hope. Living where we do now, they will never find us."

She sighed deeply. "Now we're broke and live in a ramshackle building. We've often been hungry and I'm always afraid." Tears streamed down her face. She looked into the sky and shouted. "God, why did you do this to me and my family?"

Something stirred Zach to answer. "An evil man killed my father, but good people like your husband and others helped me. We all make choices. Evil people choose to screw up this world. Good people make it a better place."

"No!" she cried. "God should just make us do the right thing."

"It would be a sad world if God didn't give us a choice. Could there even be good, if no one had a choice? I don't know, I'm not very smart about such things."

She cast a serious gaze his way. For a while they walked in silence. "You're smarter than you think. You've reminded me of things I'd forgotten."

Zach looked up at the canopy of stars. "I'd like to believe that there is a God who gathers the souls of the good people who follow him. Then someday I'll see my father and mother again, and you'll see your family."

"Out of the mouths of babes," she whispered.

"Huh?"

She smiled. "Just one more thing you've reminded me of tonight. You don't have to hold me. I'll follow you back."

A rising moon cast pale light as they arrived at the bridge. A Humvee blocked any vehicle from crossing.

As they walked onto the bridge, a voice came out of the darkness. "Halt. Zach is that you?"

He did as commanded. "Yeah, I found Mrs. Hollister. We're heading home now. I guess we need to see the doctor. Right?"

"Yeah, but the doctor left for the night. There won't be one here until 0700 tomorrow."

"What about a nurse?" Zach gestured toward the tent. "I saw one in there earlier."

"She stays in the isolation ward." Sergeant Hill said as he came onto the bridge. "Only the doctor can let someone into town." Hill rubbed his chin. "Even though it's against the rules, I'd let you in Zach. I know you had the Kern flu and recovered. You won't infect anyone, but the woman...." He shook his head. "I'm sorry."

He thought about phoning First Sergeant Fletcher and asking him to send a medic, but decided against it. Ten hours under the night sky wouldn't hurt either of them. Perhaps it would help Mrs. Hollister to appreciate the hotel. However, he did need to make one call. Zach borrowed the sergeant's phone. "Hello, DeLynn?"

"Zach! Where are you?"

"Beyond the North Bridge. I found your mother ...."

"I'll get Dad. We'll be right there."

"No don't. She's fine, but the checkpoint is closed for the night. They won't let us cross. I'll have her there at 0700."

"When?"

"Seven in the morning." After a bit more persuading he said

goodbye and turned to the sergeant. "Can we borrow a couple of blankets and a tarp?" Zach planned to use the tarp to keep them off the damp ground. He turned to Mrs. Hollister. "Let's hope it doesn't rain."

Chapter Twenty Eight

Hansen Armory, Monday, October 5th

Tired and rubbing his neck, Caden walked into the office. Hearing a perking sound he looked to his left. Someone had plugged in the long unused coffeemaker and water stood in the pot. "Do we have coffee?"

A corporal stepped hesitantly into the room. "Ah, no sir. I was about to prepare some ... well, it's sort of tea."

"Sort of tea?"

"Yes sir. It's a herbal recipe that my wife's family has been making for years. They sold it at the Library Park market until the flu shut it down. It's hot and tastes ... well, better than plain water."

"You had me at hot. When it's made, pour me a cup." He continued on to his office.

Moments later Brooks stepped into the doorway. "Here's the latest roster."

Caden motioned for Brooks to enter, took the paperwork and read the report. Half of his men were sick or recovering. Ten had died since the outbreak and he knew more would follow.

A knock snapped him away from the melancholy report. The corporal delivered a cup of pale tea. He took a sip and the warm mint eased the discomfort in his throat.

Taking another sip, Caden turned to the routine minutia of the day. Several minutes later another knock diverted his attention. Hoover stood in the doorway. "Well, are you here to arrest me?"

"No, and you're not funny either."

"Okay." Caden shrugged. "What do you need?"

"The funeral homes are no longer taking bodies." Hoover

stepped in and sat. "They say the danger of infection is too great. The morgue is full. We need to start mass burials."

Caden sipped the tea as he wondered how dangerous the dead bodies were. He decided to call Dr. Scott and ask, then recalled she had Kern flu. He needed to call about her prognosis.

"We could dig trenches in unused parts of the pioneer cemetery," Hoover suggested. "We'll need a chlorine solution, or at least lime, heavy equipment for digging, and personnel to wrap and handle the bodies."

They discussed the planning and logistics of the operation for several minutes and then Hoover nodded. "I think we have a plan. On a better note, we recovered several .270 bullets from an attempted robbery near your home last night."

Caden smiled. "What do you want to bet at least one will be a match with the Wilson murder?"

"The state crime lab is barely running, but when we get the ballistics check I'm sure it will match. That's what I came here to tell you. I would have phoned about the burial situation."

"So, you believe me now?"

"I always believed you and when this case is closed, no one will be able to say you received favorable treatment. I have gone by the book and hopefully we'll soon have the real culprits in custody. I've done you a favor. I hope someday you see that." The sheriff stood and left.

Caden sighed. He knew the importance of doing things the right way, following procedure and not showing favoritism. So why did this investigation anger him? He took a long drink of tea. Perhaps part of the anger rose from his father being part of the inquiry. Also, he trusted Hoover, and thought that the sheriff had come to trust him, but the investigation made him feel like a suspect.

Like most men, Caden didn't often examine his feelings, but this time it had revealed the source. It hurt him that, after so many months of working together, the sheriff treated him as a suspect—even if Hoover had to do it.

Caden sighed, felt embarrassed and small. The cause for those last feelings would not require examination. He leaned back in his seat, took another drink, and reached for his phone. Hoover deserved an apology. He set the phone on his desk and tapped the screen with one hand, while rubbing his sore throat with the other.

Brooks burst into the office. "On the radio...." He waved for Caden to come. "You've got to hear this."

*   *   *

North of Hansen, Monday, October 5th

Zach pulled the blanket tight around him. The first glow of morning illuminated the rough campsite near the riverbank. He didn't have a watch, but knew it was too early to expect the doctor. He sat up and yawned.

The top of Mrs. Hollister's head protruded from the other end of the cover, revealing a wild mop of brunette hair. She fidgeted and softly moaned, but otherwise remained covered. She probably hadn't slept well.

Zach stood, stretched and yawned again, before going to the edge of the forest to take care of morning matters. When he returned he sat with crossed legs and pulled the blanket around him. He imagined he looked like a Tibetan monk waiting for the sun to rise for morning prayers. Actually, he waited for the sun to warm his chilled body.

As the morning glow grew, birds chirped in the trees and flew overhead. Eventually the path of the sun crossed the small river valley and the first direct rays of warmth bathed him. Unlike the hustle and bustle of the world he usually lived in, this one remained peaceful.

A grocery truck rumbled down the road and stopped at the edge of the bridge.

Zach stood and wondered when he might eat breakfast.

Mrs. Hollister pulled the blanket down. Beads of sweat dotted her face.

Zach ran to her. "Are you sick?"

She nodded and tried to stand.

He reached out to help. Her arm felt clammy.

She crumpled to her hands and knees and seemed content to stay there. A moment later she crawled to the edge of the tarp and vomited. Then she rolled on her back.

"I'll go get help." Zach ran toward the soldiers on the bridge.

As he crossed a private yelled, "Halt."

"It's me, Zach … ah." He stopped about twenty feet from the private and pointed to the campsite. "I need to get Mrs. Hollister to the doctor. She's sick."

"You both need medical clearance. The doc will be here in about an hour."

"But she's sick. I need to get her to a doctor."

The soldier made a sweeping gesture toward the camp. "Everyone on your side of the bridge has Kern flu or, like you, knows someone who has it, but none of them gets in without medical clearance."

Sergeant Roy trotted on to the bridge and Zach explained his situation.

"When we came on duty, Sergeant Hill told me you had crossed to the other side looking for a woman." Roy sighed. "Sorry, but I agree with Hill's decision. If you want to enter, fine, but the woman will need to be cleared."

"But she won't be cleared," Zach protested. "She's sick and needs treatment."

"Yeah, her and thousands of others. The hospital's overwhelmed. Most sick people need to have family or a friend bring them in for treatment. Ambulances and EMTs don't respond for Kern flu."

"But she can't get to the hospital if you won't let her in town."

"The doc will be here in less than an hour. He treats those he can and, for the few who can get a bed at the hospital, we shuttle them. That's the best I can do."

"I've seen how this flu kills. If she's going to have any chance of living she needs to receive treatment."

"Yeah." Roy nodded. "I've seen how it kills. My oldest boy died last week."

"Oh ... sorry." Zach's gaze dropped as his face flushed.

"It's not personal." Roy frowned. "It just has to be this way. I'll get you anything you need until the doc gets here."

Zach asked for bottles of water and then returned to Mrs. Hollister. He tried to explain why it would be nearly an hour before help arrived.

Tears welled in her eyes. "I've been so sad. I wanted to die, but I was afraid to act. Maybe I succeeded."

"Don't talk like that." Zach shook his head. He folded his blanket into a pillow and offered her water, then stared across the river at the checkpoint, hoping the doctor would soon arrive.

Minutes later a car pulled up to the medical tent followed immediately by the Hollister vehicle. "Your family is here and I think the doctor is also."

After what looked like a huddle with everyone on the other side of the bridge, Mr. Hollister and DeLynn moved along the opposite side of the river until they were across from Zach.

His girlfriend looked up and down the bank. "Where's Mom?"

Zach pointed to the pile of blankets. "She's sick. Get the doctor."

"We know." DeLynn nodded. "He's coming." She stepped closer and shouted. "Mom, we're here."

"I tried to get her to a doctor," Zach shouted. "Really, I did."

DeLynn ran back to her father without a word. Moments later an older man in jeans and plaid shirt jogged across the bridge.

Zach thrust out his arm as he neared. "Don't come any closer. I think she has Kern flu."

"She probably does and so did I. That's why I'm the doctor working here."

The gray-haired man opened a medical bag, then pulled out two face masks and sets of gloves. "Here, put these on." Then he turned to his patient. "Can you hear me ma'am?"

She gave a feeble nod.

"What's your name?"

She mouthed the word, "Karen."

Zach repeated her name.

The doctor checked her heart, blood pressure, and temperature.

"Is it ...." Zach couldn't finish the sentence.

"Yes, I think so." The doctor nodded. "But we can't be certain without tests." He pointed across the river. "Your friends over there told me you've been sick and recovered."

"Yeah, just a few days ago."

"That's almost certainly why you're still healthy. You're very lucky."

"I didn't feel very lucky when I was sick."

"No." The doctor grinned. "Neither did I. I'll get a stretcher and we'll move her to the medical tent."

When the doctor returned, Zach took one end and they

carried her across the bridge. With a deputy, the soldiers blocked Mr. Hollister and DeLynn from the tent as their mother passed by. Zach didn't know what to say to either one of them in such a situation so he kept his eyes cast down.

"Mom, I love you. Get better, please," DeLynn shouted as they passed.

Zach and the doctor continued into the tent and through to the isolation section. A nurse stood over a patient at the far end. As he gazed at the sick and dying patients, Zach imagined the virus crawling over him looking for a way into his body. Although certain he remained immune; he still closed his mouth and tried not to inhale. Together with the doctor, Zach lifted Mrs. Hollister into a bed. The nurse soon joined the doctor, and Zach sat nearby.

About fifteen minutes later the doctor approached him. "We've hydrated her and given her antiviral medications, but this flu comes on so fast ...." He shook his head. "We've done all we can. I don't think she has long. Could you stay with her?"

"Sure. Would you tell her family?"

The doctor nodded and left.

Zach moved his chair nearby and clasped her hand. For several hours he talked to her, watched the IV fluids drip down, and thought about how a few terrorists started a long chain of events that caused so much pain, suffering and death. Would evil ever end?

Mrs. Hollister's gaze seemed to stare so far beyond Zach that he looked over his shoulder, but he saw nothing except clear plastic and green canvas.

With her eyes still fixed beyond, she said, "Thank you, for finding me."

"Ah ... sure," Zach said.

Her gaze shifted to him for a moment and then back to something beyond. She smiled. "I'm glad you both found me. I'm ready." She closed her eyes. "I'm not afraid."

Over the next hour her breathing slowed and then stopped. Zach checked for a pulse, but felt nothing.

*　　　*　　　*

Hansen Armory, Monday, October 5th

Three different radios stood in a corner of the office, a SINCGARS army transceiver, a rarely used shortwave, and an AM/FM radio tuned to the local station.

Brooks turned up the volume.

"… get any closer to the area, but reports are coming in of troops landing in the Iroquois Point area and at the airport. From our position near the golf course we hear constant gun fire and several explosions. Fires are raging in the … wait!"

With the announcer quiet, Caden heard the gunfire and shouts of battle.

Brooks shook his head. "Where do you think this is happening?"

"We are now receiving reports of more troops landing unopposed along the Kamehameha Highway on the north shore."

Caden nodded. "Oahu."

"Go to William on the north shore," the voice on the radio said. "The fighting is coming this way. We need to move."

The sound of battle returned for a moment, and then a brief silence, followed by a familiar voice. "This is breaking news from KHEN, Hansen's news station. We've been listening to a live report of battle on the island of Oahu, Hawaii. We hope to return there momentarily."

Soft elevator music filled the room.

Two enlisted men stood nearby. "Find a television," he ordered. "Set it up in the conference room on the double."

"We now return you to the situation in Hawaii." The sound of gunfire and the voice of a reporter filled the room.

Caden pulled up a chair and sat in front of the radio.

Fifteen minutes later the two soldiers brought in an old television and turned it on. Amid the sound of gunfire, jets, and explosions Caden saw what he had been looking for, the red flag of the People's Republic of China.

Within minutes, radio checks and questions came over the SINCGARS radio. "All stations on this net, this is Command. Unless you are under attack, monitor this channel, but maintain radio silence."

Caden drank several cups of tea while he continued to gather the news on television and radio. Around noon a private brought sandwiches to the room, but Caden had no appetite. "Leave the television volume up," he said and retreated to his office with another cup of tea. He stared out the window for nearly a minute, unable to focus. Then he recalled that Dr. Scott remained in the hospital and called for an update.

"Hold please." Click.

Caden sat in frustrated silence, listening to classical music while in the next room the sounds of war raged.

"Who are you holding for?"

"This is Major Westmore. I'd like an update on the condition of Dr. Scott."

"Ah ... I'm sorry. She died last night. Did you need anything else?"

"No. Thank you." Again he stared out the window, but this time in dazed silence. He turned at the sound of footsteps.

"Is everything all right, sir?" Brooks asked.

"Yes ... fine." Still absorbing the news of Dr. Scott's death, Caden felt detached and numb.

Brooks gestured toward the conference room. "The radio announcer just said that acting President Harper will speak before new congress in a few minutes. Governor Monroe is already in Denver and will hold a press conference with other constitutionalist leaders immediately after."

"I'll be right there." Caden stood, swayed, and stumbled. His head ached, and his throat felt like sandpaper. He knew the cause. Kern flu.

Chapter Twenty Nine

North of Hansen, Monday, October 5th

The washing and scrubbing of decontamination took a while, but after that Zach received quick clearance from the doctor. As he hurried from the medical tent he spotted DeLynn slumped forward as she sat on a log, softly crying.

Mr. Hollister stood a few feet away with his gaze in her direction.

Still fearing some blame, Zach hesitated to go to them. Then after a sigh, he approached. "I'm sorry I couldn't do more."

Hollister nodded, but his red puffy eyes stared at the medical tent.

"They won't release the ... ah, her." The sound of sobs cut off Zach's words

DeLynn cried and covered her face.

"Ah ... The doctor said the funeral homes weren't taking...."

Mr. Hollister gave a slight nod as his shoulders sagged. "The deputy told me they won't release her ... body. Come on, let's go home."

Together the three moved toward the car a few yards away.

"Would you like me to drive?" Zach asked.

Mr. Hollister handed him the keys without a word.

Driving into the parking lot beside the hotel, Zach recalled how Mrs. Hollister disliked the hotel and didn't think of it as home. He decided never to mention it.

As they exited the elevator on the top floor, Zach touched DeLynn's arm. "Tell me if there's anything I can do."

She nodded and walked away.

Zach retreated to his room, but the silence allowed too much thought. He turned on the radio. An announcer commented on snippets from some speech that had just finished. The guy talked of an invasion and called for a declaration of war.

Zach shook his head. What was all that about? Weren't they already in a civil war?

The guy droned on about a full mobilization.

He had no idea what he meant. Zach turned off the radio. It had nothing to do with him.

*   *   *

Hansen Armory, Monday, October 5th

Caden steadied himself. Without a word he walked through the conference room to the armory isolation ward on the floor below.

One soldier sat up in bed. "You should be wearing a mask, sir."

"That is the least of my concerns right now. Where's the medic?"

The young man pointed to the office at the far end.

Caden spoke to several others as he made his way across the ward. A television hung in the corner near the door. He turned it on.

Every station carried the live feed from the congress in Denver. Caden watched as John Harper, strolled into the assembly to thunderous applause. He might be only the acting president of about half the country but, Caden felt certain, the future of the nation would hinge on what Harper said to congress. Knowing it would take several minutes for him to reach the podium, Caden continued to the medic's office.

Medic Jackson scraped back his chair and stood, then saluted, as Caden entered. "You should be wearing—."

Caden held up his hand. "I don't think that will be necessary. I think I already have it."

"Sit down, sir. Tell me your symptoms."

A radio in the corner carried the news from Denver.

Jackson took his blood pressure, checked his heart and throat, as Caden described how he felt.

Finally, the medic leaned back in his chair and sighed. "Without tests I can't be certain, but your symptoms do indicate Kern flu."

Caden had reached that conclusion on his own, but the words still hit like a fist to the gut.

"The good thing is we've caught it early. We'll keep you hydrated and get started on antivirals. I survived it. You can also, sir."

Caden noticed Harper's speech had begun. "Well, if I'm going to be a patient, I want a bed across from the television."

Jackson glanced at the radio in his office. "Yes sir. This is shaping up to be a worrisome day."

While he waited for a bed, Caden returned to the ward, sat near the television, and phoned his XO.

"I've been looking for you sir. One minute you were here with us and then——."

"I've checked myself into the isolation ward. I've got Kern flu. You're in command."

"Ah …."

"You were acting as CO when I arrived, and you've been a great XO. Start combat preparations. I'll be back on the job in a few days."

"Yes, sir."

"Oh, one more thing, Dr. Scott died last night. Find out what's going to happen with her body. I don't want her buried in a mass grave."

The medic came along side Caden with a tray, pills, and a cup of water. "Let's start with these."

Caden took them and then phoned Maria.

"No!" Tension and tears streamed from her voice. "I should be with you."

"You shouldn't risk it."

"But——."

"No buts. If you are exposed you could infect Adam and everyone else at the farm. I'm in good health and we caught it early. There's no reason I can't beat this, but it will take a few days. Then, I'll come home for final recovery."

He hung up and returned his attention to the TV as the aged John Harper spoke.

"… year of crisis and tribulation, America has endured brutality at its most blatant. Terrorists laid waste to cities. Hunger and pestilence sweeps the land, and now the rulers of China seized the opportunity to steal territory. As I speak the fight continues in

Hawaii, but the aggression did not end there.

"Last night the rulers of China attacked Guam, but their aggression did not stop there.

"Last night the rulers of China launched attacks on Taiwan, Siberia and many islands of the South China Sea."

As the assembly gasped, the camera swept the spectator gallery and focused for a moment on Governor Monroe. Harper would soon ask for a declaration of war, but Monroe would quickly inherit the fight.

Harper pounded the lectern. "This is aggression at its most blatant and, regardless of our differences in the past, this challenge must be met with America's total resolve. I call upon congress to authorize a full mobilization against this flagrant attack on our people and that a state of war be declared against the government of the People's Republic of China."

Congress thundered with applause.

Caden sighed. Not since World War II had civilization seen a conflict like this. Everyone would be involved.

*　　　*　　　*

Westmore Farm, Rural Lewis County, Monday, October 5th

Maria sat staring out the front room window into darkness. Work often kept Caden away, but today there seemed to be a void in the house without him there. Normally she would talk with Lisa, but she had taken dinner to David, because, as the acting CO, he couldn't leave right now.

"God, please help Caden." Maria had repeatedly offered little prayers during the day, but Caden's parents were still in the kitchen praying with a belief and intensity she had never seen before. David and the medic tried to reassure her every time she called, even though Caden's temperature continued to climb. She resolved to go to him if death seemed near.

All these thoughts made the living room seem so empty. She lifted Adam from the floor and squeezed him tight. He whimpered and she loosened her grip, then kissed his plump cheeks and tried to smile.

Sue strolled into the room with baby Peter.

As they talked Maria became distracted by the squawking and bocking of the chickens. "Something must have frightened them."

Nikki climbed the couch to look out the window, sniffed the

air, and growled.

Figuring it might be a weasel or feral cat, she passed Adam to Sue, grabbed the shotgun, and stepped out onto the porch. Just outside she paused, giving her eyes time to adjust to the night.

The chickens continued to squawk and Nikki barked from inside the house.

Maria couldn't see much of anything or hear anything useful. She stepped off the porch into the blackness of a moonless night. Thinking she heard a voice, she put the shotgun to her shoulder and moved forward with caution.

The darkness remained deep, but a gray and black world gradually emerged. The chickens continued to complain, but no threats were apparent. She lowered her gun at the barn door and pulled it open with a loud creak. "Trevor?" she said hesitantly. "Are you in here?"

Only the squawks of agitated chickens answered.

Maria let the door squeak shut and then crept around the barn toward the hen house.

Halfway there a shot blasted through the air.

Fiery pain like fire streaked along the left side of her head. Maria stifled a scream. The side of her head felt wet and warm. She lunged left to the barn wall, and stood tight against it. "It's me, Maria!" She hoped a familiar voice would come from the night with words of apology.

Immediately a shot rang out, then another.

Anger flared within Maria. Someone had tried to kill her. She wiped blood from her eye, turned, and fired a blast from the shotgun in the direction of the shots. Then she darted behind Trevor's pickup.

Only Nikki and the chickens disturbed the silence.

She stood there, trying to control her breathing, as she figured out what to do next.

"Trevor?" Sarah walked onto the porch. "Trevor? What happened? Are you okay?"

Maria's heart pounded in her ears.

Nikki barked frantically. Then the dog pushed the screen door open and ran into the dark beyond the clothes line.

Maria eased forward with the shotgun ready.

"Do you see Trevor?" his wife asked.

Maria shook her head.

Somewhere up ahead Nikki whimpered.

Maria stayed in the shadows of the barn as she moved forward. She spotted the dog up ahead. "What do you see, Nikki?" As she bent down Maria realized why the dog whimpered. "Sarah! Someone help!"

Blood soaked the ground in a growing pool around Caden's father.

Chapter Thirty

Westmore Farm, Rural Lewis County, Tuesday, October 6th

Maria sat on the front porch, oblivious to the movement of law enforcement and others around her. She had killed Trevor, the father of the man she loved. Sobs from Sarah in the living room thundered in Maria's ears. She wiped tears from her eyes and doubted she could ever face Trevor's wife again. What penance could she perform? What words could she say, that would heal such a rift? If he survived the flu, how could she face Caden? She had killed his father.

An EMT pushed a gurney along the rocky driveway. A bloodstained sheet covered the body ... Trevor's body ... that he loaded into the back of the truck.

Maria slumped forward as he drove away. A few minutes later she stood and stepped into the living room. Lisa and Sue huddled around Sarah with long, sad faces. Maria gently lifted Adam from the playpen, kissed him several times, and then set him back. Then she turned and wandered into the darkness.

She walked along the rocky driveway until she reached the asphalt of Hopps Road, then turned toward the highway. Minutes later she heard a car come up behind her and pull onto the gravel edge. She continued walking.

A car door shut. Footsteps crunched in the gravel behind her. "Why did you walk away? Where are you going?"

She hesitated at the sound of Sheriff Hoover's voice. Perhaps he thought she had fled the scene of her crime. Perhaps she did. "I'm walking. I'm not sure where."

Hoover came alongside her. "I think we've figured out what happened, but I want to ask you a few questions."

Maria shrugged. "Whatever you need. Can I keep walking?"

"I suppose." Using a flashlight he looked at his notes. "What type of firearm did you have tonight?"

"A shotgun."

"Did anyone else have a firearm?"

"I don't think so."

He nodded. "The deputy that first arrived said you confessed to killing Trevor. Did you actually see him when you shot?"

"No." Tears flowed again. "I know I should have seen what I shot at, but someone shot at me. I shouted my name and they shot again. I fired back. Then, I went in that direction and found his body."

"Did you actually examine Trevor?"

She shook her head. "There was a little light coming from the house … I tried to find a pulse. All I could see was blood. Then I knew I … I—"

"Shot him?"

Tears rolled down her cheeks.

"He died of a rifle shot to the chest."

"Rifle? Huh?" She stared at him. "Not a shotgun blast?" She stopped and turned to him. "I didn't have a rifle."

He faced her. "That confused the deputy and so he called me. We searched, but your dog put us on the trail."

"Nikki?"

Hoover nodded. "It's still dark so I can't be sure, but I think she followed a blood trail that led to another body further out in the field. I recognized the guy immediately. His name is … was … Bachman, a career petty criminal living in a trailer about two miles down the road. He still had a .270 rifle in one hand."

Maria gasped.

"The way I see it, after you left the house to investigate the noise, Trevor did also. He may not have known you were outside until Bachman fired his first shot and you shouted your name." Hoover took a deep breath. "Well, I think Trevor stalked, and shot Bachman, but only wounded him. Bachman returned fire and hit Trevor in the chest. That was the second shot you heard and that was the one that killed Trevor. You fired, but apparently missed both."

She sobbed and fell to her knees.

Hoover knelt beside her.

Several minutes passed before she could speak. "Does Sarah know?"

"I told her what I suspected, but I had to confirm a few things with you before I could be certain." He stood and held out a hand. "Let's go back to the house."

Maria took a deep breath, let it out, and then took his hand. One burden had been lifted, but Trevor had still been murdered, and Caden remained gravely ill.

*   *   *

Hansen Armory, Tuesday, October 6th

Reveille hadn't yet sounded when Acting CO, Lieutenant David Brooks, walked into his office. Immediately the phone rang.

"This is the hospital morgue. I've been told you put a hold on the transfer of Dr. Scott's body."

"Yes." Since he had no official reason, Brooks felt it best to say as little as possible.

"Ah, there's a pandemic in progress. We don't have room to hold bodies."

Anger flared in Brooks. "I know about the Kern flu. I also know that mass burials will commence in a few days. Send out the other bodies, but hold Dr. Scott's." He hung up the phone.

When he felt calm, Brooks called and asked the medic about Caden.

"He's slipping in and out of consciousness. His temperature is one hundred and one, but we're working to bring that down. We'll know more in the next 48 hours."

"Keep me informed." He had been in the office only minutes and the situation depressed him. As he rubbed his forehead, he wondered if Caden felt that way sometimes. Caden had been more than a commanding officer; he had been a friend and mentor. Now death lingered beside him.

Brooks read the two orders received during the night. The first established draft boards in each county, called up all guard units into the armed forces, and allowed the military to seize fuel, transport, and other resources necessary to fully mobilize for the war effort.

The next one ordered Major Westmore to establish two platoons of up to a total of 100 soldiers for a special mission. The order specified that all unit personnel were to be Kern flu survivors or those who had demonstrated immunity. Brooks would assemble the unit and pray Caden would recover and command it.

*   *   *

Hollister Hotel, Tuesday, October 6th

Zach awoke early and wondered what he should do. He didn't expect Mr. Hollister to continue rehab work on the stores so soon after his wife's death, or for DeLynn to help with food distribution. Vicki would work, but she didn't know anything about the deliveries. So that left him with no clear direction. He decided to read near the apartment door and listen for movement in the hallway.

Vicki awoke and prepared breakfast for both of them.

With a mouth full of scrambled egg Zach asked, "Do you know what we're doing today?"

Vicki shook her head. "No, and I don't want to ask."

"Neither do I."

As he finished his breakfast, a few minutes later, he heard a noise in the hall. Zach hurried the last few mouthfuls and, with Vicki close behind, hurried to the elevator in time to see the numbers count back to one. He pressed the button for the lift to return.

"I'll clean up and meet you down there." Vicki headed back down the hall.

The whine of a circular saw filled the lobby. Zach stepped to the door of the general store. Mr. Hollister stood inside cutting plywood. Movement caused Zach to look left and through an unfinished wall he spotted DeLynn as she sat at a table near a window in the bakery. He went to her. "Mind if I sit down?"

She nodded.

Zach wasn't sure if that meant yes, she minded, or yes, sit. He hesitated.

"Go ahead." She pointed to the seat across from her.

When he sat, he tried not to stare at DeLynn's puffy eyes. A plate with three slices of buttered toast sat before her. One slice had been nibbled. Zach seemed always to be hungry and the smell of bread only made it worse. He would have loved some of her bread, but he wondered if it might be her first food since the death of her mother.

She stared at the toast, but it pleased him that she had eaten some and spoke with him. "I'm sorry."

"You tried to help. I appreciate that."

Vicki entered and turned the radio on while she worked at the counter.

"You don't blame me for not getting your mother home sooner?"

"No." DeLynn shook her head. "Of course not."

Zach sighed with relief.

"She left and traveled through a camp full of sick people. I'm glad you found her. She could have died and been buried in a mass grave. We'd never have known what happened to her."

Vicki stood by the radio toasting and buttering bread. Then, she placed a fresh plate of it at the center of the table and sat next to Zach. "I just heard some weird news on the radio."

"What?" Zach grabbed a slice.

"The announcer said the government is drafting guys for a war with China. When did we go to war with them?"

Panic filled DeLynn's eyes. "Don't leave me."

Zach shook his head. "There's no way."

Chapter Thirty One

Hansen Armory, Monday, October 12th

Weird dreams of blood, death, and specters haunted Caden's mind for what seemed an eternity. Pain lingered in a black void when the demons withdrew. The torments retreated gradually, leaving a restful nothingness.

Aware of an annoying beep, Caden forced his eyes open. Hardly moving his head, he gazed from side to side at a tiny room filled with hospital equipment. Sunshine poured in from an unseen window behind him. Just a few feet from his bed, a door opened. A woman wearing a breathing mask and bio-hazard suit entered. Their eyes met. She hurried to his side. Despite the mask and gown, he thought he recognized her. "Maria?"

"You've come back to me." She leaned down and kissed him through the mask.

While he gazed into her eyes, sleep overcame him.

*   *   *

Lieutenant David Brooks spoke with General Harwich on the landline phone while the head of the new draft board sat across the desk from him, waiting impatiently. As Brooks tried, unsuccessfully, to end the conversation with the general, the cell phone in his pocket vibrated.

He decided that frustration lurked in the cosmic fabric of Monday mornings. "Yes, sir. I'll get those numbers to you today."

The general grunted. "How is Major Westmore doing?"

"I haven't heard today. Last night he was still unconscious, but his fever had declined to almost normal." The annoying vibration in his pocket continued. "However, he seems to be resting comfortably."

"I need to talk to him," the general said. "Let me know the minute he wakes up."

"Yes, sir." He grabbed his cell phone and it stopped vibrating. He pulled it from his pocket with an exasperated grunt, but noticed the call came from Maria. That early in the day her call would probably be a status update on Caden. Brooks held up one finger asking the gray-haired man from the draft board to wait as he returned her call. "Maria, this is David. What do you need?"

"Caden's awake! Or at least he was. He's gone back to sleep now."

"That's great news." He sighed as worry for his friend flowed away. "Thanks for letting me know." He wondered if he should call the general, but decided to wait. "Call me when he stays awake."

He hung up and looked to the chairman of the draft board. "What have you got for me?"

The old veteran pulled two sheets from a briefcase and handed them to Brooks. "We thought we'd start by identifying the men eighteen to forty-five years old that were recently discharged, but still have reserve time. Once they're called up, the service can use a stop-loss order to keep them in."

"Probably a good idea." Brooks ran his finger down the list. Almost at once he noticed, 'Brennon, Zachery.'" He pointed to the name. "This one wasn't in the service."

"There are a few like that, young men with ROTC training either in high school or college. In Brennon's case he worked here, virtually as a soldier, and fought in two battles. We thought it a good idea to get such people in quickly. We do have a two-front war to fight."

Brooks nodded. The war with China had flared red hot even as the civil war with Durant in the east quieted because of the spreading sickness. Brooks signed the list as acting military commander and handed it back. "Okay, it's official. Draft them."

*　　　*　　　*

Hansen Armory, Tuesday, October 13th

Caden rested somewhere between sleep and awake as snoring gradually entered his consciousness. His eyes fluttered open and adjusted to the sunlit room. A vague memory emerged. He had awakened here once before. No beeping annoyed him this time, and less equipment cluttered the room. A single intravenous bag sent a slow drip into his arm. Maria, the source of the snoring, dozed, slumped over in a chair to his right. She wore no bio-hazard protection. Perhaps he had survived the Kern flu. He took a deep breath and as he let it out tension seemed to flow out with it. For several moments he stared at Maria, admiring the soft feminine lines of her face.

Her eyes opened just a hint.

He smiled. "So, am I going to be okay?"

"Oh!" Her eyes shot open. With quick flicks of her hands she brushed back her hair and wiped her eyes and mouth. "Ah … yes, your temperature has been normal for over a day. The doctor said you aren't contagious. How do you feel?"

He sighed and tried to sit up. "Like I've been in a knockdown, drag-out fight." With his shoulders barely on the pillow, he stopped and groaned. "I think I lost that bout."

"You've been in a fight, but the virus lost." Maria stood. "I'll be right back." She left, but returned a minute later with a medic.

The soldier gave Caden a quick check. "You're one of the lucky ones, sir." He removed the last IV. "You'll need a few days to regain strength, but you should be fine."

"I'd like to rest up at home."

The young man nodded. "That sounds like an excellent idea. I'll inform the XO that you're awake."

Maria turned toward the door. "I'll get a wheelchair."

"No." Caden shook his head. "If I'm leaving here I'm walking out. Help me get dressed."

When he finished, Caden stood, swayed and stumbled. He clutched Maria's hand. "Maybe we can walk with my arm resting on your shoulder."

A grin wrinkled the corners of her mouth, but sadness lingered on her face. She put an arm around him. "I certainly don't mind but, before we get home, there's something I need to tell—."

The door opened and Brooks entered. "Good to see you up, sir." He turned to Maria. "I need to speak with him alone about some operational matters."

Caden slumped into a chair.

"Already?" Anger flared in Maria's eyes. "Can't you let him recover first?"

Brooks blushed.

Caden raised his hand in a stop motion. "It's okay, Maria."

"No, it's not. Two days ago you were on the verge of death and I had to watch you, wondering every moment if you would live or die. Now you're back, but you can't even rest a couple of days?"

He looked at her for several moments. "You're right." Caden turned to Brooks. "Is anyone going to die if you don't talk to me?"

Brooks glanced at Maria and then back at Caden. "General Harwich has been very eager to speak with you. I told him you would probably be well enough today."

"What does he want to talk about?"

Again Brooks glanced at Maria, then returned his gaze to Caden. "Ah … he hasn't told me much. I received this order six days ago." He handed a paper to Caden.

Maria sat on the only other chair in the room and fixed angry eyes on Brooks.

Caden read the order, folded it, and handed it back. "I'll phone him … soon."

"Yes, sir." Brooks saluted. "Welcome back." He glanced at Maria. "I'll see you in a few days then."

With his own glance at Maria, Caden said, "Maybe longer."

Brooks turned and left.

Maria stood and helped Caden to his feet.

He placed a hand on her shoulder. "Okay, take me home. I promise to stay there while I recover and regain my strength before coming back here."

Maria slipped her arm around Caden. As they walked from the room she turned to him. "There's something I need to tell you before we get home. Something important."

*   *   *

Hollister Hotel, Wednesday, October 14th

Zach and Vicki rode the elevator down to the lobby after breakfast. The sound of Mr. Hollister cutting a board in a far corner greeted them as they exited.

Vicki shook her head as they walked. "All Mr. Hollister does is work. He's practically been living down here since his wife died."

"He just wants to get the place fixed up. When things get back to normal—."

DeLynn came out of the office holding a letter. "This was in with some business mail." She handed it to Zach. "It looks all official. I never thought of this before, but we should set you guys up with mailboxes."

Vicki looked at the envelope. "What's the War Mobilization Board?"

Zach shrugged as he examined the envelope. "I don't know." He shoved it in a pocket. "I'll deal with it later."

DeLynn turned to Vicki. "Could I get your help in the bakery for a few minutes?"

"Sure, I'll be right there." When DeLynn turned the corner Vicki pointed to the letter that barely protruded from his pocket. "I can see the concern on your face. What is the letter about?"

Zach pulled it from his pocket and tore it open.

Greetings, a local board composed of your neighbors has determined that you are available for training and service in the armed forces of the United States. You are hereby notified that you have been selected for training and service in the Army. Under the War Mobilization Act recently passed by Congress, you are hereby ordered to report for duty at 0800 on Monday, November 2nd at Joint Base Lewis-McChord.

Zach stuffed it back in his pocket. His mind raced as he tried to figure out what to do.

Vicki's eyes narrowed and she frowned. "What is it?"

"Don't say anything to DeLynn." Zach shook his head. "I've got to talk to Major Westmore. I've been drafted."

*　　　*　　　*

Westmore Farm, Rural Lewis County, Wednesday, October 14th

A blue sky and yellow sun gave no warmth. Near an ancient Douglas fir tree on the far side of the Westmore farm, two simple coffins rested on boards above open graves. Caden sat in a lawn chair nearby unable to stand for more than a minute or two. He wanted to grieve for both of the dead, but felt only numbness.

His mother sat on his right, wiping tears from her face. He leaned over and hugged her. Maria stood on his left, dabbing at her eyes. She had broken the news of his father's death on the way home yesterday. The pain of that news still twisted inside of him.

There had been so many tears this year. Telling loved ones about death was a duty he had come to know. Such a thankless job. He gently squeezed her hand.

A joyless smile crossed Maria's face as she squeezed back.

As a young man Caden's greatest wish had been to escape the rural county of his birth and the farm where he lived. He had never hated, and rarely disliked his father, but he had dismissed him as simply a farmer with only a high school diploma. Since the terror attacks and the collapse of the economy, he had come to respect his father's farming and carpentry skills. Those talents had fed the family that year. Why had he never said that to his father? He stared at the coffin and prayed for a heaven where he might get the chance.

His gaze drifted to the coffin beside his father's. Dr. Scott had treated most of the people he knew in the community. Briefly he wondered if she had delivered him, but decided it unlikely. Dr. Scott had been in family practice, not obstetrics. Being a doctor in the town of Hansen had been her life. There was no family that he knew of, except the community. Caden couldn't let her be buried in a mass grave, so she would be buried here with his family.

He looked around, nodded to Zach and a few others from the armory. Most of the town should have been there for his father and Dr. Scott, but few attended. Fear of the flu, he told himself.

He glanced at the low marble marker of Peter's grave and then at Sue. Her sad red eyes looked down at little Peter in her arms.

Lisa stood nearby holding hands with Brooks.

Across from the new graves stood the old headstones marking the resting places of his grandparents, an uncle and two aunts. These weather worn markers, made from local granite, displayed their age like a badge of honor. It gave the place a sense of dignity.

Caden looked at Hoover in the dress uniform of a sheriff. Normally the eulogy would have fallen to the pastor, but Kern flu had stricken him, too. Perhaps it then would have fallen to Caden, but his recovery had only begun. Thankfully, Hoover had asked to speak.

The sheriff stepped up to the edge of the graves and looked to the family.

Caden nodded.

Hoover coughed to get everyone's attention, which in a time of pandemic flu probably wasn't the best idea, but it worked.

"I'd like to say a few words about my two friends." Hoover paused for a moment as he stared at the graves. "I met Trevor

Westmore my first year on the force."

Caden winced, thinking Hoover was about to tell the story of arresting Caden for underage drinking. He hung his head as he recalled phoning his father to bail him out that night.

"Trevor had been a volunteer only a few months when twenty-five year old deputy Higgins died in a traffic accident. Trevor met with his wife and family, prayed with them and organized the department donation drive. Over the years, I learned that was his way."

Caden relaxed a bit.

Hoover told other events during Trevor's years at the department. The sheriff also praised his father's years in the army and how he rallied the community during the most recent crisis. Several were stories Caden had never heard before.

"Unlike Trevor, Dr. Scott wasn't born here. She chose this community after medical school. When she came here forty-two years ago, what we call the hospital stood as nothing more than a large clinic. She led and molded it into the legacy that stands today.

"Dr. Scott lived her life for others and died treating Kern flu patients. How many people are alive today because of her work?" Hoover shook his head. "We'll probably never know.

"Neither of them hid their faith, nor did they see it as a cause for pride. It was part of them and determined how they acted. We all benefited and both were examples for me as I matured. I'm saddened that these two pillars of our community were taken from us during this time of suffering, but I know that they are now in glory."

From years of Sunday school, Caden caught the Biblical references. He had never seen this side of Hoover before.

"Trevor Westmore and Dr. Scott are not ghosts lingering among us. They knew their ultimate destination and I am confident they are now at home with the Lord."

Others shared memories. When all had finished, Caden stood on shaky legs, walked to Hoover and shook his hand. "Thank you for being a friend."

Chapter Thirty Two

Westmore Farm, Rural Lewis County, Friday, October 16th

Caden sat on the front porch two days after the funeral, trying to enjoy the sun of an unusually warm autumn morning. The house had always been so full and active. Now the silence and stillness reminded him of a morgue. His mother sat in the living room and stared from grieving eyes. Caden tried to comfort her, but such gestures felt awkward to him. Maria and Sue did a better job of providing solace. Caden wanted to be of help, both physically around the farm and emotionally for his mother and sister, but he knew his efforts in both areas had been mediocre at best.

Movement caught Caden's attention. A lone figure walked along Hopps Road. Unusual, but not cause for alarm. He leaned back and tried to relax. His own walks had grown longer with each day and he did additional chores around the farm. He would be well enough to return to the armory on Monday, but wondered if he should. General Harwich phoned Brooks each day inquiring about Caden's recovery. Each day Brooks put his progress in the worst terms possible, short of an outright lie. This had brought Caden some down time, which he appreciated, but he knew the time had come to phone the general. He tapped out the number.

"Are you near a secure terminal?"

"No, I'm still at home."

"Are you well enough to go to the armory?"

"I think so." Caden didn't want to appear overly ready for work in light of the more negative reports Brooks had provided the general.

"Get to the secure phone this morning and call me."

"Yes, sir." He set down his cell, but remained seated on the porch. He felt well enough to go to the armory, just not well enough to hurry.

In a time of pandemic and lawlessness unscheduled visits to the farm made Caden nervous. The walker, a male with auburn hair, turned from Hopps Road onto the long driveway. He didn't know many people with red hair and none had cause to be coming to see him. His heart pounded. He laid his hand on the holster and gun beside him.

Caden recognized the stress that led to irrational actions and heaved a slow, deep breath. Things were better now. His recovering continued. Hoover had pushed the state crime lab to examine the bullets found at the Wilson and Harper farms. They matched the one that killed his father. He'd never met Bachman, the felon that killed his dad, but the criminal had torn through Caden's life and those dear to him, like a tornado. That storm had died, but the destruction remained for the living to deal with.

Caden squinted and though he recognized the hiker, now halfway up the driveway. He stood and leaned on the rail for a better view and relaxed. It was Zach. Feeling his legs wobble, Caden sat and waited.

*   *   *

Hansen Armory, Friday, October 16th

Brooks had worked to provide time for Caden to recover over the last few days. He told his boss only the most pressing news and kept General Harwich at bay with slanted medical updates.

The general clearly didn't want to talk with Brooks about the mission Caden would lead, so he had only learned that the command officers were eager for him to recover.

While Brooks gained little information regarding Caden's mission, news from the various fronts dominated television, radio, and military message traffic.

Kern flu had slowed the civil war in the American heartland to a series of skirmishes. In Hawaii the war waged hot. The Kern flu ravaged the Chinese population, but they had a vastly larger pool available for the war effort. So, after days of conflict the Chinese controlled most of Hawaii. Only scattered American resistance continued. Half of the American Pacific fleet had been destroyed before retreating to safer waters.

News commentators called for a quick return to liberate Hawaii. That combined with the ongoing civil war and the destruction of the Pacific fleet led military planners to decide on defeating Durant, before taking on the Chinese. Reporters seemed to think the next major push against New America forces would occur in the spring. Brooks heard rumors that something would happen sooner and wondered if Caden would be a part of that.

*　　　*　　　*

Westmore Farm, Rural Lewis County, Friday, October 16th

Caden stood again as Zach approached. "Hi. It's good to see you." They exchanged pleasantries, shook hands, and Caden motioned for him to sit beside him on the porch. "Why did you walk all the way out here?"

Zach sat beside him. "Actually I walked out to the Armory first thing this morning. I thought you'd be there, but Lieutenant Brooks said you hadn't returned to work."

"I'll be back on Monday."

"I didn't want to say anything at the funeral, but … well I got this on Tuesday and I've been wondering what I could do." Zach handed an envelope to Caden. "I'm not a coward, but I don't want to fight and kill anymore."

Caden knew the contents before he opened the letter. "No sane person wants war, but sometimes evil people bring the fight to us." He read the document. "You could apply as a conscientious objector but, considering your combat record, I doubt the board would accept that." He sighed, wanting to say something hopeful and encouraging. "You might be able to serve as a medic, but you'd need to be in before that was determined. I could help you get a deferment, but that would only be a delay." He locked eyes with Zach. "You're young, healthy and have military experience. Sometime, somewhere, you're going to be in the fight."

*　　　*　　　*

"I won't be long but I have to do this." Caden picked up the keys from the bedside table.

Maria crossed her arms. "You're not well enough and you know it."

He frowned. "I'm well enough to talk on the phone. The general needs to tell me something classified. I have to use the secure phone at the armory. I won't even be in uniform."

"Oh?" Maria huffed. "That makes all the difference. I'll drive."

"I can drive."

She gave him 'the look' and held out her hand for the keys.

He groaned and dropped them into her hand. "Okay, you drive."

Silence reigned during the trip until Maria pulled into Caden's parking space at the armory.

He opened the passenger door. "I'll only be a few minutes."

She nodded. "Should I wait here or do you need help with the stairs?"

Upstairs. The KY-68 secure phone they had received during Operation Hellhound, sat in a locked cabinet in the conference room, on the second floor. He didn't have the energy to be climbing steps, but male pride forced him to say, "No. I'll take them slow. It should be easy."

Minutes later Caden stood just inside the stairwell on the second floor breathing deeply and wiping sweat from his forehead. When he felt composed, he continued on to the office.

Brooks and two enlisted soldiers came to attention and saluted as Caden entered.

"At ease. I need to make a secure call to General Harwich."

"Should I be with you?" Brooks asked.

"No." Caden continued across the office toward the conference room. "I think the general wants to talk with me alone."

Brooks nodded.

Caden walked into the room and shut the door behind him. He sat at the large table and caught his breath before dialing the general's secure number.

An unrecognized voice came through the phone first. "Washington Military Command Center."

"This is Major Westmore. General Harwich is expecting my call."

It took less than a minute for the general to come on the line. "I'm glad you made it to the armory so I can share additional details about the operation. The first part of the mission will be recon along a certain portion of the Mississippi. Most of your men will remain in areas we control, providing backup and assisting as needed. When you've found a good location, you and a few of your men will infiltrate territory controlled by Durant's New America forces and retrieve an important package."

Caden shook his head. Considering he remained weak and Maria was still upset that he left the house, he wanted more details for his effort. "Is there anymore you can tell me, sir?"

"No, not now. NSA developed the KY-68 we're using and they remain under Durant's control. I'm reluctant to go beyond secret in this briefing."

"Many soldiers could lead an op like this. Why am I so critical to this mission, sir?"

"The answers will have to wait until you're healthy enough for us to meet in a SCIF. Then, I'll answer some of your questions."

The secrecy surrounding the mission, that General Harwich would be briefing him, and that it would be conducted in a room designed to prevent any form of eavesdropping, piqued his interest. "Yes, sir. I'll update you on Monday."

"Can you be ready by then?" General Harwich growled.

"Yes, sir." He stood and his legs wobbled beneath him. "I'll be ready."

*　　　*　　　*

Hollister Hotel, Saturday, October 17th

Zach needed to rest at the end of a long day. Vicki had been the first to mention how hard DeLynn's father had been working. All he did was labor on the hotel since his wife died. How could he work so long? Zach had left him last night at eleven and returned before eight to find him already covered in sawdust. Mr. Hollister took most of his meals while working and rarely talked to anyone. He didn't seem angry, just brooding.

He entered the elevator and reached for the penthouse button, then changed his mind and pushed the number five. Exiting, Zach walked toward carved double doors. He had noticed the extended patio on the roof of the fifth floor when working in one of the nearby hotel rooms. A quick search revealed the entrance. Wrought iron railings and tiled floor told him this had once been used for gatherings or parties.

The rusty hinges protested as he pushed the door open and stepped outside.

Pleased he could be alone there, he breathed deep the crisp autumn air. Many places in the mostly empty hotel provided privacy, but he preferred to be outside. Looking about, he imagined the deck with tables, chairs and happy people.

Somewhere nearby an engine backfired.

The party image dissolved into worry. He would soon be training for war. With a sigh of resignation he leaned against the railing and recalled the first combat he'd experienced. Everyone called it the Battle of Hansen, and thought he fought in it. He had been there, but had cowered behind a tree.

He had killed people while rescuing DeLynn at the ranger cabin, in the riot on East Bridge, and just days ago during Operation Hellhound. All those faces still haunted his dreams. He didn't think he was a coward, but he didn't feel particularly brave either.

The door creaked behind him.

Zach glanced over his shoulder.

"I've been looking for you." Vicki walked to the railing and leaned beside him. "Nice view."

He nodded. "Why are you here, Sis?"

"You're going to have to tell DeLynn about the draft notice."

He certainly didn't want to go to war, but more than anything else he feared DeLynn's reaction to his departure. She had lost her home, her mother, and perhaps she was losing her father. Would he lose her when he had to leave?

Vicki placed her hand on his shoulder. "She deserves to hear it from you."

"I know."

Chapter Thirty Three

Hollister Hotel, Sunday, October 18th

Zach looked into the sky and thanked God for a mild, cloudless day. Earlier he had found old Christmas lights, a metal table, two chairs, and a few plastic plants to adorn the fifth floor patio. He wound the lights along the railing and in the plants. Then he took a bedsheet, and with Vicki's assistance folded it for a table cloth.

With his sister's help, he prepared a meal of chicken, potatoes and corn. It wasn't fancy, but it would have to do. Finally, he added the cutlery and hurried to the penthouses.

Zach entered the elevator with DeLynn in tow and pressed five on the control panel.

"Where are you taking me?" she asked.

"You've never been on the fifth floor?"

"No. None of the rooms have been renovated. What's there?"

The elevator dinged, stopped, and the doors slid open. "You'll see." Zach led her down the hall and held opened the wooden door. When she walked onto the patio, he followed her.

"Wow!" She put her hands to her face. "What's this for?"

"You!" He clasped her hand and continued on to the table. "We haven't had a regular date this year."

"Well ... these last few months have been...." She shook her head.

Zach smiled and pulled out her chair.

Her eyes were on the table as she sat. "You didn't cook this, did you?"

"Don't worry the food is safe. Vicki cooked most of it."

She giggled. "I'm sure she did a great job."

Zach worked to keep the chat on light topics as they ate, but war, plague, and chaos had replaced the weather as common subjects of conversation. "When do you think school will reopen?"

DeLynn swallowed a bite of chicken. "Maybe in the spring. That's the rumor going around."

Conversation ebbed and flowed until they finished the meal. DeLynn smiled and held out her hand. "You look like you have something serious to say."

He clasped her soft hand. "Yeah, I've got something I really need to tell you."

She smiled, but said nothing.

"There's no easy way to put this so, I'm just going to say it."

He felt her tense.

"I've been drafted."

She gasped and her eyes shot wide. "Into the military?"

He nodded.

She yanked her hand back. "Tell them no."

"They're not asking." He frowned. "I can't say no."

She shook her head. "But you've been in the military. You fought."

"I wasn't in the Guard or army, I just helped out."

"But ... but you quit."

"I could quit because I wasn't really in the military. Now they've drafted me and I'll actually be in the army."

"You sound like that's what you want." Her voice went from incredulous to angry.

"It isn't, but I've talked to people." He reached out to hug her. "This is something we need to accept."

"No!" She shoved away from the table. "No! It's not. You can't do this." Tears and sobs burst from her and she ran back inside.

*   *   *

Westmore Farm, Rural Lewis County, Sunday, October 18th

As Caden lumbered down the stairs on Sunday morning a strange mixture of feelings occupied his mind. It would be days before his stamina returned and he felt reluctant to encourage General Harwich with reports of his growing health. At the same time his curiosity about the mission made him eager to call. He reached the bottom step and stood there for a moment. All he knew for sure was that he would be at the armory on Monday morning.

Multiple voices and the smells of breakfast wafted from the kitchen into the vacant living room. His stomach grumbled as he followed the aroma.

Pushing the door open, the smell of bacon tickled his nose. Maria stood with her back to him at the stove. Sue sat at the table slicing and buttering bread. His mother sat beside her with an open Bible. Adam pounded on the tray of his highchair. Little Peter somehow slept nearby in the playpen. Curled up under the table, Nikki lifted her head as Caden entered.

An echo of greetings filled the air.

Caden walked over to Maria and kissed her on the cheek. "Nice perfume. It smells like breakfast."

She smiled. "Well, you're feeling better."

"Hungry, that's what I'm feeling." His gaze dropped to the dozen strips of bacon sizzling in a pan. "Where did we get that?"

"I traded eggs, milk, and butter for bacon and chops. I wanted a couple of live pigs, but the farmer wouldn't go for that." She shrugged. "At least we'll have some variety for a while."

He admired her ability to figure out such trades at a time when so many were going hungry.

She flipped a couple of eggs over. "Sit down. Breakfast will be ready in a minute."

Sue and Maria filled plates with food and slid them in front of everyone at the table.

"Will you go into the armory tomorrow?" Maria asked as she fed Adam.

Caden already had egg in his mouth, but swallowed quickly. "I think I should."

"Will you meet with the general?" Maria sat across from him.

He didn't want to lie, but he suspected General Harwich would ask him to travel to Olympia for a meeting soon. He also knew that would upset her. Stillness came over the room. Even Adam stopped whacking things and now stared at him.

"Ah, I will need to call him, but we don't have a meeting planned."

That seemed to placate Maria and she continued with breakfast. When they were nearly done the phone rang.

Since the only phone for the house hung on the wall near her, his mother answered it.

"Hello. Yes. Is everything okay?" Her face paled and her shoulders slumped. "Oh, no. I was praying so hard for him. Sure, I'll talk to you later." She hung up the phone and for a moment stared out the window. Then in a soft voice said, "Pastor Higgins died last night. They were going to try and get services started when he recovered, but now ... well, Ken, the youth pastor may be recovering, but they don't know for sure yet."

This had become such a year of death: his father just days ago, many soldiers at the armory, friends like Dr. Scott and now the pastor of the church. Caden knew him, but not that well. However, looking at his mother, he saw the impact on her. This year her son, Peter, had died, then her husband, and now an old friend and spiritual counselor. He feared for both the mental and physical health of his mother.

He glanced at Sue. She still grieved for her husband. Maria had lost her entire family. Caden rubbed his forehead. He had lost a father and brother this year. Those around him were survivors, but death lurked nearby.

Caden sat in the living room after breakfast.

Nikki curled up by the fire.

Minutes later Maria sat close to him on the couch and held his hand. "I'd been talking with Pastor Higgins about our wedding." She sighed. "Will we ever be married?"

He pulled her closer. "I asked you to marry me once and you said yes. I admit the world seems to be fighting against us, and I guess I've procrastinated some—"

She shook her head. "Remember, I said no to getting married earlier this year."

"You didn't want to marry me in order to survive." He nodded. "Yeah I remember that. Well, do you *still* want to marry me?"

She held up her hand with the engagement ring still on it. "Yes."

He kissed her and in that moment forgot all else. "Okay then let's not worry about the right date, the setting or anything else. As soon as we can get a pastor, or even a judge to do the ceremony, we should go ahead."

She smiled. "I like that idea."

*   *   *

Westmore Farm, Rural Lewis County, Monday, October 19th

"I won't be doing anything stressful today." Caden pulled the key from his pocket as he neared the old pickup.

Maria frowned. "You haven't fully recovered; remember the general wants you to do that secret something."

Caden hadn't forgotten, he just wished Maria would. "I'm sure we will only be talking about it today. I still have a lot of work for whatever this turns out to be."

They kissed before he climbed in the truck and started the engine. His thoughts were a jumble of Maria and the mission as he drove to the armory. Both were compelling and enticing in their own way, and both demanded his attention. He felt like a juggler attempting to keep two objects in the air at the same time. Not a difficult task for a real juggler, but he had never found it easy.

He entered the main building of the armory and took the stairs one step at a time. It pleased him that he didn't need to catch his breath on the landing. Certainly an improvement over Friday, but his heart thumped in his chest, and he felt the stress in his legs. Still he pushed on to the office and the conference room where he picked up the secure phone's receiver and dialed.

The general answered and Caden said, "When and where shall we meet, sir?"

"As soon as you can get here."

Caden had expected the general to say, "Meet me tomorrow morning," or perhaps to meet in the afternoon. "Ah … yes, sir. I'll be there in an hour." As he hung up the phone he winced, Maria would not be pleased. Exiting the conference room he spotted Brooks. "I'm going to meet General Harwich."

"When?"

"As soon as you get me a car and driver."

Brooks raised an eyebrow, and then called the motor pool.

The jumble of responsibilities continued to fester in Caden's mind as he traveled to Olympia. He was a military officer during a time of war. He had duties. Like any military wife, Maria needed to understand that. He rubbed his chin. Wait a minute, she wasn't a military wife; she wasn't even a wife. He sat in frustrated silence as that thought rolled around in his head. He needed to make a commitment to Maria before placing expectations on her. "Okay, I'll do it," he mumbled.

"What's that sir?" the driver asked.

"Nothing." Caden spotted the off ramp to the capital plaza. "Pull off at the next exit and park at the Wainwright building."

Caden took the long stone steps one at a time. As he entered a soldier saluted. "Who are you here to see, sir?"

"General Harwich."

"May I see your ID?"

Caden pulled it out and waited as the soldier checked his list. Two guards, in full combat gear, stood watch behind him. The nurse's station of partitions and plastic sheets remained off to the right. He wondered if he would be going through that once again.

The soldier in front of Caden dialed a phone and said, "Major Westmore is here to see you sir. No, sir, he can come straight up. Yes, sir. Right away."

Caden glanced to his right. Apparently he would not be getting his temperature taken.

Another soldier trotted across the lobby. "If you'll follow me sir, General Harwich is waiting." The soldier led him to the elevator and up to the third floor. Caden knew his destination before he arrived, room 315, the SCIF conference room.

The soldier tapped the combination on the keypad. "The general is already inside."

General Harwich sat at a table in the center of the room. A single chair stood vacant across from him.

Caden saluted. "Reporting as ordered, sir."

"Yes, come in. Sit down."

A moment later as Caden looked across the table at the general, he said, "All this secrecy is intriguing, but I hope you can clear up a few things."

The general leaned back in his chair. "I'll be as honest as possible without jeopardizing the mission. There is a package that could change the course of the war with Durant, but the courier will deliver it only to you."

"What's the package? Why only me?"

"The contents are too sensitive for me to say what it is. If you are captured during the mission many lives would be at stake." He leaned back and sighed. "To answer your second question I would have to reveal the identity of the courier, and that is almost as sensitive as your first question."

"How will I know the courier if—."

"More answers will be provided once the operation is underway and you will understand more as it moves forward. Have you gathered your team?"

"My XO assembled a rifle platoon."

The general pursed his lips. "I'd like you to have more support. I'll have another platoon waiting for you when you arrive."

"How long do you expect us to be deployed?"

"This mission will need to wrap up quickly, a week perhaps." The general shook his head. "But with the current situation, who knows what will happen after that."

Caden felt relieved that the mission wouldn't take long, but felt he should be honest about his health. "I'm getting stronger daily, sir, but I'm still not one hundred-percent."

"I suspected that would be the case, but we've lost time due to your illness, so we need to move rapidly."

"What exactly does that mean?"

"I need you and your team at Joint Base Lewis-McChord tomorrow at 0800."

Chapter Thirty Four

Olympia, Monday, October 19th

Caden flinched at General Harwich's directive. "Tomorrow at 0800?" A glance at his watch showed 1100. Less than a day to prepare in so many ways, pack his rucksack, ensure the soldiers had all their gear, and arrange transport. Also, he would need to talk with Maria and his mother. He had no idea what to say. However, he had been a soldier long enough to know what to tell the general. "Yes, sir."

They stood and moved toward the door.

"Ah, sir? A couple of men who have been serving at the armory have new orders to Lewis-McChord. Another young man has been drafted and ordered there."

"They'll be training for the Pacific war against China."

"They all have experience that I'd like in my unit."

"Give me their names and I'll have the orders waiting when you get back to Hansen."

He wrote the information and then hurried back to the car. As the driver merged onto the freeway Caden's mind raced with all the things he needed to complete. After several minutes he grabbed the phone from his pocket, started to dial, and then stopped. He couldn't say much about the operation over the device in his hand. Reluctantly he shoved it back in his pocket and then planned and worried for most of the ride home.

As the driver exited toward Hansen, Caden thought of one call he could make without compromising the mission. When Hoover came on the line he asked, "Can you find me a priest or pastor?"

"Why, who's dying?"

"No one. I have to get married right away."

"Who did you … nope, none of my business."

"What? No! I … It's Maria, she's not pregnant, but I can't—.""

"I was just kidding. You're in the military and there's a war on. I can guess why you might be in a hurry."

"I know a lot of people are hunkered down waiting for the flu to burn through the area, but do you know someone who can do the service?"

"Yeah, I think I do. Let me make a call."

"Thanks." When he hung up the driver said, "Congratulations, sir. I'll have to let the pool know."

"What?"

"Most of the guys at the armory are in on a pool for the date you get married. We have one for Lieutenant Brooks and your sister also."

Heading east on the state road toward Hansen, Caden said, "I want in on that one."

"So, which way sir, home or work?"

Caden glanced at his watch. Nearly noon and he hadn't even started with mission preparations. "It looks like we're both eating good army chow for lunch."

They pulled into the armory. Caden hurried to the motor pool and ordered trucks to be fueled and ready. Afterwards he went to the office and collapsed into the chair behind his desk. Gradually his strength had grown, but not fast enough for the mission.

Brooks stuck his head in. "They told me you were back. We received some new personnel orders." He handed the papers to Caden. "Is there any mission news that you can share?"

Caden leaned back in his chair and rubbed his chin. "I'm leaving tomorrow at zero dark thirty with the platoon you assembled for me. I still don't know many details, so I can't tell you much more than that. Oh, and I'll be taking First Sergeant Fletcher with me."

Brooks bit his lip, but said nothing. "He has valuable experience. I'd hoped to—."

"That's why I need him." Caden leaned forward. "On another subject, Maria and I may get married tonight. I'd like you to be my best man."

"Of course. I'm honored."

"If this does happen have First Sergeant Fletcher fill in for you."

"Will do." Brooks headed for the door.

"Send Fletcher to see me," Caden called from his desk.

When the first sergeant arrived, he motioned for him to sit down. "I know you weren't in the platoon going out on the mission with me, but I'm adding you."

The slightest hint of a grin creased Fletcher's face. "I thought you'd never ask, sir."

"Well I'm glad that's settled. Allow the men a couple of hours to say goodbye to their families. When they're back conduct the pre-combat inspection. Ammo up, bring all MOPP gear and let me know if there is anything you think we need. I'll do an inspection tomorrow just before we depart."

"It would help if I knew where we were going and what we were doing."

"Yeah, it sure would. All I can tell you is Missouri and that is classified."

"Missouri?" he grunted. "Okay, leave the arctic gear and snowshoes behind."

Caden grinned. "And the desert camo."

As Fletcher left, the cell phone in Caden's pocket blared with the music of *I Fought the Law*. He sighed and pulled the phone out. Maria must have set more ringtones. Sure enough, Hoover had returned his call.

"Were you able to find someone to perform the ceremony?"

"It appears the community has lost a lot of priests and pastors," Hoover said flatly. "They worked with the sick and dying. I guess such mercy has a price."

Caden thought of Dr. Scott. She had paid the price of mercy. "So, you couldn't find anyone?"

"No, I found someone, and discovered that sad fact about the deaths. Am I invited to this shindig?"

"Yes, of course." Caden glanced at the clock on the wall. Already 1300 hours, and he still had much to do. "The service will probably need to be late this evening. I should talk to Maria."

"Yeah, talking this over with her is probably a good idea."

"Thanks for all your help." Anxiety churned within him. "I'll call you when it's time."

*   *   *

Hollister Hotel, Monday, October 19th

Zach glanced into the shadows as a knock echoed through the empty lobby.

Mr. Hollister continued to measure the next board without looking up.

"I'll get it." When Zach turned the corner, into the main area of the entrance, he spotted Fletcher and hurried to open the door. A Humvee stood parallel parked on the street.

"Hi, First Sergeant. What brings you here?" Zach grinned. "Have you come to see my new home? I can give you a tour."

"No, sorry. I'm here on official business."

Fletcher held a limp ruck sack in one hand as he stepped inside. Then he handed Zach a sheet of paper.

In the dim light of the lobby Zach held the document close and read it carefully. "I've been assigned to a new unit under Major Westmore?"

"Yeah, new orders." Fletcher nodded. "You'll need to come with me now."

"Why so sudden? Why me?"

"Ours is not to question why, and in this case I really don't know much."

He frowned. "Should I pack anything?"

"Sure." Fletcher handed him the ruck sack. "A toothbrush, underwear if it's plain white, things like that, but don't bother with a comb." He smiled. "This time you get the haircut with the job."

Zach hurried upstairs to his room with the bag.

Fletcher followed.

As they entered the penthouse, Vicki's eyes grew wide. "Has there been a change of plans?"

"Yeah, there sure has Sis. I leave tonight." Zach continued to his bedroom.

A door slammed in the main room.

"Your sister just ran out of the apartment." Fletcher stood in the bedroom doorway. "I hope that isn't a bad sign."

Zach had no idea why Vicki ran, or why DeLynn or Mrs. Hollister had dashed from him earlier. "I guess I should be used to women running away from me." He shook his head and grabbed more underwear. A couple minutes later the few things he needed were in the ruck sack. He wanted to say goodbye to everyone, but didn't know if he should try to find them. Perhaps he would see Mr. Hollister on the way out.

The door to the penthouse opened as Zach stepped into the living room. Vicki entered, followed by DeLynn and her father.

Fletcher turned to Zach. "I'll wait in the hall."

Zach hugged his sister and shook hands with Mr. Hollister. "I don't know where we're going or when I'll be back, but I'll try and write to you—if the mail works wherever I end up."

"The military is good about getting letters in and out of war zones," Mr. Hollister said squeezing his shoulder. "Write when you can."

"Yeah, you'd better send me letters." DeLynn smiled at him, but tears filled her eyes.

"I didn't know how you felt, or even if you wanted to see me before I left." Zach reached out to her.

DeLynn threw her arms around him and hugged him tight. "Of course I do. Just promise me you'll come back."

He had seen enough combat to know that wasn't a pledge he could make, but every part of him wanted to return to her and she needed his assurance.

For the first time in front of her father, they kissed. He didn't want that moment to end, but he had to reassure her before he left. "Nothing could keep me from coming back to you."

They kissed again and then held each other in a lingering embrace.

Fletcher led the way as they all headed for the lobby. On the sidewalk beside the Humvee, each embraced Zach and he kissed DeLynn again before saying goodbye.

Silence dominated the short ride to the armory. Fletcher pulled up to the main building and stopped. "Go to the office. Major Westmore wants to see you. Then find me, and I'll get you uniforms and a weapon."

Zach climbed the stairs two at a time. He wanted answers. A dozen soldiers hurried along the hall. Seeing the major just outside the office, Zach hurried to him. "I was told you wanted to see me, sir."

"Yes, but I wish the circumstances were better." Caden motioned for him to follow and together they strode through the office to the conference room. "Shut the door."

Zach did and then stood near the table.

"The First Sergeant may have told you that I had your orders changed." Caden sat. "You'll be inducted into the army in just a minute."

"He didn't tell me it was you that changed the orders." Zach stepped closer. "Why would you want to change them? Why would you need me?"

"It's not so much a case of need." Caden took a deep breath and stood. "I can't keep you out of the war, but I'm hoping to save you from the bloodbath that's coming in the Pacific."

"Bloodbath?"

Caden held up a laminated sheet from his desk. "We don't have much time. Raise your right hand, and repeat after me. I, Zachery Brennon, do solemnly swear that I will support and defend the Constitution of the United States against all enemies…."

*   *   *

Westmore Farm, Rural Lewis County, Monday, October 19th

Caden pulled into the driveway just before 11:00pm. He had called Maria and told her he found a pastor willing to do the service. He hadn't told her that a convoy was already preparing to leave the area with him, and that a flight to the war front would take off with him in nine hours. He anticipated little sleep tonight. As he parked the pickup near the porch, Maria hurried out the front door.

Caden stepped from the car and she rushed into his arms.

"I was just upset yesterday." She kissed him on the cheek. "When I asked if we would ever get married I certainly didn't expect you to go out the next day and arrange a wedding."

"Well, I hope you still want to marry me?"

She kissed him. "Of course I do." She relaxed her grip and turned to go inside.

Caden held her. "I know you'd want a perfect wedding and a honeymoon, but that just can't be right now."

"I know that. Your mom has been hemming and stitching her wedding dress all afternoon. Lisa and Sue will be maid and matron of honor … well maybe you can take a few days off? We can spend some time together as a couple."

"About those days off." Caden sighed. "I'm leaving on a mission tomorrow before dawn."

"Tomorrow?" He mouth gaped.

He nodded.

"When will you be back?"

"I don't know for sure."

She held his hand and led him toward the house and up the steps in silence. Instead of going inside she went to the porch swing and sat.

Caden joined her, still holding her hand.

For several moments Maria looked straight ahead without speaking, and then she nodded. "If tonight is all there is, then we'd better get on with it."

"You go in. I've got to use the phone." The call with Hoover took only a moment. "It's on. Get the pastor." He then phoned Brooks. "How are preparations going at the armory?"

"We're doing well, maybe a bit ahead of schedule."

"Good. Pass down what needs to be done to Fletcher and get here ASAP." After hanging up, he walked through an empty living room, and headed upstairs. The voices of all the women of the house could be heard down the hall. Caden went to his room and changed into his class "A" uniform and then returned to a still empty living room. Exhausted by the events of the day he sat in a recliner. He didn't have time to sleep and with all that still needed to be done even a nap seemed impossible, but he could rest for a few moments. He exhaled slowly and tried to relax. He eyes grew heavy.

Caden's eyes shot open. It seemed like only moments had passed, but Brooks sat across from him on the couch. His mother, now in a nice blue Sunday dress, chatted with Hoover as they walked through the front door. A young man followed behind them. Caden rubbed his eyes and jumped to his feet.

His mother smiled at him. "Are you ready?"

With both hands he brushed his uniform. "Yes."

"I'll get the bride." She darted up the stairs.

Hoover stepped close to Caden. "You probably know Pastor Ken."

"No." Caden shook his head. "Sorry."

"He's the youth pastor at your church."

"I knew your father." Ken thrust out his hand and they shook. "He was a good man and I was sorry to hear he died. I also know your mom, Lisa, Maria, the whole family really."

His mother hurried down the stairs fast enough to cause Caden concern. Lisa and Sue followed, dressed in their best, and stood on either side of the banister.

Caden felt like the eye of a hurricane as everyone scurried around him.

The sound of creaking boards and slow steps came from the stairs.

His mother hurried to an old record player and turned it on. The Bridal Chorus filled the room.

Caden turned as Maria, dressed in a white sleeveless lace gown, appeared. He had seen pictures of his mother in it, but never seen it worn until now. It had been a horrible year, but Maria had come through everything strong, and beautiful. Her dark hair and olive skin radiated beauty like a diamond in the light.

As Maria came alongside, Pastor Ken began. "We are gathered here today to join Caden Westmore and Maria Lopez in holy matrimony."

After combat, Caden often had trouble recalling details. He attributed that to adrenalin and stress. As Pastor Ken finished, Caden's eyes remained fixed on Maria, but he struggled to remember the ceremony.

"You may kiss the bride."

He willingly obeyed.

After shaking hands with Hoover and Brooks and kissing the ladies, Caden walked to the porch with his bride. He hugged her tight and once again kissed her, savoring the moment, committing it to memory, for as long as would be necessary. "I've got to go."

Chapter Thirty Five

Whiteman Air Force Base, Missouri, Tuesday, October 20th

Caden woke as the C-130 transport plane bumped down on the runway at Whiteman. He yawned and looked about. Soldiers were packed into the plane, five seats across the middle and the web jump seats on either side. As the plane rolled to a stop he stood and rubbed his eyes and sore neck.

The loading ramp at the rear dropped, and the soldiers jogged onto the runway. As Fletcher assembled the men, Caden looked over the area. Large portions of the runway had been recently patched. The base of the red brick control tower remained, but most of the building had been blown to rubble. A dozen nearby structures, including several hangars, stood as burnt ruins. Camouflaged netting covered the few remaining hangars. He doubted that would be effective in stopping future attacks. How many times had the base been fought over during the war?

"All present sir." Fletcher saluted.

Again, Caden's eyes swept the nearby destruction. "Let's move out, First Sergeant. I'm feeling exposed." As everyone jogged from the tarmac, Caden thought of his new wife, Maria, and the rest of his family and friends. He hoped they would remain safe and far from the front lines.

A young lieutenant walked up and saluted as they reached a grassy area. "Are you Major Westmore?"

"Yes."

"I'm Lieutenant Rookman and I'll be assisting you." He pointed to a building. "Your men can get food at the mess over there. Beside it is an open bay barracks where they can rest until transport is ready."

Caden called Fletcher over. "Make sure the men are fed and ready to go. I don't think we'll be here long."

When Fletcher jogged off the lieutenant said, "If you will come with me Colonel Hutchison will brief you."

"Hutchison?" Caden didn't budge. "From Washington state?"

"Yes, sir. This way, please." Rookman gestured toward the bombed control tower. "The colonel arrived a week ago as part of your operation."

Caden winced recalling how he had argued with Hutchison regarding the handling of Kern flu patients, and the flow of refugees. At one point, Caden even believed the colonel might be a traitor. He followed, wondering how this reunion with the senior officer might unfold.

The lieutenant led him to a backdoor of the ruined control tower. Rookman entered and they walked into a room with blown out windows, crumbling walls and a roof with gaping holes. Together they continued through another door, and down two flights of stairs. At the bottom landing he tapped numbers on a keypad and a buzzer sounded. He pulled open the heavy metal door and waited for Caden to enter.

Just inside Caden paused and surveyed the large concrete room. On the far wall hung several large television and computer monitors. Other computers lined the walls and along a table before the huge screens. Old fashioned paper maps filled most of the remaining wall space and were spread out on a large table near the rear.

Rookman entered and continued on.

Caden hurried to catch up.

"Major Westmore is here to see you," the Lieutenant announced.

Forcing a smile to his face, Caden saluted.

Hutchison returned it and then thrust out his hand. "I was glad to hear that you survived the Kern flu and were coming to join us."

"I'm glad I survived too." Caden gestured toward the room. "This operations center is quite impressive."

Hutchison shrugged. "It wouldn't survive a bunker buster

bomb, but the Durant loyalist forces aren't interested in the ruined building they see from above."

"No, I guess not." Caden glanced as another door opened and three soldiers entered.

"To maintain the illusion of total rubble most people come here through an old cable shaft from another building about fifty yards away."

"How long have you been here?" Caden asked.

"Over a week." He walked toward a table with a map laid out on top. "Command is putting every officer with combat experience in the field, but our group has been waiting for you practically since you came down with the Kern flu."

"Why am I so important to all of this?"

"I was hoping you'd tell me."

Caden shook his head. "I've been told very little and nothing about when, where or why."

"Well, I hope someone tells us something soon." Hutchison shook his head. "At first I thought Command might be planning an offensive."

"A winter offensive? With the Kern flu still decimating the ranks?"

Hutchison shrugged. "Both sides are equally affected. But now, since they told me to wait for you, I'm thinking somehow you are the key." He shrugged. "Anyway, my orders are to get you, and your men, to the front." He pointed to a location on the map. "I'm supposed to get you here, just south of Cape Girardeau. There's a regional airport nearby. That'll be your staging area."

Caden nodded. "Where are your men stationed?"

"Most of them are in Cape Girardeau." Hutchison moved his finger along the map.

"So, you'll be covering the north flank. Who's stationed to the south?"

Hutchison drew a line across the Mississippi into Tennessee. "Regular army units and elements of the Arkansas and Tennessee guard."

"I thought Tennessee was under Durant's control."

"Most of the ground is, but not all. Several military units are fighting with us."

Caden examined the map. "Okay, so, neither of us are sure

what we're doing when we get to the staging point."

Hutchison shook his head. "Get you there and hold Cape Girardeau while you're south of me. That's my orders and all I know." He stared at Caden. "I sense you have additional information."

"Not very much." General Harwich had told Caden he would be doing some recon and retrieve a package. He shook his head. "I can't say anything."

"Okay then." Hutchison stepped toward the door. "Let's make sure the men have some hot chow, a shower and maybe some rest. I doubt they'll be getting such things in the days ahead."

*   *   *

Somewhere in southern Missouri, Tuesday, October 20th

Zach stared out the back of a Deuce-and-a-half as it rumbled along a highway somewhere in Missouri. His platoon from the Hansen armory, along with hundreds of other soldiers, left in a long convoy from Whiteman airbase late in the afternoon. He knew from the position of the sun that they were headed southwest, but this had changed several times. For a while they had journeyed east, then changed roads and gone south. Then they turned again. He had no clue as to the final destination.

As day turned to dusk, his limited view filled with dark shadows. He hadn't slept well in the web seat of the C-130, and the hard seat of the truck, combined with the rifle slung on his shoulder, promised little rest in the hours ahead. So, he stared at small towns, farms, and a growing number of stars.

As the miles bumped by, his eyes slipped shut.

A roar so loud it hurt, reverberated through Zach's body. His eyes shot open to near total darkness. Overhead, jets shot past, so low and fast their engines overwhelmed all other sound.

The Deuce-and-a-half swerved to the side of the road.

Soldiers jumped from the truck. Someone bumped against Zach, thumping the rifle barrel against his head. He fell to the ground.

Like a huge Fourth of July display, the sky exploded into fire.

Zach followed the others into a nearby meadow. He could see officers shouting orders, but jet engines and explosions were all he heard. He trailed the others into the field. Behind him came the boom of another explosion. A wave of heat and wind knocked him to the ground. Lifting his face from the dirt he looked back as the truck he had been in fell to the earth in pieces.

He crawled along the field away from the fire looking for others. Gradually, he noticed bumps in the dirt. Realizing they were fellow soldiers he scurried toward them on hands and knees.

The roar of jets continued overhead.

Nearing the group, he spotted First Sergeant Fletcher.

"In the future private move faster—if you want to live," Fletcher shouted.

Zach nodded and, with the others, waited for the aerial nightmare to stop. More trucks burst into flame and more explosions dotted the sky.

Then it stopped as the roar of jets faded.

Zach's ears rang.

Fletcher stood and swept his arm forward. "Come on people, back to the convoy."

Other voices shouted. "Find a working truck and climb aboard."

Zach held back not wanting to be inside the next target.

A sergeant urged him on with a string of profanity.

Within minutes the remaining vehicles rolled down the road, this time with Zach in the middle. He struggled to listen for the jets as the convoy continued toward the front.

The first rays of sun peeked over the horizon as the vehicles pulled off the freeway.

Zach stared out the back. He noticed most of the other trucks continued on the highway. His Deuce-and-a-half rolled down one street and then turned on to another smaller road. A few minutes later it stopped.

"Everyone off the trucks," Fletcher shouted from somewhere outside.

Just two of the original vehicles had journeyed to this place. Along with Zach, about forty soldiers stood beside rubble that had once been a building. Only a covered entryway remained. Big letters on the side read, "Cape Girardeau Regional Airport."

Zach had no idea where that might be.

"Get comfortable." Fletcher picked up his rucksack. "This is our new home."

Zach surveyed the rubble of the airport as a strange

realization came to him. His whole life seemed to lead him here. As a child he played many computer war games. As a teen he hunted game in the forest. Recently he had experienced real combat. He recalled the attack on the convoy just hours earlier and surveyed the bombed buildings, burned out hangars, and plane wreckage that surrounded him.

This would be a new level of violence and destruction.

Chapter Thirty Six

Cape Girardeau County, Missouri, Wednesday, October 21st

Zach stepped into the first rays of early morning sun that shone between two nearby buildings. After hours of sentry duty on the road leading toward their position the added warmth felt good. Yesterday the platoon had built an S-shaped lane of sandbags and moved concrete blocks onto the road to slow any vehicle coming toward them. Finally, they built a wooden gate and painted "STOP" on it. If anyone drove down the road they were supposed to wait there while he radioed the platoon HQ for instruction.

He spotted Private Meyer about a hundred yards away checking perimeter defenses. Zach turned his gaze back to the HQ building at the end of the road behind him. Those inside were warm and probably had already eaten breakfast. He stomped his cold feet and slapped his hands. He glanced at the two machine gun positions closer to the base. That seemed like a neat job, but instead he had an M4 and a wooden gate.

No one had ventured down the road during his watch. He yawned. Army life had turned out to be a lot like working with the guard, except he wasn't learning anything new, and with the armory he usually went home to a warm bed and home-cooked food. It wasn't actually that cold, but after hours on watch he looked forward to his cot, sleeping bag and hot MRE breakfast.

His radio crackled. "Sentry one, report."

Zach yawned again, and pressed transmit. "Sentry one, all quiet." He walked back and forth, as the radio calls went out to other posts along the perimeter.

After several minutes he glanced at his watch. Finally, relief time neared. He hoped Private Waller didn't oversleep.

Several minutes later the sergeant and another soldier left the HQ. The sergeant seemed to be inspecting defensive positions. The other soldier walked straight toward the gate.

Zach thought he recognized him. "Ryan? Is that you?"

"Yeah." He spread his arms wide and grinned. "Private Nelson—here to relieve you."

"Steve is supposed to have the next watch."

"I traded with him, but I could go back to my cot if you don't want me to relieve you."

"No." Zach shook his head. "You'll do fine." He pulled the radio from his pocket and handed it to Nelson. "There's nothing to pass down."

"What about that car coming toward us?"

Zach spun around. For four hours no one had come near, but now a black SUV approached. "Cover me."

As Nelson used the radio to report the traffic, the sergeant and Meyer hurried to join them at the gate.

The vehicle slowed as it neared the winding line of sandbags and concrete. Zach stood behind waist-high blocks with his rifle ready. The vehicle braked to a stop at the gate.

The clear windows allowed Zach to see the four people inside, three soldiers and one civilian. The driver kept his hands on the steering wheel; the other two soldiers made their empty hands visible. The civilian in the back rolled down a window.

"My name is David Weston. I'm here to see Major Westmore."

Nelson radioed the information back to HQ.

*   *   *

Caden sat at a metal desk eating his MRE breakfast. The building had been an administrative center for the airport. Maps were laid out on a conference table, and tacked to the walls. Static and hiss called from the radios of the communication center next door.

First Sergeant Fletcher walked over holding his own breakfast. "Mind if I join you?"

Caden chewed a mouthful of bread and peanut butter. He gestured for him to sit.

Fletcher pulled over a chair.

After Caden swallowed, he held up a muffin. "I've been

trying to decide if I should eat this or use it as a hockey puck."

Fletcher glanced at it. "Eat it. There's no ice for a rink."

Caden took a bite and nodded approval. "Once you break the crust, it's not bad."

A soldier trotted in from the next office. "Excuse me, sir, an SUV just drove up to the gate. The passenger says he's David Weston, here to see you."

Caden stood. What was the governor's chief of staff doing at the war front? Could it be a ruse? "Get the ready squad out there. Let the vehicle enter, but keep it in the holding area away from the main building."

"Yes, sir." The soldier hurried away.

Fletcher stood. "Don't I know this guy?"

"If it's really him, yeah, you do." Caden motioned for Fletcher to follow. "He's the guy who impersonated Governor Monroe during Operation Hellhound. I met him at Fort Rucker while trying to get home after the first terror attacks."

"You really think it might not be him?"

Caden shrugged. "Why would he be in the war zone?"

Together they stepped from the building as the vehicle moved slowly toward them. Twelve soldiers crouched behind a semi-circle of sandbags with M4s at the ready.

The SUV stopped well back from the soldiers. The two men in the front seat kept their hands visible. Both backdoors opened. A soldier and a civilian exited the vehicle.

"David?" Caden relaxed and stepped over the sandbags. "What are you doing here?"

They walked toward each other.

Caden thrust out a hand to greet his friend.

Weston smiled and leaned close. "I'm the lucky guy chosen to update your orders."

The soldier with Weston stayed near the car.

"Ready squad," Fletcher called out. "At ease."

In a quiet voice, Weston asked, "Is there somewhere we can meet in private?"

Caden nodded. "First Sergeant, show the guys in the vehicle inside and—."

"That's not necessary. Most of us won't be staying long."

"Most?"

"I'll explain in a moment."

"Okay." Caden led Weston to a small office with a cot on one side, a metal desk on the other, and a couple of chairs. "Welcome to my home."

"Cozy."

Caden sat and motioned for Weston to do so. "I don't see a briefcase, satchel, envelope or sheet of paper. Where are these orders?"

Weston shook his head. "Nothing has been written down. This will be verbal and for your ears only. Tell others only what they need to know."

"General Harwich told me this is a recon-and-package retrieval mission, but the secrecy surrounding it tells me there is something more."

"You will be doing recon on the east bank of the Mississippi, in contested territory. However, one of the soldiers who came with me will be your guide crossing the river and in Illinois."

"A local guy?"

"Yes." Weston nodded. "And I will provide more details about the mission—later."

"If I'm going to be spending much time across the river, this base camp should be closer to it."

"This area has been quiet for weeks, and we don't want to attract attention. In two days units from St. Louis, and north to the Canadian border will launch a major offensive." Weston pulled a blank slip of paper from his pocket and wrote on it as he continued to speak. "Use the next two days to recon the area on the other side and find this location. Memorize the coordinates and then burn the paper. Use the guide to determine several ways to that position and escape routes back."

Caden waved the paper. "If you don't want to attract attention then I shouldn't go anywhere near this location until it's time to go and ... what's at this place?"

"An abandoned farmhouse."

"Okay, and what's inside the building?"

"The package you need to retrieve." Weston sighed. "I know that it's dangerous to do recon in the area of the farmhouse, but ... well, the package will only be there for a short time. You must be there at 0100 zulu on the 23rd."

In his head, Caden converted the military time to 1900 local.

"The package will not … ah, there will be no pick up if you are late or if you," he pointed at Caden, "are not there. Retrieve it and return."

"How will I identify the package?"

"You will." Weston held up his hands. "I can't say anymore now."

"The secrecy for this recon mission is annoying."

David frowned. "But necessary. If you're captured we don't want the package compromised. In the meantime, figure out your routes to the farmhouse and back to here, but don't draw attention to your team or the farmhouse. I'll return in thirty-six hours with your final orders." He stood.

"Really? Caden frowned. "You came all this way for a five minute meeting?"

"I've been in the area for a couple of weeks now working on parts of … well, things." Weston held out his hand. "I'll see you soon."

They shook and Weston departed.

Several hours after darkness settled on the region, Caden climbed into a Zodiac boat at the edge of the Mississippi for the first recon mission. Plans had been made, weapons, radio and gear checked.

Three of his own soldiers, Sergeant Hill, Corporals Franklin and Jackson, were with him. Lieutenant Shaffer, the local guide left behind by Weston, joined them in the boat. As they started across the black water, Caden thought of all the secrecy surrounding the mission and the answers he didn't have. His gut tense, and mouth dry, he stared into the night. What waited for them on the other side?

Chapter Thirty Seven

On the Mississippi between Missouri & Illinois, Thursday, October 22nd

Caden and the other four soldiers paddled and used the currents of the river to maneuver across the dark waters of the Mississippi. As they crossed, he gazed into a sky of cloud and fog. It occurred to him that, if he hadn't come down with Kern flu, the mission would have unfolded on moonless nights. That would have been nice.

Tonight, the sliver of moon glowed faintly through the clouds and provided no useful light to their enemies. Infrared sensors and radar might still detect the boat, but at least the fog made spotting them difficult. Perhaps the clouds would hold for the next twenty-four hours and provide their natural concealment.

On the eastern bank, the five men lifted the Zodiac, climbed the forested levee, and hid the craft under limbs and leaves. Lieutenant Shaffer, the local guide left by David Weston, steered them through the trees to a slough. They followed it up a gradual slope till the trees and marsh thinned, revealing a highway ahead.

Shaffer held up his hand in a stop motion. "The New America forces patrol along the river and nearby bridges." His whispered words were picked up by a throat mic.

Each of the other soldiers heard him over an earbud speaker. "We need to cross Highway 3, then travel northeast through the state forest."

"Roger." Caden nodded, leaned forward, and used a red light to study the map.

Minutes after Weston departed, he had located the farm on

his chart. That presented no problem. Finding the location in unfamiliar territory at night would prove a bit more difficult. Weston trusted Lieutenant Shaffer, but Caden remained unsure how much he could rely on the man. Caden didn't know him, and clearly, Shaffer had ties to regions controlled by Durant.

Corporal Franklin scouted north, while Sergeant Hill scouted south along the highway. Several Humvees passed in both directions, but when no headlights remained, the five rushed across the pavement into the forest. For the next hour they hiked along the tree edge in a north and east direction, roughly paralleling a branch of the Mississippi.

Shaffer motioned for the group to stop.

The team huddled near a large stump.

"We're beyond the routine patrols." Shaffer pointed into the darkness. "We need to cross a small road," he whispered. "Beyond that is a railroad bridge. When there aren't any trains coming, we need to hurry across."

Caden held the red light close to the map. "That should bring us within a mile of the position."

Shaffer nodded.

"Okay, then." Caden stood. "Move out."

As they neared the railroad bridge, the irregular chop-chop sound of helicopters disturbed the quiet of the night.

Holding his fist up, Caden signaled the others to stop. He looked up through the trees, but saw nothing.

"They're right over our heads," Sergeant Hill said into Caden's ear.

He nodded and pointed, signaling the men to retreat into the woods.

As they hurried, the sound shifted, coming through the trees to the north. The chop-chop sound slid lower and then slowed.

Caden and his team continued deeper into the forest until they stumbled into a gully. "Spread out along here."

"Camouflage yourself with branches and leaves." Caden moved along the line, helping others. "Do not move or shoot unless fired upon," he whispered.

With slow, cautious steps, Caden positioned himself so the men were lower in the gully on his right and carefully gathered tree branches and dirt over him. He laid on the bank with his M4 clutched in his right hand, while he waited and listened.

Several minutes later a twig snapped and then another.

Caden tensed.

The sounds came from different angles. It seemed two, and probably more, people crept toward them. Even though he only heard them, he felt certain they were soldiers moving forward in a line with weapons ready. He hoped they didn't have infrared gear and were equally blind.

Gradually the sound of footsteps neared. The vague outline of five men appeared a mere ten feet away. Caden stared through the grass and leaves before him as the crunch of boots came closer.

A foot landed on two fingers of his left hand.

*   *   *

Cape Girardeau County, Missouri, Thursday, October 22nd

Zach wondered why he had been selected. He stared into the darkness of the Mississippi River from his foxhole on the levee. He had once heard war described as, "hours of boredom punctuated by moments of terror." That described his life since being drafted. For several hours on the transport plane he had tried to sleep in an uncomfortable webbed seat. Then at Whiteman, they gave him food and told him to rest in the nearby barracks. By the time Zach finished eating, all the bunks were taken. He tried to sleep on the floor, and did—for a few minutes. But soon the first sergeant returned and ordered everyone into trucks for the next part of the journey. Zach found it difficult to sleep sitting upright in the truck, but almost managed it. Then jets attacked the convoy. He stumbled out of the truck and ran into the field. The truck blew up behind him throwing him to the ground.

His heart still pounded thinking about those moments of terror.

When they arrived at Cape Girardeau base camp, Zach pulled guard duty the first night. Later in the day the first sergeant told him he and twenty others had been selected for a special duty.

"You're being sent to the Mississippi," Fletcher said like it was an honor. "You'll construct defensive positions along the bank and guard the area."

While filling sandbags he saw Major Westmore and others leave in a Zodiac boat and disappear in the fog. After that he did eat some cold food and slept a couple of hours, but then found himself back along the Mississippi, and again on night guard duty.

If the New America forces didn't kill him, the lack of sleep would.

The radio clicked twice signaling a friendly approaching. Boots on gravel broke the stillness of the night.

Zach turned to face the person. "Halt. Who goes there?"

"First Sergeant Fletcher."

Zach recognized the voice. "Advance."

Fletcher strode out of the black and stood beside him overlooking the water. "Have you seen anything?"

"Nothing." Zach looked back at the river. "Except water, fog and clouds."

"That's what the other sentries are telling me."

Zach wondered why such reports didn't make him happy.

"The situation may change at any moment. Be ready. We need to hold this position until Major Westmore returns."

Zach nodded, but had no idea why this place was so important, or where Major Westmore had gone. The tension on Fletcher's face told him there would soon be more moments of terror.

*   *   *

Alexander County, Illinois, Thursday, October 22nd

A second foot slid in loose dirt nearby. The nearest foot pressed hard on his hand.

Caden clenched his teeth and held his breath.

The soldier steadied himself and then continued into the gully and up the other side.

After all sound of the soldiers faded, Caden rubbed his bruised fingers. Then he motioned for the team to huddle. "Somehow they know we're here or think we might be." He glanced at Shaffer, pondered his loyalty, and returned his gaze to the others. "I suspect soldiers are positioned along the roads and bridges. It's too dangerous to continue to the position tonight." He looked again to Shaffer. "Can you get us from here to the location tomorrow?"

"Yes."

Caden didn't want to stay in enemy territory for eighteen hours, but that seemed the best plan. "We'll wait in this area." Peering into the black forest, he said, "Let's find a good location to hide."

Chapter Thirty Eight

Alexander County, Illinois, Friday, October 23rd

Caden watched from the tight stand of trees where the team waited. The sun rose, crossed the sky, and once again slid low. Hours had passed since they heard soldiers or helicopters. That made him smile, but a clear sky meant a clear moonlit night. When the team moved into the open they would be visible. He huddled over his map and used the last rays of daylight to confirm the route they would use to the farmhouse. Then he waited for the sun to sink below the horizon. They would need as much darkness as nature could provide.

A couple hours later, Lieutenant Shaffer moved close. "We need to go," he whispered.

Caden nodded, and motioned for the others to follow.

For nearly an hour, the five men moved in a northeast direction, and then reached the edge of the forest not far from their position the previous day. The road they had followed yesterday stretched out before him.

Holding his fist up, Caden signaled the others to stop. He moved behind a tree, huddled over the map and held the red light close.

Shaffer came alongside.

Caden pointed to a spot on the map.

Shaffer nodded.

They were less than two miles from their objective.

Caden turn off the light and listened for vehicles, helicopters or soldiers, but he heard only the breeze and the waters of the nearby river. Confident no hostile forces were nearby, he motioned for the men to follow.

They continued northeast along the forest edge with the road on their right for several minutes. Following the highway as it turned east, Caden spotted four soldiers guarding the crossing.

He signaled the team to back up.

Out of sight of the soldiers, Caden and Shaffer studied the map.

"Can we avoid the sentries by going this way?" Caden whispered as he traced the route with his finger.

"Maybe." Shaffer nodded. "But there could be others."

"We'll deal with that when it comes." Caden led the team across the road and into the forest on the south side. Only a few yards wide, the narrow band of woods sloped down to the river edge, and in other spots the waters reached through creating sloughs and wetlands.

Trudging through cold marsh and dark forest, progress slowed, and they struggled to remain silent. The cold waters soaked Caden's pant legs and boots. Soon he couldn't feel his toes.

Wet and behind schedule, they came to the edge of the woods as it sloped up toward the railroad bridge.

Caden snapped his fist up. Six soldiers, three on each end, guarded the span. They moved back, out of sight, into a grove of trees.

"Is there another way across?" Caden asked.

"No." Shaffer shook his head. "Well, several miles upriver or back down it."

"We could swim it," Corporal Franklin suggested.

"Nope." Shaffer frowned. "If hypothermia didn't kill you the current would drag you under."

Caden glanced at his watch. Shaffer was right about the river, but the orders were clear, he needed to be at the farmhouse in less than an hour. "Franklin, scout down river for a good crossing point. Hill, go upriver."

Several minutes later Hill's voice came over the radio. "Three Humvees less than a mile north and headed toward you."

"Roger." Caden replied as he hunkered down with Shaffer and Jackson.

Seconds later the vehicles pulled to a stop at the railroad bridge.

"What's up sergeant?" The voice of the sentry carried on the still night air.

"We're moving north. The traitors just launched an offensive."

The sentry waved his arm and all six climbed into the Humvee.

The convoy continued on.

Caden warned Sergeant Hill the trucks were nearing. "After they pass, each of you make your way to the bridge and meet up with us on the other side."

Clicks came back to him over the radio.

When the vehicles disappeared from view, Caden motioned for Shaffer and Jackson to follow, and then raced onto the span. As he neared the opposite side the sound of trucks rumbled across the night air.

"Humvees turned around. They're coming back toward you," Hill reported on the radio.

Caden pressed transmit. "Everyone get across the bridge as fast as possible."

Jackson passed Caden near the end of the crossing. He followed the medic into the nearby trees. Breathing hard, Shaffer sprinted into the forest seconds later.

Franklin raced across the road and onto the span.

Caden heard vehicle engines race, but still couldn't see them. Then automatic weapons thundered.

Franklin paused for a moment, then dashed across the bridge and into the woods.

"They spotted me." Hill's breathless report came over the earbud.

Alone, he raced along the forest edge toward the team.

Humvees followed.

Shots rang out.

The lone soldier fell.

The vehicles emptied. Soldiers surrounded the fallen man.

He would mourn the loss of Sergeant Hill, but now was not the time. Caden pushed the anger, sadness and self-doubt aside. He had a mission to complete and they were behind schedule. "Everyone change to the backup radio channel and move out."

Seconds later, Franklin came alongside him. "Will the New America soldiers search for us?"

"Probably," Caden whispered. "So shut up and move faster." He didn't know how far or wide, but they would search for infiltrators. Caden and his team needed to reach the rendezvous position first and then disappear into the forest—or they all might die tonight.

For several minutes the four remaining members of the team ran just inside the tree line, weaving around forest obstacles as they held a rapid pace.

Shaffer slowed and pointed to a dirt road. "Three hundred yards in that direction is the farmhouse."

Caden breathed deeply. "Let's go."

The team hurried along both sides of the narrow rutted road toward the lone building ahead. Only shards of glass stood in the dark windows of the two-story wood building. Broken boards punctuated the porch railing.

Caden pulled his GPS from a pocket and checked the position. "Secure the area. This is the place." The others spread out around the home. The wood creaked as he climbed the steps to the house. The front door stood open, but not inviting. He pushed his trepidation aside, along with the door, and stepped in.

A gun clicked near his ear.

*　　　*　　　*

Cape Girardeau County, Missouri, Friday, October 23rd

Darkness fell before Zach finished digging another defensive position. He had started counting the sandbags as he filled them, but lost track. Finally, Sergeant Garcia told the work party to get food and rest.

Yeah, like what else would Zach do with his off time? Play video games and update his social media status? He signaled to the sentries on his right and left that he was leaving the area. The guards waved them on, and returned their eyes to the river. He pulled a small knife from a pocket and punctured his new blisters as he walked to the makeshift campsite. Slowly his eyes scanned the depression in the ground that served as his new home. He sat on the barren cold earth and pulled an MRE from his rucksack. A couple minutes later he yanked it from the heating sleeve and shoveled semi-warm chicken mystery meal into his mouth.

Sleep would have been his usual next choice, but tonight a small group sat nearby reading and talking. He lay on his sleeping bag listening.

"If we can help change the course of the nation, then I think we should fight to do it," a soldier said.

"No, Kevin, there aren't that many of us." A black soldier about Zach's age protested. "What can we do?"

Kevin flipped the pages of the book in his hand. "What's that verse in Second Chronicles say? 'if my people, who are called by my name, will humble themselves and pray and seek my face and turn from their wicked ways, then I will hear from heaven, and I will forgive their sin and will heal their land.'"

Zach sat up, and pulled a blanket around him.

"Durant's New America isn't going to humble itself, pray, or change," another soldier said.

"I'm not sure a lot of people on our own side would."

"God's not asking the unbelievers to do anything." Kevin shook his head. "It says if *my people*, which are *called by my name*. We're the ones that have to stand in the gap as it says in Ezekiel."

Zach stood, and with the blanket still wrapped around him, moved closer. "Mind if I listen in?"

"Please, join us." Kevin motioned for him to sit.

Zach did and immediately the black soldier introduced himself as Derrick. "Where's that verse you mentioned?"

"Chapter twenty-two, verse thirty." Kevin flipped through pages. Others did the same.

"I don't have a Bible," Zach said.

"Here take this one. We got a bunch more from a chaplain." Kevin handed his own to him.

Zach held the pristine book to his nose. It even smelled new. "What was the verse you guys were talking about?"

Derrick helped Zach find the place.

Kevin pulled another book from his rucksack and turned the pages until he found the verse. "I sought for a man among them, that should make up the hedge, and stand in the gap before me for the land, that I should not destroy it: but I found none."

With a pen Zach marked the verse, but he wasn't sure what "stand in the gap," meant. He continued to listen as the conversation turned to end times, tribulation and apocalypse. He didn't understand most of it, and wanted to hear more, but long hours of night sentry duty, digging foxholes and the semi-warm meal all fought against him. His eyes drooped. He used an unfinished letter as a bookmark. The words of Ezekiel would have to wait for another day.

* * *

Alexander County, Illinois, Friday, October 23rd

Caden froze.

"Who are you?" a woman's voice whispered. "And there is only one right answer."

He considered ducking and grabbing for the gun, but the woman's voice seemed familiar. He decided to try the truth. "Major Caden Westmore," he said praying that was the right answer.

"They told me you were coming." The arm with the gun relaxed. "But when you were late … I thought…."

"Becky? Is that you?" Caden turned and shook his head in disbelief. His old fiancée, the press secretary for Durant, stood before him. Old feelings leapt into his mind, along with anger at her choice to follow Durant. She was a traitor, but what should he do? Arrest her? "Are you the courier?"

"Courier?" She stepped closer and her long blonde hair shimmered in the moonlight. "What did they tell you?"

"Not much. There's been a lot of secrecy." The heavy coat, jeans and hiking boots seemed appropriate for the stealth rendezvous this night. In the time he had known her she had always dressed stylishly and feminine. Where did she get the farm clothes? He remembered her face as soft and gentle but, at least in the moonlight, he saw coldness there now. "Do you have the package?"

"I am the package!" she growled.

Chapter Thirty Nine

Alexander County, Illinois, Friday, October 23rd

"What?" Caden frowned. "I was sent here to get a package, not a person."

She shook her head. "You were sent to get me."

A whispered voice came through the bud in Caden's ear. "This is Guide. Soldiers approaching from the south."

Caden acknowledged Shaffer's report, and then leaned close. "So, you were everything ... the only thing ... I was sent to retrieve?"

"Yes." She nodded. "I've got everything that you were to get."

That answer hinted there was something else, but he had no time to question her. "Stay close to me."

Gunfire erupted.

Caden grabbed Becky's hand and ran to the back of the house. He pressed transmit on his radio. "Team, rendezvous back at the bridge." Then he turned to Becky. "I need both hands for the rifle. Grab my jacket and hang on." With weapon at the ready he led her from the house and into the forest.

For several minutes he continued deeper into the woods, and then turned south to arc toward the bridge. With each step he hoped Durant's New America dragoons hadn't left guards.

Becky panted, slowed and pulled on his jacket.

"We're nearly there." Caden steadied her then wrapped one arm around her waist. "You can do this. The rendezvous point should be near." With his free hand he double clicked the radio.

A triple click came back to Caden. He took several more steps.

"Who goes there?" came over the earbud.

"Team Leader."

"Advance," Shaffer whispered from the darkness. "Come this way."

As Caden drew near, the lieutenant stepped from the bushes, reached out an arm to Becky, and helped carry her to a nearby low spot.

The depression provided cover for the group. At the bottom, about five feet below the surrounding earth, Jackson leaned over a prone Franklin and wrapped a bandage around his abdomen. Shaffer and Becky sat nearby.

Caden slid closer to Franklin. "What happened?"

The wounded man's eyes fluttered.

"Shot in the gut." The medic glanced at Caden, and then continued his work.

Shaffer moved closer to Becky and drew his pistol. "Aren't you Durant's press—."

Caden grabbed his arm. "She's the mission. That's all you need to know." Still not entirely sure of the lieutenant's allegiance, he reluctantly ordered him to guard the perimeter.

For the next several minutes, Caden listened to Franklin's labored breathing. "Is there anymore you can do for him?"

Jackson shook his head. "He needs a hospital."

Becky found a canteen and drank deeply.

"Are there guards on the railroad bridge?"

"Yes." Shaffer nodded. "Four on each end."

Caden tried to formulate a plan.

"We've got to go." Becky tossed the empty canteen aside. "We'll need to leave him."

"No!" Caden snarled. "And either whisper or shut up."

"You've got to get me back safely," she said softly.

"I will, but we're not leaving him." Caden replied.

"He made the decision for us." Jackson stood. "He's dead."

Becky stared at Caden, but said nothing.

"Movement in the forest." Shaffer's voice came in his ear.

"Roger." Caden stood and checked his rifle. "Guide, return to camp, and we'll head out."

Jackson removed Franklin's radio gear and offered it to Caden.

He looked away. "Give it to her."

"Team Leader, this is Guide. I'm coming in." Shaffer's words came over the radio, and then he appeared at the top of the depression. "Can we move Franklin?"

"That's not necessary. He's gone." Jackson said as he put the mic on Becky.

Caden pointed west. "If we get separated meet at the Zodiac no later than 1100 zulu." He grabbed Becky's arm. "Move out."

For nearly an hour the four weaved a general southwesterly course through unfamiliar forests and marshes.

"Stop." Becky stumbled. "I can't breathe." She collapsed to the ground. "My feet hurt. I've got to rest."

"We shouldn't stop." Shaffer continued on several steps.

"I'm the reason for this mission and I can't go on."

"Whisper," Caden ordered. "Or use the throat mic."

She huffed at him and pulled off her boot and sock.

Medic Jackson shined a red light on several large blisters that dotted her toes and heel.

"Don't run many marathons, do you?" Shaffer mocked.

Becky glared, but said nothing.

"Jackson, do what you can for the blisters. We need her able to run." Then he turned to Shaffer. "Scout ahead. We'll catch up." As the medic worked, Caden climbed from the depression, and circled the position as a sentry. For several minutes he heard and saw nothing.

Twigs snapped.

"Team this is Leader. Movement to the north."

Gunfire erupted.

Becky screamed.

Footsteps thundered in his direction.

Becky darted out of the darkness.

Caden reached out and yanked her down beside him.

She screamed again.

Jackson fell inches away.

Caden knelt, returned fire, and checked the medic for a pulse.

Jackson was dead.

Caden fired again, clutched Becky's arm and darted through the forest. He called over the radio as he ran. "Guide, rendezvous at the Zodiac." He heard no reply.

Comforting darkness embraced them as the moon slid below the trees. For many minutes they hurried through the forest toward the Mississippi.

"Got to stop." Becky pulled on his arm. "I don't care if they shoot me, I've got to stop."

Caden slowed his pace, and found a spot where a stream had cut a gully.

They hid behind a few rocks in the gulch.

"Where's your pistol?" Caden asked as he looked her up and down.

"I dropped it earlier when you threw me to the ground."

"Really?" He shook his head. "Do you know how many men have died to get you this far?"

"Huh? What?"

"You drop your gun and say you don't care if you're shot, but good men have died to keep you alive."

"They're soldiers. They fight. Some die. That's what they do."

"I'm a soldier."

"You made that choice. You could have been someone of influence."

Caden shook his head in disgust. "Why did you defect?"

"Because Durant is going to lose this war."

"All of this is so you can be on the winning side?"

"Yes." She shook her head. "I mean no. I've got valuable information. You should be glad I defected."

"Maybe." He sighed. "But why did you ask for me?"

"Most Constitutionalists want me dead, but I knew you wouldn't shoot me."

He stared at her and just for a moment pondered the possibility. "I hope the information you have is worth the lives of the good men who died to save you." He handed her a canteen. "Drink some water, and then we need to go."

She drank and returned the canteen to him. "These last few weeks Durant knew there was a spy in his midst. When I slipped out of New York three days ago they started 'wanted dead or alive,' announcements about me. I've been terrified since even before then, and the fear makes me … well, like I've been." She breathed deeply and let it out slowly. "About whether the information is worth it or not, I'll let you decide.

"The Chinese first encountered the Kern flu last year. They've been working on a vaccine since then and succeeded in producing one about the same time it broke out in this country. They passed the vaccine to Durant, but he's been using it to keep people in line. If you're a loyalist, you get the vaccine. If you're a troublemaker you don't."

Caden shook his head. "Your boss is playing god."

"Former boss. Word about his tactics has leaked out. Dozens of senior military leaders are willing to defect because of what Durant is doing. I have the vaccine formula and the names of those willing to defect."

Caden looked her up and down. "Where are you hiding the information?"

"Ah ...." She stared at him hesitantly.

He grinned. "I'm mad and disappointed with you, but I won't kill you and take it."

"Here." She pointed to her mouth. "One of my back teeth has dental floss tied to it. The other end is tied to a microchip in plastic that I swallowed."

"Wow, like a drug mule."

"I'm not thrilled with the comparison, but yes, something like that. Is the information worth the cost of this mission?"

Caden sighed. "Come on. We've got to get you to the other side before dawn." As they continued he called on his radio hoping to hear Shaffer. Occasional static came back. He adjusted the squelch, but heard no words.

The sound of traffic rumbled through the trees before they reached the forest edge. The main north-south highway ran atop an earthen embankment fifty yards ahead. Between them, and the road, stood a grassy clearing.

The vehicles drove without lights, making it difficult for Caden to judge, but it sounded like steady traffic lumbering north along the highway.

"What are all those vehicles?" Becky stared at the vague forms moving on the highway. "Where are they going?"

"Reinforcements for the battles north of St. Louis." A check of Caden's GPS and map confirmed what he already knew. "The boat is on the other side of that highway and just over a mile north."

"If we try to cross they'll either see us and shoot or we'll get hit by one of the trucks." She stared at the dark road. "The traffic thins, but never stops. How do we get across?"

"I'm not sure."

They scouted north, toward the hidden Zodiac, as worry grew in Caden's gut. He looked in the direction of the Mississippi river, less than a mile away. On the other side were friendly, Constitutionalist forces, but all too soon, daylight would arrive making them visible. He needed a way over or—.

His foot slid in the mud beside a stream.

Under. He could go under the highway. Caden followed the stream to the forest edge and smiled. Two hundred yards away he spotted the black circle of a culvert under the road.

He turned to Becky as he recalled their first day together. "Did you ever learn how to swim?"

"No."

"Too bad." He pointed to the pipe. "That's how we're getting to the other side."

Becky frowned.

"Since they're driving without lights we should be able to reach the highway before going in the water, but I don't know how deep it is. Stay low in the gully, and follow me."

She shuddered, nodded, and followed.

Huddled over, Caden left the trees behind as he weaved along the gulch. He tried to stay on the bank. His feet would dip into the chilly water soon enough. Static crackled in his ear. He glanced back over his shoulder. Becky raced just a few feet behind him.

"Team leader …."

The words came through the earbud as Caden eased into the icy water flowing into the culvert. "Try not to splash."

Becky splashed. "It's deep."

"Shhh!" Caden stopped and held a finger to his lips. "Not that deep." He held his rifle over his head as the cold water rose to his shoulders. "You can do this."

"I'm on my tip-toes," she whispered.

In the darkness he couldn't see Becky, but heard her following.

Caden paused at the west end of the pipe and looked around. Vehicles still rumbled overhead, but the waning darkness would hide them. "Stay low and follow me into the woods."

She nodded.

"Team leader … Guide … read me."

Caden recognized Shaffer's voice. As he ran into the forest he pressed transmit. "Guide this is Team Leader. Change to frequency three." When they were again talking he asked, "What's your position?"

"I can see you. I'm coming in from the north."

If Shaffer wasn't loyal this would be an excellent place to trap them. No, in the culvert would have been a better ambush. Still, Caden huddled down behind a tree, while he waited and listened.

A wet and tired soldier emerged from a nearby stand of trees.

Caden remained behind his tree until Shaffer stood next to him.

"Did Jackson make it?" Shaffer raised an eyebrow as he looked at both of them.

"No." Caden frowned.

Shaffer sighed. "I scouted south looking for a way under the highway. Nearly two miles from here I spotted about a hundred of Durant's New America thugs moving this way."

"Yeah." Caden frowned. "We've seen a lot of vehicles heading north."

"No." Shaffer scowled. "These soldiers were stationing guards, using drones, and boats on the nearby streams. It's seemed to me their mission is either to seal off the area or push us north into a trap." He leaned close to Becky. "And I'll bet you're the cause of all the trouble."

"Yes." Caden touched Becky's arm. "She has important information."

Shaffer pursed his lips.

"We need to keep moving." Caden pointed ahead. "Let's find our boat."

They hurried north, staying in the forest, trying to remain silent, and unseen.

Becky struggled to keep pace. She stumbled, and her breathing grew more labored.

"Are we near?" She asked.

"Stop for a moment." Caden whispered.

Shaffer slowed, but signaled he'd scout ahead.

Caden checked his map and GPS. They were within a

hundred yards of the boat.

Shots rang out.

Dirt flew in the air.

Shaffer stumbled firing his rifle. He fell back against a tree and continued to shoot. "Go." He pointed and fired again.

Becky ran in the direction Shaffer pointed.

Caden fired as the first soldiers came into his view.

"Go." Shaffer shouted. "I'll …." Bullets hit and he slumped to the side.

Caden ran toward the boat.

Becky was doing her best to push the Zodiac into the water with limbs still on it.

He slammed into the boat and it floated free.

Becky jumped in and paddled.

Caden followed and together they rowed the black zodiac into the waning darkness. He sighed, changed the frequency on his radio, and pressed transmit. "Delivery service with package to drop off. Do you copy?"

"Roger." Fletcher's voice came over the radio. "I'll summon the welcome wagon."

Gunfire thundered from the eastern shore.

Becky yelped, collapsed to the bottom of the boat, and covered her head with her hands.

"If you're hit, stay there. If not, get up and paddle!"

She paddled.

He glanced over his shoulder. They were firing into darkness, but that wouldn't last long. Caden spun around in the seat, returned fire and started the motor.

*　　　*　　　*

Cape Girardeau County, Missouri, Saturday October 24th

Zach woke to gunfire. He grabbed his rifle, and helmet and joined others as they ran toward the levee.

"Everyone hold your fire." Fletcher snarled over the radio. "Do this just like we practiced. If you shoot before I give the order I will kill you myself."

Zach reached the river and spotted Major Westmore and a woman as they jumped from a Zodiac and ran up the embankment.

"More boats!" Zach pointed.

A dozen Zodiacs skipped downriver.

Multiple explosions boomed to the south.

"Drones," Fletcher hissed. "Shoot at anything on the water."

"Boats coming in from the south," a panicked voice reported.

Zach glanced in that direction. Smoke and flames obscured his view downriver. Thirty yards away Major Westmore helped the woman into a jeep, then he ran back to the levee as the vehicle sped away.

"Shoot at the boats!" Fletcher ordered. He fired off several bursts.

Zach aimed at the nearest boat and shot.

Dirt sprayed around him.

Something hot cut his cheek.

Zach returned rapid bursts of fire.

A weird looking jet with a gun in the nose swooped low over the river and peppered it with bullets.

"That's a Warthog," a nearby soldier shouted. "And it's from our side."

The plane continued along its deadly path as a cheer rose from the men on either side of Zach.

An awful roar hurt Zach's ears.

The plane exploded and fell into the water. Flames, wreckage, bodies, and sinking Zodiacs dotted the water.

"Fall back," Major Westmore shouted over the radio. "Fall back to the vehicles and regroup at the airport."

Jets darted back and forth overhead.

Zach jumped into the back of a Humvee and it sped away.

He slipped the rifle onto his shoulder and felt a three-inch long cut on his cheek. He gazed at bloody fingers.

Fifty feet ahead, a deuce-and-a-half exploded.

The Humvee driver cursed and swerved around the flaming wreck.

Minutes later the vehicle slid to a stop at the Cape Girardeau airport.

He jumped from the Humvee and tried to figure out what to do. Soldiers seemed to be running in every direction. Helicopters waited on the runway. Three jets circled overhead.

"Zach!" Major Westmore shouted and pointed to the helicopters. "Get on the middle chopper . Guard the woman."

"The jets." Zach pointed. "They'll shoot the helo down."

"They're ours. Go!"

He nodded and ran to the waiting craft.

When he jumped aboard, Zach immediately spotted the lady. "Don't worry ma'am, Major Westmore sent me to guard you."

A ghostly pale face peeked from under several blankets. Soggy boots and a wet coat lay on the floor beside bloody, bare feet.

Zach sat across from her. Could she be the cause of all this death and horror?

The chopper lifted into the air.

Chapter Forty

On the road to Hansen, Saturday, December 24ᵗʰ

Even if he wasn't on duty, Zach Brennon couldn't have slept. As the Humvee rolled south he recognized more roads, rivers and buildings. He leaned back in the seat and smiled. He would soon be home.

After two months of fighting in Missouri, Illinois and Indiana, the unit had been rotated to the rear. Several days of hot food and eight hours of sleep had been great, but then it got better. Durant asked for a ceasefire and peace negotiations.

The surviving soldiers of the platoon received orders back to Washington state. He would be home for Christmas.

The vehicle exited the freeway and turned toward Hansen. He noticed the convenience store by the exit. His father had been murdered there years ago and, after the terror attacks, it had been looted, but someone had fixed it up. Lights were on. Windows had been replaced. Cars were parked outside.

He knew he should be pleased that some sort of life had returned to the store, but sadness came to him.

So much had changed during the year. Death, despair and depression had taken a heavy toll.

He had changed.

Early in the year he wanted to fight in the Battle of Hansen, but when he arrived he huddled in fear. Thinking of that boy now caused him to smile both in amusement and embarrassment. Back then he didn't understand the terror of war. He wasn't a coward, but it took him months to figure that out.

At some point he had changed. Grown up? Perhaps there

was no one moment. He had learned how to fight and that gave him confidence. But he had learned to hate killing, even when he knew he must. Only later did he understand that someone must stand in the gap.

He pulled the little Bible with its bent and frayed cover from a pocket and flipped through the pages. The night the book had been given to him seemed long ago. He found the verse marked with a pen. "I searched for someone who would build the wall and stand in the gap for the land."

Yes, that was him. He nodded inwardly. That was the change. He hated war, and killing, but he would stand in the gap with his fellow soldiers to protect the land, his family and those he loved.

Was that the difference between a boy and a man? He shook his head. Such thoughts were way too philosophical for Christmas Eve.

"Stop at the road up ahead," Major Westmore said from the back seat.

The convoy parked at the turn to Hopps Road.

"Sergeant Brennon."

"Yes, sir?" Zach turned in his seat as the major opened the door.

"Come with me."

Zach followed Major Westmore to the deuce-and-a-half behind them in the convoy.

First Sergeant Fletcher stepped from that vehicle and saluted. "Will you be leaving us here, sir?"

"Yes." Caden looked down the road. "Tell Lieutenant Brooks I'll be … no, don't bother. Let him find me."

"Yes, sir." Fletcher smiled. "After all there is a ceasefire. The war can wait until after Christmas."

"Exactly." Caden turned to Zach. "And deliver our new sergeant here to his home. I think we can spare him for a while."

"Yes, sir." Fletcher nodded. "We just might be able to manage over Christmas without him."

"Thank you, sir!" Zach grinned.

"Merry Christmas." Caden grabbed his rucksack from the back and walked toward home.

*　　　*　　　*

Hollister Hotel, Saturday, December 24th

Zach pushed opened the door to the bakery.

A bell overhead jingled.

DeLynn's familiar voice called from the back, "I'll be right out."

Near one end, he leaned against the counter and took in all the dough and fresh bread smells. He had kept his promise and come back to her, but would he be able to keep that promise till peace reigned? Only God knew.

DeLynn came from the back with her eyes fixed on the tray of buns in her hands. Then she looked at him with a flour-smudged face.

Zach stood straight and smiled. "Hello, beautiful."

"Zach!" She dropped the tray onto the counter and ran to him with open arms. "I've been worried sick about you." She ran a finger along the scar on his face. "Are you all right?"

"I am now."

"Do you have to go back?"

He shrugged "I don't know, but—."

She smiled. "We'll worry about that later." She pulled him close and kissed him.

*   *   *

Near the Westmore Farm, Rural Lewis County, Saturday, December 24th

The clouds in the distance foretold snow. It might be a white Christmas this year. During his school days, Caden had walked this road many times and enjoyed the stroll beside the creek, but today he held a quick pace.

Home called to him in the distance. He adjusted the rucksack on his back and marched faster. It only took minutes, but it seemed like forever before he turned up the long driveway to the farmhouse. No vehicle could be seen, but smoke rose from the chimney.

The front door stood unlocked. He pushed it open and hurried into the living room. An ample fire warmed the space. Peter slept in the playpen near the television. Caden walked over to the baby. "Where's mommy?"

The kitchen door creaked slowly open.

Adam stepped out still holding the door.

Caden looked beyond the toddler and spotted Lisa working in the kitchen.

Adam giggled.

Caden held a finger to his mouth. "Shhh."

Adam stumbled back pushing the door behind him, and then went toward a box of toys.

From inside the kitchen came his sister's voice. "Adam where did you go?" The door swung open. "I told you to stay in the kitchen with me."

Lisa stifled a scream, gaped at her brother, and then ran to him.

Caden threw open his arms to embrace her. "I'm glad you don't have a shotgun this time."

She feigned disapproval. "Don't surprise me, and I won't shoot you. What are you doing here?"

"I pulled a few strings to get my platoon home for Christmas."

She hugged him tight. "When did you get here?"

"Just now." They talked for a few minutes just standing in the middle of the living room. Then Caden asked, "Where is everyone else?"

"Mom and Sue are at the church. They're helping prepare for the candlelight service tonight. It's the first service in ... well, a long time. They'll be home soon."

"Where's Maria?"

"The barn. I think. We should give you two some privacy. Adam, come with Auntie, back in the kitchen." She took the child's hand, but fixed her eyes on Caden. "We've all been worried, but I think it was hardest on Mom and Maria. Go find your wife."

"Thanks, sis." He stepped back through the door. "I will."

The hinges squeaked as he entered the barn.

Nikki darted toward him but stopped, growled, barked, and then seemed to recognize Caden. Wagging her tail, she ran to him.

Caden knelt and petted the dog.

In a denim jacket and jeans Maria stepped from the tool room. Seeing him, she gasped. Then a smile grew on her face. "Is it over?"

"No." He frowned and slowly stood.

"How long can you stay?"

"That depends upon the peace negotiations. A few days ... a week maybe."

She ran a hand through her hair. "Then, let's not waste it." She stepped close to him.

"I agree." Caden reached down and swept Maria off her feet. "There are several things we never got to do after the wedding." He carried her out of the barn, up the porch steps and across the threshold.

GLOSSARY

ACU   Army Combat Uniform

AK-47   The AK-47 is a selective-fire military rifle, developed in the USSR, but also used by the People's Republic of China.

Fueler   An army or National Guard fuel truck

Humvee   High Mobility Multipurpose Wheeled Vehicle (HMMWV), commonly known as the Humvee, is a four-wheel drive military vehicle.

JBLM   Joint Base Lewis-McChord (JBLM) is a large military installation located nine miles south-southwest of Tacoma in Washington state.

M11   United States military designation for the SIG P228 pistol. See SIG P228.

M2   The M2 is a Browning .50 caliber machine gun.

M4   The M4 is a common U.S. military magazine-fed, selective fire, rifle with a telescoping stock.

M9   The M9 is a semiautomatic, 9mm, pistol in common use by the United States military.

M35   A military truck in the 2½ ton weight class, often referred to as a "deuce and a half."

MOPP Level   MOPP is an acronym for "Mission Oriented Protective Posture" and as used in the book it refers to the level of protective gear used by military personnel in a chemical, biological, radiological, or nuclear combat situation. MOPP Level zero means gear will be carried, but not worn.

MRE   Meals, Ready-to-Eat (MRE) are self-contained, individual military field rations.

OPLAN Operation Plan

Op Order   Operations Order often abbreviated as OPORD

PLA   The People's Liberation Army of the People's Republic of China

Recon   Military slang for reconnaissance.

RPG   Rocket-propelled grenade

SIG P228   A compact pistol in use with many law enforcement agencies and the military where it is designated as the M11. Caden is given a M11, 9mm .40 S&W, in Chapter 13 along with two 15 round magazines. Caden refers to the M11 by the SIG name.

Also by the Author

Through Many Fires (Strengthen What Remains, Book 1) Terrorists smuggle a nuclear bomb into Washington D.C. and detonate it during the State of the Union Address. Army veteran and congressional staffer Caden Westmore is in nearby Bethesda and watches as a mushroom cloud grows over the capital. The next day, as he drives away from the still burning city, he learns that another city has been destroyed and then another. America is under siege. Panic ensues and society starts to unravel.

*   *   *

A Time to Endure (Strengthen What Remains, Book 2) The exciting saga of Major Caden Westmore continues in this, the second book of the *Strengthen What Remains* series. In the first book, *Through Many Fires*, terrorists use nuclear bombs to destroy six American cities. Now, the nation's economy teeters on the verge of collapse. The dollar plunges, inflation runs rampant, and the next civil war threatens to decimate the wounded country. In the face of tyranny, panic, and growing hunger, Caden struggles to keep his family and town together. But how can he save his community when the nation is collapsing around it?

*   *   *

Titan Encounter Justin Garrett starts one morning as a respected businessman and ends the day a fugitive wanted by every power in the known universe. Fleeing with his 'sister' Mara and Naomi, a mysterious woman from Earth Empire, their only hope of refuge is with the Titans, genetically enhanced soldiers who rebelled, and murdered millions in the Titanomachy War. Hunted, even as they hunt for the Titans, the three companions slowly uncover the truth that will change the future and rewrite history.

About the Author

Hello and thank you for reading.

I grew up in the mountains of Colorado and went to Mesa State College in Grand Junction. When money for college ran low I enlisted in the United States Navy. I thought I would do four years and then use my veteran's benefits to go back to college.

While serving in the navy I wrote space opera and military science fiction. Both *Titan Encounter* and the *Final Duty* stories fall into that period.

My first assignment was with a U.S. Navy unit at the Royal Air Force base in Edzell, Scotland. Two years later, while on leave in Israel, I met Lorraine from Plymouth, Devon, England. We married the next year. Together we spent the remainder of my twenty year naval career traveling across the United States from Virginia to Hawaii and on to Guam, Japan and beyond.

After I retired from the military I taught in an Alaskan Eskimo village for several years while continuing to write. My first post-apocalyptic novel, *Through Many Fires*, became an instant hit, rocketing onto the Kindle Science Fiction Post-Apocalyptic list and eventually making it to the number one spot. The second book in the series, *A Time to Endure*, appeared on several genre bestseller lists and led to the recently released third book in the series, *Braving the Storms.* My books are available on all major online retailers.

Today, Lorraine and I live on a small farm in Western Washington State.

Visit my website at: http://www.kylepratt.me

About the Newsletter

Once a month I send out an email newsletter about upcoming books, events, specials, giveaways, promotions and more—and I give a free ebook just for signing up! Use the link below. I respect your privacy and will never rent, sell, or give away your personal information.

Newsletter: http://kylepratt.me/contact/

CPSIA information can be obtained at www.ICGtesting.com
Printed in the USA
BVOW06s0755300416

446205BV00017B/214/P